PAUL BISHOP PRESENTS... PATTERN OF BEHAVIOR

TEN TALES OF MURDER & MAYHEM

PAUL BISHOP   ERIC BEETNER   NICHOLAS CAIN

BEN BOULDEN   BRIAN DRAKE

CHRISTINE MATHEWS   L.J. MARTIN

RICHARD PROSCH   ROBERT J. RANDISI

NICOLE NELSON-HICKS

WOLFPACK
PUBLISHING
— EST 2013 —

Paul Bishop Presents... Pattern of Behavior: Ten Tales of Murder & Mayhem

Pattern Of Behavior and the other stories in this collection are a work of fiction. Any references to historical events, real people or real places are used fictitiously. Other names, characters, places and events are products of the author's imagination, and any resemblance to actual events, places or persons, living or dead, is entirely coincidental.

Published in the United States by Wolfpack Publishing, Las Vegas.

Wolfpack Publishing
6032 Wheat Penny Avenue
Las Vegas, NV 89122

wolfpackpublishing.com

Paperback ISBN: 978-1-64119-924-7
eBook ISBN: 978-1-64119-729-8

CONTENTS

PAUL BISHOP PRESENTS...
PATTERN OF BEHAVIOR

FOREWORD

It has been said writing is the best job in the world because you get to sit around all day in your pajamas playing with your imaginary friends. The problem for crime writers, however, is many of our imaginary friends are dangerous—bad guys, villains, stalkers, megalomaniacal malignant narcissists, sociopaths, psychopaths, lowlifes, grifters, deviants, femme fatales, and plain old bastards, none of whom play well with others. Those dangerous characters can drag a writer to some dark places, which is okay (even we're in our pajamas) because dark places are where crime writers feel at home.

Personally, I think writing is the best job in the world because aside from my imaginary friends, I get to spend time in person and online with some of my real friends—other crime writers. They are brilliant, creative, funny, and inspiring. They get me, and I get them. They've been where I've been, and I'm not talking Disneyland here.

I can also reach out to many of them and say I need a

great story for a crime anthology, and they respond quickly with fascinating tales of mystery and mayhem. The ten authors in this collection are good friends and great crime writers. I'm excited to share their stories with you and to also contribute one of my own. I hope you enjoy reading them as much as I did...

Paul Bishop
    North of Los Angeles
    2019

Pattern of Behavior
Paul Bishop

Pattern of Behavior started life as a spec script for a popular television series. You can probably tell which one by the structure of the story. While the script was never produced by the show for which it was designed, it did act as a strong writing example enabling me to get work on other shows. However, not wanting a good tale to go unpublished, I adapted the script to make it an original novelette for this collection. Featuring my series character L.A.P.D. homicide detective Fey Croaker, Pattern of Behavior is chronologically set after Chalk Whispers, the fourth book in the series. Like the original Fey Croaker novels, Pattern of Behavior is set in the late 90s. As such, the storyline represents the attitudes and technology relevant to the time period.

PATTERN OF BEHAVIOR

IN THE CENTER of the darkened banquet room, Anna Havilland was curled into a fetal position. Her long blonde hair was scattered across her twenty-something face, obscuring her features. Her short black skirt was rucked up around her thighs, exposing her lack of underwear or pantyhose. A rope was bound around her ankles, and a colorful man's tie secured her wrists behind her back. Across her mouth was a single slash of duct tape. A large, ornate restaurant sign proclaiming Tony V's leaned drunkenly against the wall behind her.

Whimpering, she struggled to pull her hands under her buttocks. Painfully she threaded her legs through until her hands were in front of her. She paused to rest for a few seconds—time was meaningless—before reaching up to pull the duct tape from her mouth with a swift tear. She burst into tears from the pain.

Eventually gaining control of her emotions, Anna crawled slowly toward her abandoned purse. With shaking fingers, she reached into the purse and removed her cell phone. Massive effort was required to pick out and push the proper numbers—9-1-1.

When the connection was made, a recording came on the line asking her to wait. Anna lay her head on the floor, the phone under her ear, and the recording repeated twice more. Finally, a live voice came on the line. "Operator fifteen-eighteen. What is your emergency?"

Anna sucked in a breath. "Please help me. I've been raped."

Fey Croaker sat at her desk in the Robbery-Homicide squad room and pushed keys on her computer with desultory interest.

"Do you have a minute, Fey?" The question came from Whip Whitman who was leaning out of his Captain's office at the far end of the squad bay.

Happy for any interruption, Fey stood up and grabbed her coffee cup as she left her desk. Inside Whitman's office, Whip sat in a high-backed chair behind his desk. Next to the desk stood a dark-haired man with sun-blackened skin. He was only slightly over five-six and wiry thin, but there was an inner stillness about him that was slightly spooky.

"How's your team?" Whitman asked Fey without introducing his other guest.

"What team?" Fey replied. "We still haven't replaced Hammer and Nails. Brindle and Alphabet are on vacation. And Monk is down with this damn flu."

"Situation normal, then? All screwed up?"

Whitman noticed Fey looking pointedly at the other visitor. "This is Mickey Crow," Whitman said finally. "I need you both to respond to a stranger rape on your old turf in West Los Angeles Division."

"A rape case?" Fey cut her eyes back to Whitman in surprise.

"You know that since the start of the year, RHD Rape Special has taken over city wide jurisdiction of all stranger rapes."

"Sure, but I run a homicide team."

"There's nobody available from Rape Special to handle the case. Like everyone else, they've been decimated by the flu. You don't have a team, and Mickey just transferred in. The case is down to you. Get on it."

———

FEY AND MICKEY Crow approached Officer Tina Delgado outside Tony V's restaurant. Tina's uniform shirt was pulled tight across her impressive chest, but Mickey Crow didn't appear to pay any attention. He'd talked little to Fey on the trip out from downtown. Fey had only learned he recently surfaced from a deep cover assignment with Organized Crime and Vice Division. He had nine years on the job and appeared apathetic toward his new assignment to RHD.

"How's the victim?" Fey asked Tina.

"As good as can be expected."

"She give you anything on the suspect?" Crow asked.

Tina consulted a small officers' notebook. "Male,

Caucasian, six-foot-one, two hundred pounds. Black hair, razor cut and slicked back. Paul Newman eyes—her description, not mine."

"Anything else?" Fey asked.

Tina looked back at her notebook. "The victim was coming out of a play at the Shubert last night with a female friend when the suspect approached them. He said he was a movie producer—wanted to make the victim a star."

"And she believed him?" Fey's question was rhetorical. She'd become cynically endured to the average citizen's gullibility.

"Everyone wants to be a star in this town," Delgado said. "Suspect told the victim to meet him this morning in the lobby of the Century Towers."

"How'd they get here from there?"

"Suspect told her he wanted to take some publicity stills in his studio. The victim followed him over in her own car, but once the suspect got her inside—bada-bing, bada-boom."

Fey shook her head. She looked at Crow. "You know what this country needs?"

"What's that?" Crow asked, surprisingly willing to play the straight man.

"A good twelve-step program for stupidity."

———

FEY AND CROW made their way around the building to find criminalist June Sweetwater fingerprinting the door of Tony V's back entrance. The closed restaurant occupied the lower left corner of a two-story office building. June looked up as the two detectives approached.

"Is this the POE?" Fey asked.

"Looks that way," June said with a smile for Fey. "I lifted a couple of prints from the doorknob. There's also a couple of tool marks on the jamb. Find the tool, I'll give you a match."

Crow moved forward to examine the pry marks. "You find anything inside?"

"Not much—rope from the victim's ankles, the tie used to bind her hands. The victim said the suspect used a condom, but he must have taken it with him."

"Done this before, then?" Fey said.

June shrugged. "Probably."

Crow stood back to look at the building. "How long has the restaurant been out of business?"

June shrugged again. "A couple of months. Lousy food, lousy service."

"Go figure," Fey said. "You would have thought the L.A.'s nouveau riche would embrace it."

Anna Havilland sat on a small couch in the *soft room* provided by Santa Monica Hospital's Rape Treatment Center. Vicky Torrance, the comfortable-looking rape counselor, sat next to Anna on the couch holding her hand. Fey and Crow were forced to stand as there were no other chairs in the small room.

"I know it sounds stupid," Anna told Fey and Crow. "But he was so convincing."

"Who was the friend you were with at the theatre?" Fey asked.

"Tiffany Bannister."

"Do you have her address?"

"In my purse," Anna said. She rummaged in the black leather bag on her lap and produced an address book. Crow took it and began leafing through the pages.

"Had either of you seen this guy before?" Fey asked.

"Never. He just came up to me in the parking lot and asked if I was an actress."

"Are you?"

"I've done a couple of soap opera walk-ons, but nothing major."

"This guy told you he was a producer?"

"He said I was perfect for a part in the next Mel Gibson film he was casting."

"You didn't question him," Crow cut in coldly.

Anna was close to tears. "He seemed legit—nice suit, clean cut, good jewelry."

"Did he tell you his name?" Crow asked.

"John Clark."

"He have any identification?"

"She's not a cop," Vicky Torrance interrupted, her anger showing. "Normal people don't meet somebody and ask to see their driver's license."

Fey stepped in to smooth things over. "When you met Clark in the hotel today, did you feel he was staying there?"

"I guess," Anna said. "I gave him my portfolio. He was sitting in the lobby, sorting through a bunch of papers."

"Props," said Crow.

Fey shut him up with a look. "After you left the hotel, you drove to the restaurant?"

"Actually, the front of the office building," Anna said. "He told me it was his production company. I could see movie posters on the walls through the glass doors, and the name—Lionheart Pictures."

"Why did you take your own car?"

"I'm not naive enough to come to the city without my own ride."

Fey and Crow exchanged a glance.

"How did you get into the restaurant?"

"He wanted to start taking photos in his studio around the side of the building."

"How did he open the door?"

"It was already partially open. He stood back to let me enter, but I saw it was dark. I turned back, but he shoved me inside, and then—" Anna suddenly burst into tears and buried her face into Vicky Torrance's shoulder.

Back in the Robbery-Homicide offices, Whip Whitman stood next to Fey as Crow fiddled with the remote control of an industrial VCR.

"You picked the security tape up from the hotel?" Whip asked.

"After we had an artist do a composite with the victim," Fey confirmed.

Crow finally found the right button, and the tape in the machine began to play.

"There are ten security cameras in the hotel," Crow said. "They rotate every two seconds." He suddenly froze the image on the screen. "That's the suspect. The back of him, anyway."

"And he never turns around?" Whip asked.

"Never."

"What do you think?"

"It's like he knew the cameras were there," Crow said.

"You check out the restaurant?"

Fey nodded. "The property is owned by Elgin Tremayne, the same guy behind Lionheart Pictures."

"Not John Clarke?"

Fey Shook her head. "Too easy."

"Then you better get over to Lionheart and do it the hard way."

Elgin Tremayne's office was not plush. Castoff furniture blended in functional mismatch under the framed posters of numerous B-movies. Sitting behind his desk, Tremayne was a wizened man in his seventies. His lawyer, Susan Lawrence, sat next to him like a handmaiden. Greta Martin, the Lionheart office manager, leaned against the door as Fey and Crow conducted their interview.

"Mr. Tremayne," Fey said. "The business license registry shows you own both these offices and the attached restaurant, Tony Vs."

Tremayne's voice was thin and reedy. "My company owns the property where Tony V's was located, but the restaurant was owned by two men who we are now engaged within major civil litigation. Can you tell us what this is all about?"

Fey nodded. "Were you aware somebody broke into the restaurant premises yesterday and committed a rape?"

"No! How horrible." The outburst came from Susan Lawrence.

"Didn't we change the locks on the restaurant two weeks ago, Greta?" Tremayne asked his office manager.

"Yes," Greta replied. "I have a set of keys, you have a set, and John has a set."

"John?" Crow jumped on the name. "Who's John?"

"John Clark," Tremayne said. "He's our maintenance man."

Crow slid a copy of the suspect's composite across the desk to Tremayne. "He look like this?"

"No way," Tremayne said, giving the composite a cursory glance. "He's about five foot tall, bald, and sixty. He wishes he looked like this." Tremayne picked up the composite and studied it closer. "Wait a minute," he turned to hand the paper to Susan Lawrence. "What do you think?" he asked her.

"You know this guy?" Crow asked.

"Maybe," Tremayne said. "It's the eyes, mostly."

Greta Martin moved in to take a look at the composite in Lawrence's hand. Her face paled.

"So, who is he?" Fey asked.

"His name is Rafe Vandermere," Lawrence said, putting the composite back on the table. "He's one of the men who owned Tony Vs."

"The guys you're involved in the civil litigation with?"

"Yes," Tremayne confirmed. "They stole all the ovens and other fixtures when we evicted them."

"But there's more," Lawrence said. "Vandermere has a prior record for rape."

Fey was in Whip Whitman's office bringing him up-to-speed when Crow entered with a sheaf of printouts.

"Vandermere is a registered sex offender," Crow said, handing the printout to Fey.

Putting on her glasses, Fey scanned the sheets. "Two priors for rape that stuck, and a forced oral cop arrest that bounced behind a reluctant witness."

Whip was reading over Fey's shoulder. "How'd he get nailed?"

Fey turned several pages. "Leaving the scene of the second rape, he hinked up a couple of uniforms. The M.O. tied him to the first rape, and the first victim then picked him out of a line-up."

"Can we get a quick picture to do a photo line-up with our victim?" Whip asked.

Crow held up a line-up card with six photos inside. "Already put the *six-pack* together. The victim is on her way in."

Whip gave Crow an assessing look. "Any idea where Vandermere is now?"

Crow nodded. "He and his partner, Anthony Picardi, have opened another restaurant called La Scala. Vandermere shows it as his parole address."

Whip checked his watch. "If you hurry, you can get the victim to ID and still beat the lunch crowd."

"Apache," Crow said out of the blue, as he and Fey parked down the street from the La Scala restaurant and exited their detective sedan.

"What?" Fey looked confused.

"You want to know what kind of Indian I am. Everyone does. I'm an Apache."

Fey stopped walking. "First of all, I didn't ask the question. Second, if you've got some kind of chip on your shoulder because you're an Indian, get over it if you want to work for me. And third, you aren't an Apache. Your facial structure isn't right."

Crow smiled for the first time. "How would you know?"

"All palefaces aren't stupid. I'd say you're either Creek or Iroquois."

"Iroquois with a little French thrown in," Crow said.

"Then why say you're Apache?"

"It's what everyone expects to hear."

"If I want to know something, I'll ask. And don't ever make the mistake of lumping me in with everyone."

"No," Crow said thoughtfully. "I stand corrected."

"Damn straight," Fey said. "Now, let's do this."

The two detectives crossed the street during a break in traffic.

"This guy is being served up to us like a pig on a spit," Fey worried as they approached the front of the restaurant. "It's almost too easy."

"So what? Let's put an apple in his mouth and send him back to jail. His pattern of behavior in this case is the same as the priors."

"I know," Fey said. "It all fits."

"Then what's the problem? The victim immediately picked Vandermere out of the *six-pack*. He's a predator."

"I'm not arguing, but I've still got an itch."

Crow opened the restaurant's front door and stood back. "Maybe you should try a little baby powder in your shorts," he said in a low voice as Fey passed through.

Inside, the restaurant was empty of customers. A busboy was setting tables, and a bartender was busy with his bottles. The bartender's nametag read, *Rand*.

"Sorry, folks," Rand said. "We don't open for another half hour."

"Tony or Rafe around?" Fey asked.

Rand gave them a look. "You friends or something?"

Crow smiled and extended his hand toward Rand. "Mickey Crow. How ya' doing?"

As Rand reflexively took the proffered hand, Crow tightened his grip and pulled Rand off balance across the bar.

"Hey!" Rand yelled.

"Actually," Crow said, maintaining his grip. "We ain't friends. We're the *or something*."

The busboy looked over, but Fey pointed a gun finger at him. "Relax. No problem here."

"Cops or leg breakers?" Rand asked.

"Glad you make the distinction," Crow said. "Now, are Tony or Rafe around?"

"Tony's in the back office."

"What about Rafe?"

"Not my turn to watch him."

Crow nodded to Fey, letting her make a start for the back room before releasing Rand. "Be a good boy," Crow said and patted Rand's cheek.

With Crow behind her, Fey walked briskly to the back of the restaurant and pushed open the door to a small office. Inside, Tony Picardi sat at a tiny, cluttered desk talking on a cell phone. He was in his thirties with Italian good looks. He looked up, startled, as Fey and Crow crowded in.

"What is this? No customers are allowed back here."

"What about cops?" Fey asked, displaying her badge.

"I'll call you back," Picardi said into his phone.

"Are you Anthony Picardi?" Fey asked.

"Yeah, I'm Tony. Why the roust?"

"Where's your partner—Vandermere?"

"He's at the bank. He'll be back any minute. Hey, does this have anything to do with those jerks at Lionheart?"

"Why do you think that?"

"It's the only thing we're into."

"They say you stole all their ovens and fixtures when you closed down Tony V's," Crow said.

"That's crap," Picardi said. "We didn't steal nothing. They wanted the restaurant space back, so they put us out of business. Cost us a fortune. We're suing them for breach of contract."

"Still doesn't justify grand theft," Fey said.

Suddenly, a slim, dark complexioned man opened the door to the office.

"Cops, Rafe!" Picardi yelled.

Rafe Vandermere slammed the door shut before Crow could react. Picardi stood up, forcing Fey to push him back to get room for Crow to open the door. Pulling out their guns, the two detectives ran for the front of the restaurant.

"There!" Crow yelled, pointing as Vandermere disappeared through the front door.

Fey was still running when Rand, the bartender, hip-checked a table and sent it skittering across in front of her. Colliding with the awkward object, Fey crashed to the floor. Right behind her, Crow tripped over Fey's legs and slammed down on top of her.

"Go, damn it! Go! Go!" Fey yelled as Crow scrambled back to his feet.

Dashing out the restaurant entrance, Crow pushed the hair out of his eyes to look up and down the street. There was nothing but a blur of traffic and pedestrians. No Vandermere.

———

FEY AND CROW stood in front of Whip Whitman's desk like children in the principal's office.

"I expected better from you, Fey. You were sloppy out there. If things had gone differently, you might have ended up with more than a few bumps and bruises."

"We screwed up," Fey said, defiantly. "So fire me."

Whitman looked about to burst.

"We did get Vandermere's car," Crow said, in a deflective action.

"Congratulations," Whip said, turning on the other detective. "You gonna charge it with rape?"

"We found a Jimmy under the front seat," Crow

persisted. "Forensics has matched it to the pry marks on the door to Tony Vs."

"Doesn't do you much good without Vandermere in custody."

The phone on Whitman's desk rang. He scooped it up with short, pudgy fingers.

"Whitman." He listened for a few moments. "I'll send them over," he said finally before hanging up. He sighed and gave Fey and Crow a dark look. "Somebody must be watching out for you two. That was Gerald Shultz, Vandermere's lawyer. He wants to surrender his client."

Shultz was pot-bellied, balding, and aging fast. He ushered Fey and Crow into his office. A willow blond in her thirties with sharp features was sitting in a client's chair. Shultz moved forward to make introductions.

"This is Janet Kent." Shultz indicated the blond. "She is Mr. Vandermere's civil counsel."

Kent loosened off a predatory smile. "I represent Mr. Vandermere and Mr. Picardi in their action against Lionheart Pictures."

"How nice for you," Fey said. "Where is Mr. Vandermere? We were told you wanted to surrender him."

"Why do you want to talk to my client?" Kent asked.

"We want to arrest him," Fey said blandly.

"Even if he's an innocent man?"

"Innocent men don't run from the police."

"Oh, please," Kent gave a harsh half-laugh. "Don't be ridiculous."

"Rafe Vandermere has been identified as the suspect in a rape investigation," Crow said.

"When did this alleged rape occur?" Kent asked.

"Yesterday morning."

"Where?"

"At Tony V's," Crow said. "The restaurant he owned with Anthony Picardi."

Shultz stirred himself. "Are you aware of the civil litigation surrounding that location?"

"We're aware," Fey said. "But it isn't relevant."

"Of course it's relevant," Janet Kent almost shouted. "Elgin Tremayne has already ruined my client's business. Now, he's trying to ruin my client's life."

Fey kept her voice level. "It's your client who has ruined a young woman's life."

Gerald Shultz put a restraining hand on Janet Kent's shoulder. "How can you be sure?" he asked. "Wasn't it Tremayne who pointed you at Mr. Vandermere?"

"And how would you know that?" Fey asked.

"It stands to reason," Kent told her. "I'm sure Tremayne, or one of his lackeys, told you about Rafe's prior criminal record."

"Let's stop playing games," Fey said. "Where is Vandermere?"

"Do you have a warrant for his arrest?" Shultz asked.

"We don't need one," Crow said. "We have more than enough probable cause—"

"All of it fabricated by Tremayne," Kent interrupted.

"That's for a jury to decide," Fey said. "Somehow, I don't think they're going to believe the victim is a figment of Tremayne's imagination."

Back in the RHD squad room again, Whip Whitman

had played the mountain to Mohammed and was standing by Fey's desk.

Whip scowled. "So they refused to produce Vandermere?" "All they wanted was a tip-off to what we had," Fey told him. Any ideas on where Vandermere might be?"

Crow slid a haunch onto the corner of Fey's desk. "We got

the impression Janet Kent is involved with Vandermere on

more than just a professional basis." "Are you doing anything about it?"

"We've parked surveillance on both her office and residence," Fey said.

"What about Tremayne? You think he's setting Vandermere up?"

Fey shook her head. "As a frame-up, it's far too complicated."

"The civil litigation is real enough, though," Whip said. "And the victim did tell you she's an actress."

"Are you saying you think the whole thing is a hoax?" Crow asked. There was a belligerent edge to his voice.

Whip hardened his gaze and shifted it to the new detective. "I'm saying let's make the case tight. Tomorrow, re-interview the victim and confront Tremayne with the accusations. Let's see what shakes loose." He paused for a moment, thinking. "And what about Tiffany Bannister, the friend the victim was with at the theatre. Let's see if she can pick Vandermere out of the photo line-up."

The next morning Fey and Crow arrived early at

Tiffany Bannister's apartment. Answering the door to their knock, Tiffany appeared to be in her early twenties. Her hair was tousled, and she wore a soft collar-brace around her neck. Fey and Crow identified themselves and were invited in.

"You'll have to excuse me," Tiffany said. "I look a wreck, but I'm still not used to this thing." She touched the collar at her throat.

"Traffic accident?" Crow asked.

"Yeah. My car was totaled. I'm very lucky I wasn't injured worse."

"Are you aware of what happened to your friend Anna Havilland?" Fey asked, getting down to business.

"Sure, but I still can't believe it. I told Anna the guy was handing her a line."

Crow gave Tiffany a look. "You didn't believe his producer story?"

"Come on," Tiffany said with emphasis. "Everybody in this town is a producer."

"Have you ever heard of Lionheart Pictures or Elgin Tremayne?" Fey asked.

"Who are they?"

"Doesn't matter," Fey said. "We'd like you to look at a photo line-up and see if you can pick out the man who approached you and Anna in the parking lot."

"I'll try," Tiffany said.

Crow held out the photo six-pack face down for Tiffany to take.

"Before you turn it over," Crow said, "I need to give you a legal admonition." His voice became more formal.

"A picture of the suspect may or may not be in this line-up. Remember, hairstyles and facial hair can be changed, and skin complexions can be lighter or darker than in these pictures. Do you understand?"

"Yes." Tiffany took the proffered line-up and turned it over. She ran her eyes quickly over the photos. "That's him," she said, pointing to Vandermere's photo in the number five position without hesitation.

"Are you sure?" Crow asked.

"Positive," Tiffany said. "It's the eyes."

Leaving Tiffany Bannister's apartment, Fey and Crow returned to Lionheart Pictures to re-interview Elgin Tremayne in the presence of his lawyer, Susan Lawrence.

Tremayne was into his Hollywood powerbroker intimidation mode. "We've shown you all of our employee records. Anna Havilland has never worked for Lionheart."

"I've checked with the SAG, which is something you should have done before coming here," Susan Lawrence said with condescension. "Havilland's acting career consists of six weeks' work on two different soap operas produced by the same company, neither of which has any connections to Lionheart."

"What about the allegations you put Tony V's out of business?" Fey asked. "Vandermere's lawyer claims you are now trying to frame Vandermere because of the civil suit."

"You can't possibly believe that crap," Susan Lawrence said. "It's crazy."

"What I believe doesn't matter," Fey said, calmly. "The question still has to be addressed."

"Rafe Vandermere and Tony Picardi sold us a bill of goods," Tremayne said. "There had been several other attempts to run a restaurant on the premises without success. We were going to convert the location into office space, but Rafe and Tony convinced us to rent it to them for another try as a restaurant."

Lawrence laid her hand on Tremayne's arm. "Elgin gave them all the backing he could," she said. "He provided advertising and other promotions, even used them to cater to our other business functions."

"None of it helped," Tremayne said. "There were health code violations, unhappy customers—the menu was a disaster."

"Picardi was the brains?" Crow asked.

"I don't know about brains," Tremayne said. "He was the head cook and busboy anyway. Vandermere was the showman, but he was all show and no do. We had no choice but to evict them when they consistently failed to meet their financial obligations."

"What do you intend to do with the property now?" Fey asked.

Tremayne shrugged. "When the civil suit is settled, we'll convert it to office space. Lionheart is out of the restaurant business."

From the Lionheart offices, Fey and Crow moved on to Anna Havilland's apartment. Both detectives had been thoughtful while driving to the location. However, walking through the entrance to the complex, Crow broke the silence.

"This whole set-up theory doesn't make sense. You saw the victim at the hospital. Do you believe she wasn't raped?"

"Maybe she's an Oscar class actress."

"You can't be serious?"

"No," Fey said. "But I learned a long time ago that trusting gut instinct was a loser's game. We check everybody's story out. We get proof."

They were now approaching the door to Anna's apartment when Fey saw it was slightly open. She tapped Crow's shoulder and pointed.

"Your gut instinct telling you something?" Crow asked assessing the situation. "Or do you need proof?"

"Shut up," Fey said, knowing he was right.

Approaching cautiously, Fey knocked on the door. It swung open slightly, but there was no response from inside. The two detectives drew their guns, holding them down by their sides.

"Ms. Havilland?" Fey called out. "Anna?"

Crow pushed the door open wide and stepped in. "Anna Havilland?" He called out loudly. "Police."

They walked through the small apartment. Fey checked the kitchen as Crow pushed open the door to the single bedroom. He looked inside and immediately withdrew his head.

"Fey," he called out softly.

Fey moved to his side and looked into the bedroom

for herself. Anna Havilland's body lay naked across the bed, a man's tie wrapped tightly around her throat.

Fey let out a deep sigh. "Oh, hell."

Deputy Coroner Elsie Manning talked to Fey as they stood next to the stainless steel autopsy table bearing Anna Havilland's body.

"Cause of death was definitely asphyxiation," Elsie said. She was drying her hands on a small towel.

"Any sexual trauma?" Fey asked.

Crow entered the autopsy room and came to stand next to Fey, picking up the thread of the conversation.

"None," Elsie reported. "But she did put up a struggle. I found a fair amount of skin under the nails of her left hand. There were some black beard hairs in the skin."

"So, you're saying whoever did this is walking around with a hell of a set of scratches on their face?" Crow asked.

Elsie nodded. "Best guess would be the suspect's right cheek."

Crow turned to Fey. "Surveillance just called in. They spotted Vandermere sneaking into Janet Kent's townhouse."

"Tell me they had a close enough look to see scratches on his face," Fey said.

"Got it in one," Crow said with a grim smile.

Fey and Crow quietly approached the front door of Janet Kent's darkened townhouse. Wearing bulletproof vests and raid jackets, they led the way for several other similarly clad RHD detectives. There were also two uniformed officers, one of them carrying a battering ram.

"Better knock and identify ourselves," Fey whispered as she and Crow reached the front door. "Wouldn't want to break the law."

Crow tapped ever so lightly on the front door. "Police," he whispered. "We have a search warrant." He looked at Fey.

"Better break it down," Fey said, continuing to whisper, "before they can destroy any evidence."

Crow grinned and waved to the uniformed officer carrying the battering ram.

The door to the townhouse burst open with the first swing of the heavy metal ram. Fey and Crow surged in followed by the other detectives, all with their guns drawn and ready.

"Police!" Crow yelled.

He and Fey swarmed down a short hallway and kicked open a door leading to the main bedroom. Inside, Janet Kent was pulling a sheet up to cover her nakedness. Rafe Vandermere had already rolled out of the bed and was heading for a window. Fresh scratches were visible on his right cheek. Fey's gun came unwaveringly to bear on him.

"Don't even think about it," she said through gritted teeth. "Just give me an excuse."

Vandermere froze in his tracks. Crow moved past Fey, careful to stay clear of her line of fire, and cuffed Vandermere.

"What's the meaning of this?" Janet Kent demanded.

"Search warrant, counselor," Fey said. She holstered

her gun before tossing a copy of the warrant fact sheet on the bed. "I'm sure you're familiar with the concept."

One of the other detectives entered the room. "Look what we found," he said, holding up a man's shirt with blood on the collar and Anna Havilland's acting portfolio.

"Let's go, Vandermere," Crow said, pushing his captive toward the bedroom door. "You're under arrest for the rape and murder of Anna Havilland."

Fey started to follow Crow. She looked back over her shoulder at a shocked Janet Kent. "See you in court, counselor."

————

ASSISTANT DEPUTY DISTRICT ATTORNEY Winchell Groom sat behind his desk. The office was utilitarian, much like Groom himself. Tall and rapier thin, the black skin of his shaved skull glinted under the fluorescent lighting. Arlene Lancaster, another, younger, DA leaned against the side wall watching Groom verbally fence with Gerald Shultz and Janet Kent.

"Our client is being framed by Elgin Tremayne." Kent made the statement in a fashion demanding it be taken as fact without further question.

"That's not what the evidence shows." Groom was unruffled. "Just insisting Vandermere is being framed accomplishes nothing."

Arlene Lancaster pushed herself upright with a shove of her shoulder. "Ms. Kent, is it possible your personal involvement with your client is hindering his defense?"

Gerald Shultz immediately responded before Janet Kent could get any words out. "I'm handling the criminal defense in this case. Due to the civil overtones, Ms. Kent is assisting me.

"Then you should know you need more than supposition and innuendo to support an affirmative defense," Lancaster told him. "There is a mountain of forensic, situational, and eyewitness testimony on the people's side."

"If you'd like to make a plea," Groom offered, "the people will accept murder-one with a life sentence."

"Out of the question," Kent said rising from her chair.

Shultz placed a restraining hand on her shoulder.

"We believe accepting a plea at this juncture would be premature," he said.

Groom made a gesture with his hands. "My door is always open."

Shultz stood up to follow Kent who was leaving in a huff. He almost bumped into her, however, when she turned on her heels in the doorway.

"This is far from over," Kent said, before storming on her way.

When they were out of earshot, Lancaster turned her head toward Groom. "She's wound a little tight."

"Tight enough to manufacture evidence?"

"Maybe," Lancaster said. "Perhaps we should get Croaker to find out."

Greta Martin, the office manager for Lionheart Pictures, took her coffee from the Starbucks service counter and carried it across to a small table. Fey and Crow walked across to join her.

"Hello, Greta," Fey said. "Do you remember us?"

Greta looked up. "Sure. You're the detectives."

"That's right. The district attorney's office has filed charges against Rafe Vandermere, but we need to ask you a few more questions."

Greta took a sip from her coffee. "It's a horrible situation, but what could I possibly tell you?"

Fey sat down in the chair next to Greta. "Vandermere's lawyers want us to believe Elgin Tremayne is attempting to frame their client."

"And you believe them?"

"Frankly, no. But I need to gather all the information I can about the situation, so the district attorney isn't blindsided in court."

"What do you want to know?"

Fey leaned back in her seat. This was the tricky part. "It appears to me there's more to the closing down of Tony V's than wanting to turn the space into offices."

Greta looked down at her coffee for a beat, fiddling with the cardboard holder.

"I have a good job with Lionheart," she said eventually.

"But?" Fey probed.

Greta appeared to weigh her options before continuing. Finally, she said, "Mr. Tremayne has some tax problems. He needs to sell the building. To do so, he needed to break the lease with Tony and Rafe."

"So he forced them to close down and get out?" Fey asked.

"Yes," Greta said. "But their lawyer got an injunction

stopping the sale of the building until the civil suit is settled."

"So, why doesn't Tremayne settle?"

Greta took a long swig from her cooling coffee. She put the cup down on the table. "I said Mr. Tremayne had tax problems. What I meant was he has huge tax problems."

Fey stood in the office of head filing deputy Owen Overmars. Winston Groom perched himself on the rolled arm of a leather couch next to Arlene Lancaster as Fey and Crow reported on her findings.

"We talked to an IRS investigator I know named Craven," Fey told the lawyers. "He said Tremayne is about to be put under indictment for tax evasion."

"And selling the building could forestall the situation?" Overmars asked.

"The building is Tremayne's largest asset," Crow said. "He needs to sell it before it is seized."

"Okay," Overmars said. "So you've found a reason for Tremayne to want to get Vandermere and his partner, but what good does having Vandermere in jail do him?"

Fey began to pace slowly. "What if Tremayne's best-laid plans went south on him? What if Tremayne manipulated Vandermere into attempting to rape Anna Havilland— wanting to catch him in the act?"

Winston Groom made a face. "You're thinking, if it happened that way, then maybe something went wrong and Tremayne didn't get there in time?"

Arlene Lancaster nodded her head, seeing where Fey was leading. "If Tremayne had caught Vandermere in the act, he could have forced him to drop the civil suit."

"Probably," Fey said. "Then he could sell the building and deal with his tax problems."

"Or make a run for the border," Crow said from his position leaning in the doorway.

"You have a nasty mind," Overmars told him. "But even if it was a set-up gone wrong, Vandermere is still guilty of rape at the very least."

"Only if Anna Havilland wasn't a willing partici-pant," Arlene said.

Overmars and Groom exchanged a glance as this sunk in.

"Okay," Groom said. "But how do you get from there to murder?"

Fey shrugged. "When everything went south, perhaps Anna Havilland did too. Maybe she turned on Tremayne — threatened blackmail, forcing him to kill her."

"If this was my idea," Groom said, "you'd be throwing a feminist fit."

"Maybe so," Fey said, smiling. She'd worked with Groom for a long time and liked him.

"Wait a minute," Overmars interrupted. "There's something that doesn't fit. What about the scratches on Vandermere's face?"

"We haven't got that figured yet," Fey admitted. "But give us time."

"Maybe we can let Vandermere explain," Groom said. "We'll get Shultz to agree to an interview after the arraignment."

The courthouse interview room was cold and feature-less. A scarred wooden table sat in the middle of the room surrounded by several rickety metal chairs. Owen Over-mars had suggested letting a male interview Vandermere, so Winchell Groom was sitting across the table from the prisoner. Gerald Shultz sat next to his client. Arlene Lancaster and Janet Kent hovered off to the side.

"Chicks like her are all the same," Vandermere was saying. "They'll do anything to get into the movies."

"Movies you have nothing to do with," Groom said.

"Since when is it a crime to lie to somebody to get into their pants?" Vandermere asked.

"Since you started tying them up to do it," Groom fired back.

Gerald Shultz entered the fray. "Isn't moralizing about sexual kinks between consenting adults counter-productive at this point?"

Vandermere leaned forward. "We were having fun. I didn't rape anybody, and I didn't murder anybody." There was no modesty in the man.

"Then what did happen?"

Vandermere slumped back in his chair. "When I found out about the rape charges, I knew this had to be a scam."

"Why?" Groom asked.

"Elgin Tremayne's lawyers found out about my past record. They've been trying to use it against me ever since to get the civil suit dropped."

"How did you know where Anna Havilland lived?"

"From the portfolio she gave me at the hotel. I went to

confront her, but when she opened the door and saw me, she went off the deep end—screaming and stuff."

"Let me guess," Groom said. "You grabbed her to calm her down, and she scratched your face."

"Yeah," Vandermere nodded. "And then I got the hell out. She was a psycho, but she was alive when I left."

"Your lawyers are working very hard to convince us you've been framed," Groom said. "But as far as I'm concerned it's a pretty pathetic effort."

Vandermere's eyes flashed. "I swear I didn't kill the girl."

"You've admitted to raping her. If you didn't kill her, who did?"

"Wait a minute," Shultz jumped in. "Mr. Vandermere has not admitted to rape."

"I told you," Vandermere said. "The sex was consensual. Kinky maybe, but consensual. She asked to be tied up."

"No jury is going to buy that line," Groom said.

"She thought she could get into the movies by taking care of me," Vandermere insisted.

"Where did she get the idea you ran a casting couch?"

"Beats me." Vandermere's grin was goading.

"But you didn't dissuade her?"

"Would you?"

"Yes, I would," Groom said. After a pause, he resumed. "So, what happened next?"

"I told her to meet me Sunday in the lobby of the Century Towers. When I suggested we go and take some pictures, she jumped at the idea."

"Why did you go to Tony V's?"

"I live in a room over the new restaurant. Like I'm really going to take a chick there."

"Okay, so what happened at Tony V's?"

"The locks had been changed, so I jimmied the door. Then I waited out front."

"How did Anna react when there weren't any cameras?"

"She didn't. She knew the score."

"What score? Sex now, movie part later?"

"Hey, she got into it. Anything I wanted. When I was done, I split."

"Quite the gentleman."

Vandermere shrugged. "I didn't need no grief."

Groom pushed open the door to his office, allowing Arlene to enter ahead of him.

"I don't get the point," Arlene was saying. "You could tell Vandermere was lying. His lips were moving."

"The point is, Shultz wants us to drop the murder charge and offer a plea on the rape."

"On the basis of their dreamed-up conspiracy?" Arlene was offended. "Vandermere hasn't even copped to the rape yet."

"Come on," Groom said. "You were there—that's what they were hinting around."

"You think they're that desperate?"

"Don't you? We go with what we've got, and a jury will slam-dunk Vandermere. It's going to take a magician to produce an affirmative defense."

Arlene pursed her lips. "I'm not so sure. I'd like to ask Croaker to take a direct run at Elgin Tremayne."

"You're asking her to spend ten dollars on a five dollar job. Go with what we have and move on."

"Not yet. I want to be sure Tremayne isn't a card hidden up the defense's sleeve."

While Crow did his usual supporting the wall trick, Fey sat opposite Elgin Tremayne at one end of a low couch in Tremayne's office. Susan Lawrence was also present. Fey fleetingly wondered if Lawrence and Tremayne were sleeping together despite their thirty-plus-year age difference.

"Sure I've got tax problems," Tremayne said in response to Fey's question. "Doesn't everybody in business?"

"Not everybody is about to be indicted by the IRS," Fey said.

"We are prepared to deal with any tax evasion allegations," Lawrence said with a lawyer's glib assurance.

"I would love to sell the building," Tremayne said. "It would free up a lot of cash, but the civil injunction is not the end of the world."

"No?" Crow asked bluntly. "I hear your company is in the dumper."

"All independent film companies are in the dumper," Tremayne assured him with a chuckle. "At least until the next deal comes along. It's typical Hollywood book-keeping."

"I take it, you have the next deal?" Fey asked.

"I have three straight-to-video teen sex-and-slasher

flicks ready for release." Tremayne scattered a collection of stills onto the glass top of the coffee table in front of the couch. Fey leaned forward to examine them.

"Not exactly material for the art house circuit," she said.

"Who cares as long as they make money?" Tremayne came back.

Susan Lawrence touched the photos before adding her comments. "Overseas feature release will recoup the production costs. Domestic, Canadian, and video sales are pure profit."

"The IRS bloodsuckers know the money is coming," Tremayne said. "They're simply saber rattling to make sure they get their share."

Fey picked up one of the stills and studied it. "Is that who I think it is?" she asked Crow, handing him the photo.

Crow grunted in recognition.

"What's the matter?" Tremayne asked.

Crow handed him the photo. Susan Lawrence moved around to look over Tremayne's shoulder.

"Is that a photo of Tiffany Bannister?" Crow asked.

"Yes, that's Tiffany," Tremayne said. "Terrible actress, but big boobs. She gets impaled on a marlin spike halfway through Hatchet Harvest."

Fey and Crow returned with their bounty to Owen Overmars' office. Winchell Groom and Arlene Lancaster were summoned to join them.

"Tiffany Bannister is the girl who went to the theatre with Anna Havilland," Fey explained.

"How did you recognize her?" Overmars asked. He was looking at the publicity still Fey had brought from Tremayne's office.

"You're a guy. You're only looking at her exposed chest," Fey said. "It's her hair."

"Her hair?" Overmars asked.

"It's a girl thing," Fey said. "I've been thinking about getting my hair cut, and her hairstyle in the photo caught my eye."

Arlene Lancaster laughed. "You go, girl. I know exactly what you're saying."

Fey smiled. "When we interviewed Bannister, her hair was a mess, and she wore no makeup. She wore a soft collar around her neck from a recent car accident. I wouldn't have recognized her as the actress in the publicity still if I hadn't been sure I'd seen the hairstyle before."

"Where?" Groom asked.

Fey picked up a remote control and pointed it at a TV/ VCR set-up on a shelf in the corner of the office. "Watch," she said, and pressed the play button.

The screen of the television lit up with the video of the security tape from the Century Towers Hotel.

Crow suddenly moved forward. "There," he said, pointing.

Fey froze the frame. "That's her standing off to the side. Anna and Vandermere couldn't have seen her, but the camera picked her up from the opposite angle."

"I still don't see how you recognized her," Overmars said.

"I didn't until after I saw her hairstyle in the publicity still. It's done the same way on the security video."

"Talk about magic tricks," Arlene said.

"There's more," Fey said.

"I can't wait," Overmars told her.

"We checked on Tiffany's traffic accident. There was a report at West Traffic because of the injuries. It occurred the day of the rape after the time on the hotel security video," Fey said.

"Where?" Groom asked, knowing the answer.

"Halfway between the Century Towers and Tony Vs."

Fey and Crow had convinced a reluctant Tiffany Bannister to talk to them at her apartment. Tiffany sat on the couch wearing her neck brace. Fey went straight for the jugular.

"Tiffany, can you explain your presence in the lobby of the Century Towers Hotel on the day Anna Havilland was raped?"

"I wasn't—"

Crow held up the security video. "Before you answer, we should explain that you appear on the lobby videotape."

Tiffany looked shocked and took in a deep breath. Tears burst from her eyes.

"Anna wasn't supposed to get raped. I thought I could stop him."

"What do you mean?" Fey asked.

Tiffany sniffled. "When Rafe approached us in the

theatre parking lot, he didn't recognize me. He only had eyes for Anna."

"You knew him?"

"We'd never been introduced, but I'd eaten at Tony V's with some of the cast from Hatchet Harvest. They all knew about his rape convictions, it was common gossip, and Rafe told me to stay away from him."

"What happened in the parking lot?" Crow asked.

"Rafe laid this crap on Anna about being a producer. I told her he was feeding her a line, but she thought I was jealous."

"Why didn't you tell her about his rape record?"

"I don't know. I thought—"

"Yes?" Crow pushed.

"I knew Mr. Tremayne was having problems with Rafe. I thought I could follow them. If Rafe tried to rape Anna, I could video it, and then stop it before it went too far."

"Why?" Fey asked.

Tiffany cried even harder, her words difficult to understand through the flow. "I thought—" she gasped for breath. "I thought, I could trade the tape to Mr. Tremayne for a big part in his next film."

Fey ran her hands through her hair as she slid into the passenger side of the detective sedan after leaving Tiffany Bannister's apartment.

"Why does everyone in this town want to be rich and famous?"

"Don't you?" Crow asked. He started the car and pulled away from the curb.

"No," Fey said. "And certainly not like that. Can you imagine allowing a friend to be set-up by a known rapist?"

"She was blinded by ambition," Crow said. "She thought she could stop the action before it got out of hand."

"It was already out of hand."

Crow looked over at Fey. "She certainly didn't plan on getting into an accident on the way to the rescue."

"I can't believe you're defending her."

"I'm not. I just don't see how it changes anything. Tremayne didn't put Tiffany up to the ruse. The set-up was Tiffany's own decision."

"And we've still got a rape and a murder," Fey agreed reluctantly, seeing the point.

"And Vandermere is still elected to take the fall," Crow concluded.

"For the rape anyway," Fey said.

"What?" Crow asked. "Now, you think somebody else committed the murder. For Heaven's sake, who?"

"The woman scorned," Fey said.

"Janet Kent? You must be kidding?"

————

ARLENE LANCASTER and Whip Whitman stood next to Fey's desk in the squad room. Fey was flipping through files.

"I knew all along this case was too easy," Fey said. "But would anybody listen to me?"

"Do you have anything at all to tie Kent to the murder?" Arlene asked.

Fey held up a sheaf of papers in triumph. "Maybe," she said. "This is the surveillance log from the team that was staking out Kent's residence. When they spotted Vandermere, they called us in, but it took us a while to get there and get organized."

Fey handed the log to Arlene, who began thumbing through it.

"And?" Arlene asked, not immediately seeing the significance.

"Look at the last page," Fey said. "Guess who arrived thirty minutes after Vandermere."

Arlene stared at the page. "Janet Kent."

"She could have followed Vandermere to Anna Havilland and murdered her after he left," Fey suggested. "Setting Vandermere up to take a murder rap in revenge for cheating on her."

"Pretty sick," Arlene said. "Murder the rape victim to punish the rapist."

"In her warped mind, she could have decided Havilland led Vandermere on," Whitman said. Fey never ceased to amaze him with the convolutions of the cases she became involved in.

Arlene nodded. "So, you're saying Kent blamed Havilland for luring Vandermere back into his known pattern of behavior?"

"Stranger things have happened," Fey said.

Crow suddenly entered the squad room, waving a file folder.

"Bingo," he said as he approached the gathering.

"You got something?" Whitman asked.

"Latents compared Janet Kent's prints to all unidentified prints from the crime scene, and they matched ten points on two prints as belonging to Kent."

"We need sixteen matching points for court," Arlene said.

"But you only need eight points to actually identify somebody. With ten points, we may not be able to go to court, but we know the prints belong to Kent."

"So you've only got half a bingo," Whitman said. "No sixteen points, no court."

"Still," Fey said. "Coupled with the surveillance log, we've got enough probable cause to haul Kent in."

Arlene smiled. "Sounds as if she's going to need a good lawyer."

Outside of the courtroom the following day, Arlene Lancaster approached Gerald Shultz. She matched him stride for stride as they walked.

"Busy day?" she asked.

"I've been like a long-tailed cat in a room full of rocking chairs," Shultz said.

"Did Kent and Vandermere come to you as a package?" Arlene asked.

"She brought the case to me," Shultz said. "But she wanted to stay involved because of the civil side."

"Her personal relationship with Vandermere causing you problems?"

Shultz stopped walking. "Where is this leading?"

"Humor me," Arlene said.

Shultz shrugged. "Okay, Kent's in love with the guy. Actually, obsessed would be a better word. I don't see it myself, but I guess the guy's got something."

"Is she advising Vandermere to fight the murder charge, even with all the evidence stacked against him?"

"Despite his record," Shultz said, "she refuses to even consider Vandermere might be guilty."

"What does he say?"

"He's not admitting to the murder if that's what you mean."

"What about you?" Arlene asked.

Shultz looked at her evenly. "Don't get me wrong, counselor. I do my best for my clients. But if it were up to me, I'd plead the bastard out and move on."

"What if I told you he didn't murder Havilland?"

"If not him, then who?"

"Kent."

Shultz's eyes widened in surprise.

Arlene sat in Owen Overmars' office discussing the case with Overmars and Groom.

"Shultz doesn't like the courtroom. He's a deal maker. He'll get Vandermere to testify against Kent in return for an offer on the rape charge."

"Did Vandermere know or suspect Kent killed Havilland?" Overmars asked.

"No," Arlene said. "But with hindsight, he's able to fill in a lot of the blanks."

"What does Shultz want on the rape?" Groom asked.

"Felony sexual battery—three to five, no strike."

"He's kidding, right?" Overmars was scornful. "Vandermere is a twice-convicted rapist."

"The question was what does Shultz want, not what will he settle for."

"Okay," Overmars said. "So, what will he settle for?"

Arlene tilted her head slightly in thought. "One count of rape. Vandermere serves eighty-five percent of a twelve-year sentence."

"What about the third strike problem?" Groom asked.

"Retrospective record amendment," Arlene said. "Change the first rape conviction to sexual battery."

Overmars fiddled with a cold pipe. "That makes this case only a second strike. It's a good deal for him."

"It's only worth it if Vandermere can make our case," Groom said.

"I'm holding the third strike over his head," Arlene said. "We don't get Kent—Vandermere doesn't get his record amended. He strikes out and gets life."

Overmars set his pipe down on his desk. "Make sure you don't open the door for Kent's defense to bring in Vandermere's record. You're also going to have trouble with the fingerprint evidence."

"Court wouldn't be fun without a challenge," Arlene said.

"Kent say anything to Croaker when she was arrested?"

"Nothing you could repeat in church. She lawyered up immediately."

"Who?" Groom asked.

"Bernie Easterbrook."

"He's a heavy hitter. He'll fight you right from the preliminary hearing."

"That's why I want to avoid it. I want to take the case to the grand jury, get an indictment, and go straight to trial."

Arlene Lancaster had checked her new suit several times before going into court. The skirt was long enough not to offend the women on the jury but short enough to give the men a glance at her nicely shaped legs. The white blouse under the well-cut jacket was tight across the bust but revealed no cleavage. Some days it pissed her off that she had to be more worried about how she looked than how strong of a case she could present, but juries were notorious for turning against the evidence based on their like or dislike of either attorney.

Fey had also dressed carefully as she was to sit next to Lancaster as the investigating officer in the case. Her role was more supportive at this point. The investigation was over.

The courtroom was Lancaster's playground.

Officer Jim Breland was on the stand being questioned by Arlene. He was young and wore a hip suit, which would have looked better at a nightclub. On the bench, Judge Julia Faversham presided over the proceedings from behind heavily hooded eyes.

"Officer Breland, what is your occupation and assignment?"

"I'm a police officer assigned to LAPD's Special Intelligence Services' surveillance unit."

"On the day Anna Havilland was murdered, were you surveilling the defendant's residence?"

"Yes."

"Previous testimony by the coroner has established the time of Anna Havilland's death as approximately four p.m. Please tell us what your log shows happening at five-thirty."

Breland briefly checked the notes on the counter in front of him.

"The subject identified as Rafe Vandermere approached the door of the residence on foot and entered through the rear door."

"Was there anything strange about his appearance?" Arlene asked.

"Several prominent scratches on his right cheek were noted."

"Now, please tell us what your log notes reflect for six p.m."

"The defendant, Janet Kent, parked her car in front of the residence and entered through the front door using a key."

"Anything unusual about her appearance?"

"She appeared upset and disheveled."

"Objection!" Bernie Easterbrook had risen to his feet to earn his fee. He was solid and senatorial. His mass of silver hair set off with piercing green eyes drew many a younger woman to him. "Calls for speculation."

"Sustained." Judge Faversham waved a hand slightly from her position on the bench.

"Prior to six p.m.," Arlene continued, "did you see the defendant at the residence?"

"We saw her leave shortly before noon. We didn't see her again until she returned at six."

"No further questions," Arlene said. She walked around the edge of the prosecution desk holding the original SIS surveillance log. "We would ask that the surveillance log be marked as people's seven."

"So marked," Faversham said, as Arlene handed the log to the court clerk.

Arlene sat down and whispered to Fey, "I miss anything?"

"Not so far," Fey told her. She then sat back as Bernie Easterbrook rose for cross-examination.

"Officer Breland, is there anything unusual in somebody leaving their house at noon and not returning until six?" Bernie's voice was full and measured.

"I guess not," Breland said.

"Did you ever see Ms. Kent anywhere else? At the market? The mall?"

"No."

"Have you ever seen Ms. Kent anywhere even remotely close to Anna Havilland's residence?"

"No."

Bernie smiled. "No further questions."

Arlene called latent print technician June Sweetwater as her next witness. After establishing Sweetwater's credentials and expertise, Arlene got quickly to the point.

"How many latent prints did you recover from the scene of the murder?"

"Twenty-seven," Sweetwater reported.

"How many of those were positively identified?"

"Fifteen."

"At some point, did you compare the remaining unidentified prints to the defendant's fingerprints?"

"Objection!" Easterbrook was on his feet again. "The prosecution is attempting to force in evidence that may be unfairly prejudicial to my client by its nature."

Judge Faversham's heavy eyelids moved a fraction upward. "Ms. Lancaster?"

"I'm simply trying to establish possibilities, your honor."

"We'll take a fifteen-minute recess," Faversham said, with a bang of her gavel. "Counselors, my office."

Inside Faversham's chambers, Arlene Lancaster and Bennie Easterbrook sat in uncomfortable, straight-back chairs.

Easterbrook was elucidating his objection. "To serve as identifying evidence in a criminal matter, a fingerprint must have sixteen points of identification."

"Do you have sixteen points, Ms. Lancaster?" the judge asked.

"No," Arlene said. "Only ten, which is two more than needed in a civil case."

"It's still six points short for criminal proceedings," Faversham pointed out.

"Two of the recovered prints each matched ten points with those of the defendant," Arlene explained. "The matching points of the two prints, however, are different. Combined, the two prints match seventeen points with the defendant."

Easterbrook snorted. "Seventeen points from two prints does not equal sixteen matching points from one print."

"He's right," Faversham said. "You don't have criminal ID from either singular print."

"I'm not trying to get a positive ID," Arlene said. "I simply want to show the possibility that the prints could belong to the defendant."

Easterbrook disagreed. "They could also come from somebody else. It's prejudicial to allow the comparison testimony."

"There are precedents for allowing the admission of partial prints in both Hays-versus-California, and Denniston-versus-Ohio," Arlene pointed out.

"Denniston was overturned on appeal," Easterbrook said.

"Yes," Arlene agreed, "but not on the print evidence."

"Both of you settle down," Faversham said. "I understand your feelings, Mr. Easterbrook, but I'm familiar with Ms. Lancaster's cites. As long as she doesn't claim positive ID, you can argue the significance of the ten points with the jury."

Back in the courtroom, Arlene started in again with June Sweetwater.

"Did you compare the defendant's fingerprints to the twelve unidentified latents from the crime scene?"

"Yes."

"And what did you determine?"

"Two of the twelve unidentified prints had ten matching points of identification with the defendant's prints."

"Not enough for a criminal ID?" Arlene asked, trying to steal Easterbrook's thunder.

"No," Sweetwater agreed.

"But enough for a civil identification?"

"Objection!" Easterbrook was on his feet again.

"Sustained," Judge Faversham said. "You're dangerously close to the edge, Ms. Lancaster."

"No further questions," Arlene said. She sat down quickly and gave Fey a smile.

Easterbrook had remained standing. He began his cross-examination.

"Isn't it true you need sixteen matching points to positively identify a print in a criminal case?"

"Yes," Sweetwater replied, unruffled. She had testified in hundreds of other cases.

"So," Easterbrook said. "Ten points doesn't cut it?"

"The odds—" Sweetwater began.

Easterbrook interrupted quickly. "Your honor, the question calls for a yes or no response."

"Answer yes or no," Faversham directed the witness.

"No," Sweetwater said sourly.

Easterbrook smiled. "Therefore, the two prints with the ten matching points of identification are worthless for identification in this courtroom, aren't they?"

"Correct." Sweetwater sighed. She'd seen this coming.

"You can't prove they belong to my client, can you?"

"No."

"As far as this court is concerned, they could belong to anyone?"

"Yes."

"No further questions," Easterbrook said and sat down.

"Any re-cross?" Faversham asked.

"No, your honor," Arlene said.

"Then call your next witness."

Arlene put Rafe Vandermere on the stand. This was make-it-or-break-it time. From her seat at the prosecution counsel's table, Fey turned to look at Janet Kent. She was pleased to see her previously calm exterior beginning to wear around the edges. Kent was looking anywhere except at Vandermere. She was uncomfortable and agitated. Maybe we're getting somewhere, Fey thought.

"During the time you lived with Janet Kent, were you ever unfaithful to her?" Arlene asked Vandermere.

"Sure," he replied in his cocky manner.

"And was she aware of these wanderings?"

"Objection!" Easterbrook broke in. "Calls for speculation."

"Sustained," the judge agreed.

"Did the defendant ever accuse you of being unfaithful?" Arlene restated her question.

"She accused me of screwing anything that would hold still long enough, and we'd fight about it. She'd threaten to kill me and whoever I was screwing."

Fey saw Janet Kent start to stand. She was immediately restrained by Easterbrook and subsided back into her chair.

"What else did the defendant do as a result of her accusations?" Arlene continued.

"She started to follow me," Vandermere said. "I'd lose her if I had something going on the side, but it just caused more arguments."

"What happened when Anna Havilland made accusations against you?"

"I went to confront her."

"Did you see the defendant following you?"

"Yeah, but I didn't care. I wasn't going over there to fool around. I wanted to get the Havilland bitch off my back."

"Was Anna Havilland alive when you left her?"

"Absolutely."

"And did you see the defendant when you left the victim's residence?"

Vandermere nodded. "She was sitting in her car, which was parked across the street."

"Why did you live with the defendant if you felt the need for other women?"

"She was paying the bills."

Vandermere smirked at Janet Kent, making the woman squirm in her seat. Fey could see Kent was on the boil.

"That's not very honorable," Arlene said to Vandermere.

"She knew I was a scorpion when she met me," Vandermere said.

"What does that mean?"

"You know. The story about the scorpion who convinces the frog to give him a ride across the pond?"

"Enlighten us."

"The frog refuses, saying the scorpion will sting him. The scorpion promises he won't. Finally, the frog agrees, but halfway across the pond, the scorpion stings the frog. As they're both dying, the frog asks the scorpion why. The scorpion says, 'You knew I was a scorpion when you gave me the ride—you knew I would sting you.' It was the frog's fault, not the scorpion's," Vandermere concluded.

Janet Kent jumped up from her chair, out of control.

"I loved you, you bastard!" she screamed. "But you couldn't keep it in your pants!"

Judge Faversham began banging her gavel in earnest as the courtroom erupted.

Bernie Easterbrook was sitting in Owen Overmars' office with Fey, Arlene Lancaster, Overmars, and Winchell Groom.

"You don't play fair, Ms. Lancaster," Bernie said. "You worked my client over deliberately."

"My heart bleeds," Arlene said.

"It doesn't matter what her provocation," Owen Overmars stepped in. "Janet Kent is guilty of murder."

"We'll plead to man-two."

"No way," Overmars said. "Murder-one. No special circs."

Easterbrook shook his head. "You don't want this to go to a jury. Premeditation isn't even in the ballpark. Manslaughter-one. Eight years."

"Murder-two," Overmars shot back. "Twelve to fifteen."

"I can sell ten to twelve," Easterbrook said.

Overmars glanced up at Fey and Arlene. They both nodded agreement.

"Deal," Overmars said.

After Easterbrook left, Arlene and Fey walked out together toward the elevator.

"We got away with one," Fey said.

"Sometimes, you have to take your chances," Arlene agreed.

"I wonder if we don't push our luck too often," Fey said.

Arlene smiled. "Hey, they knew we were scorpions when they hired us."

Chuckling, Fey followed Arlene into the elevator.

No Chips, No Bonus
Ben Bolden

Reporter, columnist, novelist, teacher, and history maven, Ben Boulden and I first came to know each other via a shared love of vintage western paperbacks. We quickly found we also admired a number of the same mystery/crime writers, such as Ed Gorman, Garry Disher, Joe Ide, and Ralph Dennis. From this basis, our friendship grew, and I was delighted when Ben began to find publishing success. His short novel *Merrick*, a hybrid crime-western-heist story, is excellent and I look forward to more of Merrick's adventures. Ben's story in this anthology is a prime example of the type of tale he does best...

NO CHIPS, NO BONUS

I WAS AWAKENED BY BOBBY HELMS' singing *Jingle Bell Rock*. An ironic ringtone because it was July and the only jingling I'd heard in months was the simulated sound of coins cascading from slots that were programmed tighter than a billionaire's wallet.

"Ford? You awake?" Jenkins' voice booming in my ear.

"Sure, I'm awake." My eyes were still closed.

"We have a problem." Jenkins was tense. A quaver of anticipation and fear and something else I couldn't label whisked into a frothy hum I imagined his imported girls heard every time he unzipped his pants.

"We?"

A gulping sound. "Yeah, *we*. The casino's been hit."

I sat up, my eyes opened. The bedsheets tumbled to the floor. Jenkins owned and operated The Desert Diamond. A casino on the Utah-Nevada border. I was his trained dog on retainer as a security consultant and general troubleshooter. A relationship I despised but was dependent on since no one else wanted me.

I said, "When?"

"A couple hours ago. Sixty grand. He—"

"Chips or cash?"

"Chips from the VIP room."

"You know who did it?"

The fat man coughed, wheezed.

"You going to tell me, or do I guess?"

"His name's Tyler Watts." Jenkins' voice, for once, sounded embarrassed, almost contrite.

"Watts?" I looked at the ceiling, its cottage cheese dirty and gray. "The kid I did the background check on? The junkie? The one I told you not to hire?"

Silence.

"But you hired him anyway?"

Jenkins cleared his throat of what sounded like a game hen. "Shit, Ford, it was drugs. If we don't hire because they use drugs, who the hell are we going to hire?"

The kid was a felon. Instead of calling Jenkins an idiot, I rubbed my eyes. "You call the cops?"

"No."

"Why?"

The digital line was quiet as death.

"The kid is my sister's nephew," Jenkins finally said. "I was hoping we could work this robbery off-the-books."

It was my turn for silence. *Off-the-books* made me nervous. Jenkins made me nervous. The way he operated his gambling empire like J. Edgar Hoover was still sitting in the FBI's big chair. But Jenkins had ignored my past, and since he was my only client, he paid my rent and bought my groceries.

"A $5,000 bonus if you bring Tyler and the chips to me on the quiet," Jenkins said, his voice tentative and unsure.

The offer made me more suspicious. Jenkins was a stingy bastard. "I can do this on retainer," I said. "It's part of the job."

"I pay for good service, Ford. If you do this—quietly, you'll be rewarded."

"Since when do you pay for anything? You stiff the carpet cleaners every month." I paused, annoyed because I'd already mentally spent the bonus on a new transmission for my worn-out Impala.

Jenkins didn't respond.

I finally asked, "Any witnesses?"

The fat man chuckled, sounding like he was back in charge—and he was.

He said, "You know Gina Sanchez?"

"She works the night shift in the VIP room?"

The line went dead.

———

THIRTY MINUTES LATER, I was showered and dressed in my regulation navy-blue FBI suit. The same one I'd worn for fifteen years as a Special Agent. A matching white oxford and a blue necktie. I walked into *Café Storm*, a tropical themed coffee shop in The

Diamond's back corner. It was mostly empty at five am, but Gina, a slim redhead with a bright smile, gave the place more life than it deserved. She waved me over to her table beneath a palm tree. Before I could say good morning to Gina, a tanned twenty-something with long black hair, a bikini top, and a grass skirt appeared and asked if I wanted anything.

"Coffee. Black."

The grass skirt said, "Sure thing, Mr. Ford."

To Gina, I said, "You okay?"

"You bet." A dimple revealed itself in her left cheek when she smiled, and at the moment, she was beaming.

"Okay, Gina, tell me about the robbery."

Gina waited for the grass skirt to set my coffee on the bamboo table and leave before saying, "Tyler had been acting weird all night."

"Weird, how?"

Gina frowned, an expression as alluring as her smile. "I thought he was high. All jumpy and wired."

"Do you think he planned to steal the chips last tonight?"

The green and brown of her eyes danced in the café's phony tropical light. "Maybe." She looked down at the table. "But it may have been opportunity."

"Something happen that gave Tyler an opening to take the chips?"

Gina shook her head and looked at me. "A normal Monday night. Quiet. The last group was gone, and we were closing. The doors were locked, and I was cleaning behind the bar while Tyler vacuumed the main room."

I nodded and held her eyes with mine. "Okay, tell me what happened."

———

SHE'D GONE into the storage room behind the bar to lock up the liquor. When she came back, Tyler was at the main table, the security drawer open, chips in one hand and a black duffel in the other.

Gina said, "What are you doing, Tyler?"

A blood vessel in Tyler's temple bounced. "I—" The skinny kid then shrugged and dumped the chips into the bag.

"Tyler?"

A small automatic appeared in his right hand. "I'm sorry, Gina. You been real nice to me."

"You can't walk out of here, Tyler." Gina's breath caught in her chest. "Security will be here any minute for the chips."

Tyler's eyes slid to the closed double doors. "I have to, Gina. I'm sorry."

He pointed the automatic at Gina's head, dropped the duffel on the floor, and pulled two black plastic cable ties from his pocket. On shaking legs, Tyler took a small step toward Gina. "I don't want to hurt you, but I have to do this."

"Why?" Gina said.

Tyler tossed the plastic ties. They landed at Gina's feet. "Pick them up, please."

She did.

"Put one through the post on the bar and fasten it around your wrist."

When Gina was done, Tyler scurried forward and tightened the cable a notch past comfortable. He grabbed Gina's left wrist and bound it to the same brass pole running beneath the bar.

———

GINA'S FACE WAS WEARY, her smile gone. "Tyler emptied the drawer and walked out."

I placed my hand on top of hers. "You're sure he said, 'I have to do this?' He used the phrase 'have to?'"

A tear glistened in Gina's eye. I thought I knew why.

"Was the security drawer locked?"

Gina looked down. She was the only employee on duty with access to the drawer. "No."

"It's supposed to be locked, right?"

She looked up with wet eyes. "Yes, but I asked Tyler to lock it while I secured the alcohol behind the bar."

I let go of her hand and leaned back in the uncomfortable chair. "It's not unusual for you to give Tyler access to the chip drawer?"

Gina shook her head, her red hair exotic in the warm light. "I do it sometimes when I want to get home in a hurry."

We both knew she could be fired for breaking security protocols, but her eyes never left mine. "I have to ask, Gina. Are you involved?"

"No." Her voice was strong.

"Did you know about it?"

"No, Jimmy. I didn't know anything. I swear."

I believed her.

"Did Tyler ever tell you about his friends?"

Gina tried to smile, a tear running down her cheek. "Sometimes."

She gave me two names.

As I stood to leave, she grabbed my hand. "Will I lose my job?"

"That's Jenkins' call."

Gina had a sixteen-year-old and a three-month-old granddaughter at home. As I walked out of the *Storm* and into the casino's early morning clatter, I felt Gina watching me. And damned if I didn't feel a sadness for the woman, and something like responsibility.

————

THE FIRST NAME on Gina's list was a junkie with a Utah address. An old aluminum trailer with rust dripping from its roof like stalactites. It was on a narrow lot between Scobie Road and the east-west train tracks. Across the road's cracked asphalt, a dirt parking lot was jammed with oxidized semi-trailers, and a little farther south, a pink-sided diner huddled at the desert's edge. Its parking lot was empty.

I navigated the broken glass and blackened knee-high weeds to the front porch. A well-traveled path curled around the back and across the tracks to a casino. The stairs wobbled and creaked. On the small landing, no more than three feet by three feet, I stopped and listened. There was nothing other than the wind and I-80's rumbling traffic.

I raised my hand to knock but thought better of it. Instead, I eased the .38 from beneath my jacket and with my other hand twisted the doorknob until it clicked. The door swung open. A refrigerator humming. The acrid smell of human waste slapped me. I gagged, my eyes watering. I covered my nose and mouth with a cupped hand and stepped inside.

A humped shadow materialized against the room's back wall. When my eyes adjusted to the pale darkness, the shadow became a woman. Her head was propped against the tattered couch, and her legs were sprawled wide across the filthy carpet. Her left arm was tied-off with rubber surgical tubing, and an empty syringe discarded next to her on the floor. Her face calm and peaceful, almost beautiful in the trailer's fuzzy light.

I walked into the small kitchen. The sink and gold-flecked counters were cluttered with dishes and garbage. The smell was worse—acrid and dank. The floor was sticky. A dust-covered painting of Jesus hung crookedly on one wall. At the back, there was an opening half covered with a torn accordion door.

On tip-toes, I moved across the kitchen and eased the door the rest of the way open on its track. I peeked inside. Dust particles floated in the tepid light and filtered through broken blinds. On the bed, a sleeping man was curled into a ball. His long hair was stringy and damp. His left arm tied-off, the same as the girl's.

In the corner, flies swarmed above a five-gallon bucket. The sides were stained black, and the smell of the sewer reeked from it. I retched, my mouth and throat scorching.

I holstered my gun and walked back to the kitchen, where I found a plastic pitcher, its bottom clogged with a green-black sludge. At the tap, I filled the pitcher, then pushed a pile of garbage onto the floor, and set it on the counter. I checked that the girl was still dreaming and went back to the bedroom.

I wrenched the kid off the bed and his head bounced on the floor with a thud. He whimpered, but his eyes stayed closed. I dragged him onto the kitchen's gray linoleum and nudged him with my shoe. When he didn't stir, I poured water on his face.

The kid gagged and coughed. He raised a defensive hand over his face. His eyes popped open. When he saw me, the kid froze. His mouth wide, his pupils jumping.

I smiled.

He said, "What—"

I slapped his face hard enough to let him know I was real and not a drug-induced specter.

He gasped.

"What, man? What do you want?"

I walked to the sink and filled the pitcher again and splashed it over his head.

The kid coughed, water cascading from his open mouth.

I kneeled next to him. My hand balled into a fist. "You awake, Zachery?"

Zachery flinched. "Don't hurt me, man. Please. Whatever you want, man, please—"

I said, "Have you seen Tyler Watts?"

The kid's eyes danced, his pupils small and hard. "Who?"

I leaned down and showed him my hand and touched his nose with a finger.

He shuttered, the fear plain on his face.

"This can work easy or hard, Zachery. You're in control. Anything that happens here is on your head." I pointed to the girl sleeping in the other room. "What's her name?"

"Hey, man, don't hurt her. She's got nothing to do with this."

"She's got nothing to do with what, Zachery?"

He said, "You're looking for Tyler?"

I pushed a toe into his ribs.

"Holy—"

I touched his nose again. "You need to focus Zachery. That's what they call you, right? Zachery, not Zach?"

"Sure, man. That's my name. But listen, I haven't seen Tyler in a few days. Maybe a week. We're not friends, really. At least not since his old man sent him away to that clinic in Salt Lake. He's like, working at a casino. The fancy one, you know, The Desert Diamond."

Once Zachery started talking, he couldn't shut up. He told me everything. "There's these two guys. They wanted Tyler to do something, something big. It had to do with the fat guy who runs the place. You know him, the fat guy, right?"

The fat guy was my boss, Jenkins.

"You know him, right?"

"Sure, the guy who runs The Diamond. But we seem to be stuck here, Zachery. What does the fat guy have to do with Tyler?"

Zachery squirmed. His eyes closed. "They had some pictures, man."

"What pictures?"

Zachery looked over at the girl on the floor. "The fat guy and Jess."

I pulled his face back to me. "The pictures."

"The fat guy and Jess."

"Doing what, Zachery?"

"You know, man. They were..." He paused to look at the girl still dreaming on the floor. A silver tear on his cheek. "The fat guy, he trades dope for sex, man. He has a thing for Jess. A few weeks ago, Brands followed Jess and the fat dude to a cabin in the Silver Islands. You know them, right?"

I knew the Silver Islands were a bleak mountain range shadowing the salt flats east of town, but I didn't know Jenkins had a cabin anywhere near them.

Zachery rushed forward to fill the silence. "The rich asshole takes Jess there." He points at the girl on the floor. "And Brand hides and takes some snaps of Jess and the guy, you know, man—"

Zachery whinnied like a horse. It took me a few seconds to realize he was crying. The girl meant something to him. For the first time, I saw him as a person instead of a junkie.

I said, "How old is Jess?"

"Nineteen, man."

"Jess is nineteen, and she trades sex for heroin with the guy from The Desert Diamond, that right?"

"Right," Zachery said. "Right, man."

"And Brands—he took pictures to blackmail the fat guy?"

"What else would it be?"

"Is Brands a first or a last name?"

"Wallace, man. Brandon Wallace."

Brandon Wallace, the other name on Gina's list.

"What happened when Wallace approached the fat guy and showed him the photos?"

Zachery smiled, all blood and decaying teeth. "The guy said *fuck off*, man, *I don't care*."

It sounded like Jenkins.

I said, "What did Brandon do?"

The kid looked at me with pleading eyes. "I ain't a snitch, man. I never—"

I pushed my toe into his ribs. He squirmed, yelping.

"What did Brandon do?"

"Man, he came up with this crazy idea. But he needed Tyler's help for it to work. The high-roller room's like a club. Not much security, you know? The chips are just sitting in a drawer."

"This plan. Was it before or after Tyler got the casino job?"

Zachery looked confused. "After, man. After he got the job."

"Anybody else know about the plan?"

"Yeah, man. Tyler and Brandon and another guy named Story. Ryan Story."

"You part of this plan, Zachery?"

He shook his head from side to side. "No way, man. I'm a junkie, I'm not an armed robber."

"Where do I find Tyler?"

"You know the ghost town off I-80, Black Mountain?"

I did.

"They're hiding in the old motel."

I stood. "You tell anybody else about this, Zachery?"

The kid hesitated and said, "No, man. No way."

I believed him.

"This stays between you and me, right, Zachery?"

The kid nodded with enough zeal to bounce his head off the floor.

I pulled my wallet from an inside jacket pocket, counted a handful of bills and dropped them on his chest. "I'd think hard about moving on, Zachery. Take Jess and go somewhere else." I paused, then asked, "You have family who can help you get clean?"

The kid stared at me with wide eyes.

I said, "I don't want to see you around here again."

Zachery sobbed.

When I walked past Jess, she was still dreaming. Whatever she was seeing, I hoped it was better than what she had.

———

I EASED the sedan from the road and down a mild

depression—tires crunching through shattered rock. I stopped next to a small juniper stand and stepped out into the uncertain afternoon. Quickly, I moved into the juniper trees and away from the corrugated dirt road. Black Mountain's emptiness beckoned from the hill's far side. The alkaline dust, pale as chalk, rose in a diaphanous shimmer with each step I took.

A large block engine thundered into life, smashing the desert's calm. I ducked, my left knee in the dirt, my right hand on the gun at my waist. The car's tires raking the earth for traction, dirt and rocks clattering. I dashed across the hill's spine in time to see a black Dodge Challenger reversing away from the abandoned motel. The car's windows dark, large chrome wheels spinning. It skidded to a halt, the driver grinding its gears before the car wrenched forward with a thud of transmission. The rear end fish-tailed and the car disappeared around the hill's fold.

I stared at the dusty track, the license plate was too blurry to read, but the rear windscreen was decorated with a U.S. Marine Corps emblem. An eagle sitting atop a globe, an anchor angling downward from right to left. A recognizable car if it stayed in rural western Utah. However, if its destination was Salt Lake City, I'd never see it again.

I turned to the broken down litter of Black Mountain. Its buildings were faded and crumbling, desert grasses and shrubs crawling from the cracked concrete drives. An old Chevy van was parked next to the diesel shop. Tires flat and windshield shattered. The L-shaped motel was arid and quiet.

After catching my breath, I scrambled down the hill and into the abandoned town. I moved behind the motel and under the faded sign painted on its back wall.

Motel Café–Vacancy

I counted seven windows and guessed the Challenger had been parked at the fourth. I stepped through broken glass, around a rusted truck axle, between two cast iron bathtubs and a toilet. Its seat was down and the lid closed, awaiting its next customer.

I crouched by the window and listened. I stood on my toes to get a sight angle into the bathroom. The main room was visible through the open interior door, the light dim.

A shadow flickered.

"God!" A terrified voice from inside.

A fist smacked wood. "Shit! Shit, man. He's dead."

The voices were disembodied, the men invisible. I shifted my feet to get a better angle, the crunch of shoe leather and sand loud in my ears.

I stopped.

The men sounded desperate.

After a moment, I moved away from the window and crept to the motel's corner.

My ears buzzing with anticipation.

The .38 slid into my hand. I eased around the motel's corner, eyes darting across the abandoned landscape. I held the Colt in both hands, away from my body. A few feet from the room's door, I took a knee and listened as the men argued in hushed tones.

I shifted to the door and peered into the room's murky interior. I let my eyes adjust, and the men appeared. One was standing at the room's center, skinny and long, his shoulders stooped and head down. The other was sitting on a bucket in the corner.

On the torn carpet lay a motionless body. A halo of brownish-red blood blossoming on the floor.

I advanced into the room, keeping low. The .38 aimed at the man standing beside the corpse.

"Hands up!" My voice was calm and deliberate, the way the Quantico instructors had taught me in the long ago—before I burned my life and stranded myself in this desolation, working for a slug-shaped hood with Bugsy Siegel's self-image.

The guy standing, skinny and emaciated, gasped and squealed. His tiny pupils said he was high.

The one on the bucket wobbled, his hands high in the air. "We didn't do it!"

I crossed to where the skinny guy gaped—eyes wide and arms dangling at his sides. I clapped his temple with an open palm. He flinched, stumbled backward. He tripped on a chair and crashed to the floor, his eyes vague with confusion and rocking from side to side. A pathetic whimpering hum escaped cracked lips. The fear and drugs had him in another place.

"What's your name?" I said to the kid on the bucket.

He opened his mouth like a drowning fish.

"I'm not here to hurt you, but if you don't talk, I will."

The kid gulped and said in a whisper, "Brandon."

I pointed to Skinny. "Ryan Story?"

"How?"

"Lucky guess." I held a finger up and advanced on the dead man lying on his back. His sightless eyes staring at the water-stained ceiling, his hair was matted and sticky. A dent on the left side of his head. The blood splattered high across a shattered mirror told me two things. The dead man had been standing when the blow came, and whoever struck him was right-handed.

The corpse was Tyler Watts, former Jenkins' employee, junkie and casino robber.

The .38 back in its leather, I said to Wallace, "Who are you working with?"

"What?"

I grimaced. "Don't play dumb. The blackmail. Jenkins. The chip heist."

"How?"

I leaned close with my right hand up, the palm open.

Wallace brought his arms up defensively, almost fell off his bucket. "No—nobody. Please, don't hit me."

"Who was in the Challenger?"

Panic in his eyes. "They killed Tyler." He pointed at Watts on the floor. "They killed him. He gave them the chips, but they killed him anyway."

I crouched. My eyes were level with Wallace's. "Who are *they*? I'm looking for names here."

"I don't know, dude."

I shook my head, a parental scowl on my face. "Not good enough, Brandon."

"Look, all I know is those dudes came here for the chips. They knew everything about last night. Everything."

I sat back on my heels. "You tell anybody about your plan?"

"No, I swear it."

"Except Zachery? Maybe Jess?"

Wallace's eyes widened. He nodded and shook his head in a single motion.

"You confused, Brandon?"

"No. I mean…" Brandon wiggled on the can like he needed to piss. "We didn't tell nobody except Zach and Jess and they wouldn't tell no one."

"They told me."

The kid cried, a quiet trembling. "You a cop, man?"

I shook my head. "Today, I'm your best friend."

Sitting on the bucket, Brandon Wallace looked like a six-year-old with a skinned knee. "I don't know how those guys knew. I never seen them before. I swear it."

I believed him. "You plan the robbery?"

Wallace looked dazed. He shook his head.

"Who did?"

Brandon glanced at Tyler's dead body, pointed with his chin. "Him, man."

"I heard it was you, Brandon."

His Adam's apple skipped in his neck. "It was Tyler's idea from the start."

"He get the idea after he started working at The Diamond?"

Brandon shook his head. "He got the job so he could rob the casino."

His answer made me nervous. I stood, thinking. The room's clutter was impressive—an empty bed frame against one wall, a splintered chest on another. The floor was littered with empty cans and bottles and used condoms. The ceiling and walls were filthy with graffiti.

"You spend much time here, Brandon?"

"Hell, no."

"Where do you stay?"

The kid looked at the floor. His stringy hair tumbled down onto his face. "Around—the airbase."

I knew the old air base. It was built at the start of World War Two as a training base, and while many of the old buildings were standing, it had been empty for decades.

I looked at Watts, the blood pool darkening around him and his face pinched with fear. I said, "The guys who killed Tyler...Do you think he knew them? He use their names?"

Wallace looked up, his face was as greasy as his hair. "Yeah." He was excited. "They wore ski masks, but Tyler called the big guy Sammy."

"You sure it was Sammy?"

"I think so, dude."

"And the other guy, what did he look like?"

"Short."

I said, "Could Sammy have been 'Sonny?'"

The kid smiled. His teeth were broken and brown, loose in his mouth. "That's it...*Sonny!*"

I knew Sonny and his height-challenged friend. We weren't buddies, but all three of us shared an employer.

"They say anything else?"

Wallace shook his head. "They wanted the chips is all. Tyler wanted to give them a share, but the short one whacked him with a bat and they took everything."

I walked past Story, who was still curled into a ball and moaning. At the door, I turned back to the junkies. "I told your buddy Zach to get lost. You should do the same."

Brandon said, "Yeah. It's time, dude." Ryan Story stared with bland disquiet.

As I walked to the Impala, anger buzzed in my ears, the day's heat unnoticed as I considered why everything pointed to Jenkins and his two goons.

BACK IN WENDOVER, I parked on Aspen in front of an aging blue mobile home. The yard was dirt. A string of colorful Christmas lights drooped from the eaves. A skinny cat was sleeping on the weathered porch steps. The trailer park was quiet and resigned, decaying bitterly in the casino's glitzy glare.

The ancient flip phone in my hand, I dialed Jenkins.

He answered on the fourth ring, breathless. A woman giggling. "What do you want, Ford?"

"I found your nephew."

His voice went soft. "He ain't my nephew, Ford."

"You want to know where he is…maybe how he is?"

Indignant now. "Okay, where is he?"

"Dead." I let it hang.

So did Jenkins, but he won.

"You're not very inquisitive today, Jenkins. Don't you want to know where the kid is? How about the chips? Any interest there?"

Jenkins said, "Where?"

"The kid, Watts. He's in room four at the Black Mountain motel. Someone used his head for batting practice."

"So where are the chips, Jimmy?"

He only used my first name when he knew something I didn't.

I ended the call and turned off the phone and stepped from my car into the airless afternoon. Sweat popped on my forehead as I crossed the slender road to a battered mobile home. Its skirting was gone, and the cinder blocks holding it off the baked ground were ugly with graffiti. An abandoned mattress and a kid's bicycle hiding underneath. The steel security door at odds with the trailer's decrepit exterior.

A black Dodge Challenger was shading itself under a carport, a Marine Corps decal visible in the rear window.

I shook my head at the stupidity and stepped to the front door.

From inside, voices argued. The television. I figured it was *Dr. Phil* or maybe *The View*.

I knocked, rang the bell.

A dog barked. Someone inside shouted. The dog whimpered and went quiet.

I stepped back and to the right. I hid the .38 behind my hip and spread my feet.

The trailer's floor creaked as someone approached the door and looked out the peephole. A few seconds passed while they tried to figure out who knocked. Then, "Yeah?"

I said, "Sonny?"

"Who's it?"

"Jimmy Ford. We need to talk. Jenkins sent me."

"Shit." A muted conversation on the other side before the door opened a few inches. Sonny's crooked nose and his livered lips appeared in the opening. "What do you want?"

"That Challenger yours?"

His lips twitched into a grotesque smile.

I tried to show interest. "It's the V8 Hemi?"

The door opened wider. Sonny's broad face florid. His belly drooping over his belt.

"Hell, no, it ain't no *Hemi*." The words were filled with scorn. He looked over his shoulder. "You believe this guy, Eric? He can't tell the difference between a Hemi and a Hellcat?"

A wet laugh from inside. "Dumbass. How many times I told you he's a dipshit?"

I whistled. "Hellcat? I've never seen a Hellcat before." Playing the fool. "What's it got, five hundred horsepower?"

Sonny shook his head and frowned theatrically. He opened the door wider. "Try 707."

"That much? My dad's airplane had fewer horses."

Sonny folded his arms across his chest and laughed. His teeth yellow, tongue stained blue.

I took a short step and extended a finger at his face. "You got something there."

He frowned. "What?"

"Your tongue's blue."

The big man looked over his shoulder again.

From inside, "Tell him to fuck off, Sonny."

As Sonny turned back to me, I smashed the .38 into the side of his head and raked the gunsight across the soft flesh under his jaw. Blood blossomed and splattered wetly on the door frame.

Sonny grunted. He clutched the wound with his hands and stumbled backward, crashing against a wall. He took a step and fell on his face. The impact shaking the mobile home.

The other man shouted, his words lost in panic. The dog barked.

I stepped into the trailer, the gun ready. The television was loud, its colors flashing in the small room.

"Hands up." My voice was even and hushed.

Eric Vaughn's eyes were wide and he had a baseball bat in his right hand.

I said, "Where's the dog?"

The little man raised a hand. "Back there, in the bedroom."

I leveled the .38 on Vaughn's chest and watched the baseball bat in his hand and said, "Is that the bat you killed Tyler Watts with?"

The short man smiled and gripped the bat in both

hands. He took half a step forward. "I'm going to kill you with it, too, fancy FBI man."

Ice clawed the back of my head, the world slowed.

I said, "Jenkins sent me for his share."

Vaughn's eyes flickered with uncertainty. He looked at his partner lying face down on the floor.

"I owed him one. It has nothing to do with this." The .38 steady on Vaughn's chest.

He looked back at me, squinting this time. "What chips?"

I laughed. The sound harsh in my ears. "The chips you killed that junkie, Tyler Watts, for." Then, "You do that on Jenkins' orders?"

"Shit. You don't know nothing." He eased a few inches away from the wall.

"Nobody gets hurt if you tell me where the chips are."

With a devil's smile, Vaughn said, "What about Sonny?"

"A scratch. He's high-strung, so he panicked and fainted."

His laugh was fingernails on a blackboard. "You're funny, Ford. A funny G-Man."

"Yeah, that's me. Funny."

Vaughn adjusted his grip and pulled the baseball bat closer to his right hip. "Sure, Jimmy. No problem. The chips are in the closet behind you." He nodded to my right, expecting me to follow his gaze, and started his swing.

The .38's muzzle flashed. Its roar crashed in the room.

My ears ringing.

Eric Vaughn's eyes were puzzled, disbelieving. He dropped the bat and put a hand on his chest where blood blossomed in a neat circle.

The little man slumped against the wall. "You shot me."

I moved forward and kicked the baseball bat away.

I said, "Jenkins part of this, Eric?"

Vaughn held out his hand, staring at the blood-stained palm. He smiled, an ugly, feral expression. "You dummy." His eyes closed. The smile stuck to his face.

I switched off the television, the silence sharp in my ringing ears. I checked Sonny's pulse. Weak, but regular.

He would bleed out in an hour, but that gave me plenty of time to finish the job.

I found the chips in the black duffel in the closet where the little man, Eric Vaughn, had pointed. I carried the bag across the street to my car and tossed the duffel under the spare tire in the trunk. When I was done, I strolled back to the goons' house. Inside, the killers were lying in converging pools of blood. The stench was a mixture of cordite, copper, and shit.

I went to the front porch and sat on the top step and pulled the cell phone from my pocket. I turned it on and dialed 9-1-1. Before the operator answered, a West Wendover police cruiser lit up like Christmas skidded around the corner and jumped the curb. Its front bumper a few feet from the house.

The officer, young and nervous, opened his door and scurried out. An automatic in his hands. He told me to raise mine.

I did.

———

I SPENT the rest of the day and most of the night explaining things. First to a couple uniforms and then to a handful of detectives. They didn't like any of it, but an anonymous caller—a couple minutes after I'd told Jenkins where to find Watts—fingered Sonny and Vaughn as part of a ring that robbed The Desert Diamond's VIP Room the night before. After Jenkins explained why he'd kept the rip-off quiet, as a favor to his sister and her beloved nephew, they released me.

But they told me to stay in town.

I said, "Where else I got to go?"

The detective, a guy named DeSpain, who was on our payroll for the odd favor here and there, knew me better than I liked. He gave me a knowing smirk. He followed it with, "You'll be interested to know, we found the stolen chips."

Trying to keep the surprise from my face, I said, "Where?"

DeSpain shook his head, the lopsided pornstache ugly on his face. "That jerk's locker at the casino."

"Right there, in Eric Vaughn's locker?" I knew it was Jenkins' work, placing chips worth sixty-grand in Vaughn's locker to keep the investigation pointed away from him and the casino. It made it look like a simple case of stupid criminals falling out.

"In a black duffel, right on the top shelf."

"And I'm the dummy."

DeSpain winked. "I've heard that." We shook hands, and I went home to my crummy casino hotel room behind The Diamond. I slept in my suit on the bedspread. Five hours later, I got up, showered, changed into a fresh suit, and went to Jenkins' suite. His rooms were in the new wing of the casino's hotel and not crummy at all. They had ten-foot ceilings and gold-foil-covered walls. High-priced oil paintings—nudes, classy and vulgar alike—hung as if they belonged. The fat man sat behind his big desk.

When he saw me, he said, "Where's my chips?"

I shrugged, shook my head.

He scowled.

I said, "Why'd you feed Watts to Sonny and Vaughn?"

Jenkins only laughed, a twinkle in his piggy eyes.

"This whole thing smells like you, Jenkins. You hired Watts against my recommendation. I bet you used Sonny to give Watts the idea for the robbery. Probably even made Watts think it was his idea. Then, after Watts steals the chips, you have your goons take them back. Then what? You file an insurance claim? That about it, Jenkins?"

That twinkle stayed in Jenkins' eyes.

His bliss confirmed everything I thought. I was the straight man in a joke I never knew about. Maybe I'd get lucky and find the junkies, a handful of The Diamond's chips in their pockets, but the rest would disappear forever because Jenkins had them. When my search went blank, Jenkins would report the theft and explain everything. Never admitting the chips were recovered. After all, his investigator, Jimmy Ford, former FBI Special Agent, lost the trail and alibis the story from beginning to end. The insurance company coughs up the claim. Jenkins pockets sixty grand, and Jimmy Ford is the asshole.

"Never could fool you, Jimmy." The fat man's leather chair creaked as he leaned back. His eyes never leaving me. "Should have known those two blunts would foul everything." He leaned forward and slapped the desk. "Good work on your part, though. Sonny will be inside for five to seven."

I wondered how much Sonny's silence would cost Jenkins, but said, "They kill Watts on their own initiative?"

Jenkins laughed, the sound wet and hard. He was a crook, but he wasn't stupid. Sixty thousand wasn't worth a murder rap. When I found Watts dead, Jenkins' plan changed from low-grade greed to high-fear survival.

And I did exactly what Jenkins expected me to do— kill Vaughn and bash Sonny hard enough so he wouldn't think right again.

And Jenkins wins, like he always does.

I said, "Too bad you found the casino chips and can't make an insurance claim."

The laugh again, like he'd swallowed a watermelon.

"That is too bad, Jimmy, but I'm sure the stolen chips will reappear once Sonny wakes up."

My first name again, and it bothered me.

I said, "But until then, you're down 60k and a couple enforcers."

Jenkins shrugged. "Easy come, easy go."

"Why Watts?"

"You're too much, Jimmy." Jenkins dismissed me by reaching for a stack of papers at the edge of his desk.

"What did you have on him? Why did Watts *have* to pull the robbery?"

Without looking up from the paperwork, Jenkins said, "You're boring me, Jimmy. I *have* to do my work." He said "have" with sarcasm—and that's what he knew that I didn't. The *why*. Why Watts joined the crew, and how the junkies' feeble blackmail attempt fit with the hook Watts had been dangling from.

"Asshole."

A whisper, but Jenkins heard it and his smile hardened. "You're forgetting your place, Jimmy. This is my kingdom. I pay your way, give you a woman here and there, and I own you. I own you from top to bottom."

Anger flashed hot behind my eyes, but I pushed it down. He was right. There wasn't anything I could do about it.

I said, "When can I expect my bonus?"

Jenkins, with his arms stretched wide and his palms up, gave his best *whattaya-do* shrug. "No chips, no bonus."

"Sure, no chips, no bonus." Then I asked, "Gina keeps her job?"

Jenkins grinned. "She didn't do anything wrong."

"Keep your hands off her, Jenkins."

A little two finger Cub Scout salute. "I wouldn't think of it, Jimmy. She's past her prime, but you're more than welcome to make a run at her."

I stood there staring at my boss, thinking about how satisfying it would be to crack his head open. Instead, I turned and walked away with more swagger than I deserved. He owned me, but those casino chips were all mine. Right there in my car's trunk where I'd left them. The conversion would take time since I'd have to make the exchange to cash in The Desert Diamond. A few hundred here and a few hundred there and no one would bat an eye. It didn't hurt my feelings the money came straight from Jenkins' wallet instead of an anonymous insurance company.

My Impala would get its new transmission. I'd find Zach and Jess, those poor doped-up kids, and give them enough for a stint in rehab and a fresh start somewhere out of the desert. Maybe they would do something with the chance. I would try to satisfy myself with the facts. Watts' killers were on ice, one in a cage and the other in a casket. Wallace and Story had escaped any punishment, but not the junk they kept jamming in their arms.

I was happier than I'd been in months.

Dark Estate

Richard Prosch

I first had the pleasure of meeting Richard Prosch via the *Men's Adventure* Paperbacks of the 70s and 80s group on Facebook—a bunch of guys of a certain age still fascinated with the books of their misspent youths. Rich and I began trading a few genre books with each other, especially Westerns to which we were both partial. As we became friends, we also exchanged books we had written. Reading his, I found myself captivated by his skill as a storyteller. Aside from the pleasures of his novels, Rich's short story collections were a joy—clever, low key, emotionally resonate, and filled with realistic small-town characters. If Meadows Ford, Nebraska, where many of his stories are set, was real, I'd move there tomorrow. Recently, Rich has been busy writing an excellent new crime series—featuring Dan Spalding, an ex-state cop turned vintage record store owner. Fortunately, he still allowed me to coax him into writing a new Meadows Ford story specifically for this anthology...

DARK ESTATE

NO TWO WAYS ABOUT IT.

Jennifer Rand wasn't dressed for running. Her jeans were just a little too tight and less than a block down the sidewalk, the pumps she wore to the estate sale that Saturday morning had flown off like unbuckled overshoes on the first day of summer. She dug deep, pounding along State Street with bare feet and a rising anger like she hadn't felt since landing stateside after two tours overseas.

In Afghanistan, she'd learned how to breathe through sand and hailstorms of smoke and debris.

The morning exhaust from two farm pickups and Mrs. Larkin's white Buick, she could handle.

But losing those pumps...

She'd spent the last of her July salary on them and payday didn't come again for two weeks.

Despite proximity to acres of agricultural wealth, a

police officer in Meadows Ford, Nebraska—population 5,100—wasn't exactly Warren Buffet.

Brittney Dale would have to pay. Or her mom would.

Jen's ponytail swung back and forth and two big dollops of sweat fell from under her arms, staining her avocado-green camisole.

Just great. Exactly the way she wanted to spend her day off.

Slim Thompson drove past in his mail truck, going the opposite direction. Honked. Jen waved and kept running.

Ahead, lanky Brittney Dale was down to a fast trot.

Tall as she was, the girl was easy to see from a distance. Like a radio tower complete with red beacon up top.

Britt's cherry-colored Elvis pompadour might've scored her some points on the trendy meter at Meadows Ford High, but it was a definite detriment in trying to elude pursuit.

Wearing a loose sweatshirt and cargo shorts two sizes too big, she wasn't dressed for running either.

Jen flexed her fingers, squeezed her hands into tight balls, and cranked hard, closing the distance between them by half. She'd already identified herself, called out for the kid to stop.

Brittney knew perfectly well who Jen was and why she was chasing her.

She knew it the minute she shoved the turquoise jewelry in the pocket of her shorts at the Willards' estate sale and, pushing past Jen at the card table checkout, made for the street, leaving a dozen eye-witnesses to the petty theft behind.

In an organized race, Brittney wouldn't stand a chance against Jen.

But Miss Sticky-fingers had a head start.

Even so, as they turned onto Broadway, only a block from the downtown business district, Jen closed in.

Near enough now to contemplate whether or not tackling the school superintendent's daughter on the brick-inlaid main street was a good idea.

Chief of Police Lyle Lindquist might frown on the idea.

Much as Jen would enjoy it, she'd have to think of something else.

As if a takedown would be necessary. Brittney was down to a stumbling jog. Jen had run her to ground.

That's when Lyle's white Chevy Tahoe pulled up to the four-way stop at the intersection of Broadway and Main.

Cutting Brittney off in mid-stride.

Look who shows up when the hard work is done.

Brittney didn't even try to continue. Lyle's arrival was the last straw, and the girl drew up fast, hands on her hips, out of wind, before bending over to stumble against the blond brick side of the Farmers and Merchants State Bank.

Lyle had his vehicle parked and crawled out from behind the wheel as Jen arrived.

"Morning, ladies," he said, his teeth working a slender unlit cigar. He pushed the bill up on his black

Meadows Ford PD cap and scratched his trim white hairline.

He checked the time on his wristwatch.

"If you were trying to make it to the bakery before the last apple fritter sold, I'm afraid you're too late." Lyle patted the extra ten pounds he carried under his sky blue work shirt. "I already got it—bought and paid for."

"Bought and paid for," said Jen, her breath slowing to normal, her temper cooling as Brittney gulped for air beside the bank. "There's a novel idea, Chief."

"Is that a new concept for some people, Officer?" said Lyle, for Brittney's benefit.

"Apparently," said Jen.

"Whatever, bitch," Brittney said between gasps, waving them both away. Reaching into her cavernous pockets to remove three rings and a bracelet. "Take the stuff. No harm, no foul."

"No harm, no foul," said Jen. She cocked her head and raised her eyebrows. "That's a new idea too."

"And 'bitch' isn't accurate at all," Lyle said. He gave Brittney his best stare of authority. "Please apologize to Officer Rand."

Brittney showed him her middle finger.

She shoved the jewelry in her other hand toward Jennifer. "You want these or not?"

Jen took the stolen items.

The little collection was primitive but lovely. Hammered pewter the color of an evening thunderstorm, flashing turquoise that caught the sun with veins of lightning. Attractive in the way only handcrafted items could be. Jen had no idea what the pieces were worth but figured the still-attached paper price tags still would help.

"Shall we walk over to the station?" said Jen.

Before Lyle could respond, a car braked to a hasty stop behind his Chevy.

Mariah Dale shoved open the angry little BMW's driver-side door and leapt into the fray, jaw set, eyes afire. "How dare you," she said.

After several seconds Jen realized the older woman was talking to her. She rolled her eyes, deflecting the criticism toward Lyle.

"I'm officially off duty here," said Jen.

"Nice to see you, Mrs. Dale," said Lyle, showing off a confident row of teeth. "I'm glad you could join us."

Mariah Dale wore a crisp beige suit with a white cotton blouse and a pendant of amber. Her hair was dark chocolate with silver streaks, so it looked like it was casually flowing through a breeze that wasn't there. Her cheeks were heavy with foundation, and her lipstick a challenging black smear. She smelled of cigarette smoke.

Jennifer couldn't remember ever being quite so made up on a Saturday morning.

"Are you okay, sugarplum?" said Mariah. "They didn't hurt you, did they?"

"You got an evidence bag?" Jen asked Lyle. She held up the loot.

"Evidence bag?" cried Mariah. "Evidence of what?"

"Brittney didn't pay for this jewelry," said Jennifer. "She took it off the table at Ms. Willard's sale."

"She did not," said Mariah. "I was right outside, waiting in the car."

Jen held the other woman's gaze. "And I was inside, watching her do it."

"You're talking about a future academic All-American here. We've already signed a letter of intent for Harvard," said Mariah.

"Why don't we walk over to the station and talk about it?" said Lyle.

"We will not," said Mariah. "I've got to be in Lincoln this afternoon on business, and that's a three-hour drive. Plus, Brittney has a pool party at her friend's house."

"I'm sorry, Mrs. Dale, but this really can't wait," said Lyle.

"Of course, it can."

"Oh, Christ, mother," said Brittney. "Will you just shut the hell up?"

"I don't think, I—"

"Can I take this, Chief?" said Jen.

Hiding a smile, Lyle nodded.

"How about the four of us walk back down to Ms. Willard's house and we sort it out there?"

Mariah Dale had her phone out, staring at the screen.

"I don't think so," she said. "I need to be on the road."

"That or we go to the station," said Lyle. "Lots of paperwork over at the station."

"I imagine the Chief would rather go fishing this afternoon than fill in all that paperwork," said Jen. "But I guess that's up to you, Mrs. Dale."

"I did have a nice little pond in mind," said Lyle.

Everybody was quiet, and Jen shifted her attention from Mariah Dale to the lazy street.

Mrs. Larkin's Buick purred past once again, moving in an opposite direction from its earlier run. Slim Thompson and the mail truck. A guy on a John Deere tractor.

Finally, Mariah gave in.

"Oh, alright," she said. "But I'll drive myself, thank you."

"It's just past the big oak tree on State Street," said Jen. "Look for the green sale sign."

Mariah went back toward the BMW, opened the door. "I know where the Willards live, Jennifer. I told you I was there waiting on Brittney this morning." She settled into the leather upholstery. "By the way, dear. While you're there, why don't you look for some shoes? I'm sure they'll have something you can afford."

Jennifer looked at her bare feet and smiled.

After her Army stint, complete with a medal of commendation, she'd had a job offer from Homeland Security.

Some days she wondered why she hadn't taken it.

———

ON STATE STREET, past the sign, a white ranch house with blue shutters rested on an acre of grass, its two open garage doors offering a candid display of its occupant's everyday life. Amateur oil paintings hung from the rafters, and ceramic ashtrays filled two card tables next to several pieces of mid-century furniture that were loaded down with ratty paperback books and brazen piles of lacy lingerie.

This was the estate of the late Herb Willard, curated by his daughter, Nora.

Six or seven familiar faces from the community browsed through the merchandise, including Sam Miller from the market and Mrs. Larkin. Jen glanced toward the street and saw the white Buick parked at the curb.

Edna certainly got around to all the weekend sales.

On the other hand, Lyle Lindquist wasn't the estate sale type.

"Estate sale, garage sale, flea market," he said around the soggy tip of his cigar. "It's all the same collection of smelly kids clothes, old garage tools, and broken tchotchkes."

"Tchotchkes?" said Jen as they followed Brittney Dale up the driveway past a series of potted wildflowers to the front door where Brittney's mother waited impatiently.

They hadn't taken the time to retrieve Jen's shoes, and the cement was hot on her bare feet.

"What?" said Lyle. "You don't know what tchotchke is?"

"I know. I'm just surprised that you know. It doesn't sound right coming from you. It's not a word a small town Nebraska cop would use."

"You don't think us hick cops got culture?"

"I've never seen any evidence of that, no."

"Everybody knows Tchotchke is the kid on that seventies TV show," said Lyle. "With Joanie?"

"That was lame. Even for you," said Jen.

"Game face," said Lyle as they got close to the door.

Jen pulled the stolen merchandise from her pocket.

Lyle nodded at Brittney and Mariah Dale. Now he was all business. "Let me offer Ms. Willard a quick explanation of the facts. Then Brittney will apologize. We'll see where we go from there."

They went inside.

Less than fifteen minutes later, the situation was resolved.

Knowing Nora Willard, Jen figured it would be.

A silver-tongued septuagenarian who identified as a Sixties flower child with alert blue eyes and waist-length white hair, Nora dressed in a flowing tie-dye poncho, stretch pants, and strappy black sandals. After more than a year caring for her late father, Herb, she was selling off his estate and going back to Santa Fe.

"It's a haven for us enlightened types," she'd told Jen.

After listening to Brittney's reluctant apology, and once the jewelry was back on display, Nora wrapped both arms around the teenager and sang a Native American song of forgiveness.

"That was lovely," said Jen.

"It sure was," said Lyle.

"Whatever," said Brittney, pulling away from Nora's embrace.

"Are we done here?" said Mariah.

"We are indeed done," said Lyle.

"Why don't you stay a while?" said Nora. "I've got Matcha tea in the fridge. Or any number of other varieties. I can fix you whatever you like." She settled back down behind the card table checkout, flipped open a plastic cashbox and started tending to a line of five chattering customers. A stack of old Meadows Ford Chronicle newspapers sat on the floor beside her chair.

"I'll take you up on that iced tea," said Jen. "So will Chief Lyle."

Nora nodded and pointed toward the kitchen.

"We're leaving," said Mariah. "Come along, Brittney."

The teenager slunk toward the front door.

"You get to college, you ought to go out for the track team, Brittney," said Jen. "You're a fine runner."

"She'll do no such thing," said Mariah.

Brittney and her mother left the house, door closing hard behind them.

"There goes a troubled pair," said Edna Larkin as Nora made change and then started wrapping a set of steak knives in tissue paper.

Edna quickly stopped her. "Don't use your nice paper for these old things," she said. "Newspaper is fine."

Nora smiled and took a sheet of newsprint from the pile.

"I agree with Edna," Jen told Lyle. "The Dales are a troubled pair."

"Hard to be a single mother," he said. "And the school super on top of it. Mrs. Dale has a lot of responsibility."

"She doesn't wear it well," said Jen.

"Says the girl without shoes," said Lyle.

"I think the force ought to reimburse me for those," said Jen.

"We've got a whole bedroom filled with shoes," said Nora. "Just down the hallway."

"Let's look around," said Jen, catching hold of Lyle's shirt sleeve, guiding him through the other shoppers.

"The garage entrance is down there, too, Chief," said Nora. "Take your time. You never know what you might find."

"That's what I'm afraid of."

"Maybe there's some fishing stuff," said Jen.

"Sorry," said Nora. "Dad wasn't much of an outdoorsman. No fishing stuff."

However, it turned out Nora was wrong.

When they got there, Jen and the Chief had the garage all to themselves. Jen drank some of her iced green tea and took a mental inventory of the place. Nora was right. Herb had been an indoor hobbyist. The heavy wooden workbench was covered with woodworking tools. Carving knives and chisels. A pair of wood burning kits, both well-cared for and stored in the original cardboard boxes. More than a dozen small hand saws.

"No gun rack. No shovel. Not even a lawn mower," said Jen. "You sure Herb Willard was from Nebraska?"

"He worked as a clerk over at the county courthouse his whole life," said Lyle. "Retired when I was a kid. I never really knew him. I don't know anybody who did."

Lyle poked around at the tools on the bench. "It's a cinch he never went fishing."

When Jen pushed aside a folding lawn chair an aluminum tackle box poked its padlocked face out.

"Maybe he did go fishing," she said.

The top of the gray box had been spray-painted black. Jen lifted the handle, picked it up, and carried it to the center of the garage. "Nora didn't put a price on this," she said.

Lyle whistled with admiration. "Industrial strength," he said.

"You want it?"

Lyle bent over and examined the padlock. "Depends on what's inside it," he said. "Need to get the lock off."

"What if it's packed with vintage lures?" said Jen.

"Could be."

Jen picked it up. "I think a big tackle box like this would be nice all by itself. Let's see if it's for sale," she said. "Then you can buy me some shoes."

———

AFTER A LUNCH of microwaved burritos and coffee at his desk, Lyle logged George Hutton in on the duty roster and watched through the station's front window as the veteran officer drove away in his Crown Victoria. First stop on his Saturday afternoon patrol would be the high school. Then up and down Main Street a few times.

The Chief was just about to pick up his new tackle box and try to open the padlock when the phone rang.

Mrs. Thompson had a coyote prowling around her back yard. Could Lyle come over personally?

On the way to the Thompson house, Jake Matthews called in from the drug store, having caught Irene Raymond boosting a greeting card intended for Edna Mae Voss's funeral. "She may have sympathy, but I don't," said Jake.

Then Linda Warbler's security system went off for no reason. "I only have the damn thing because of my insurance," she said.

Meanwhile, somebody had vandalized Merv Salmon's construction site. "Stripped out all the copper wiring to sell."

Finally, the sewer drain backed up on Elk Road, and by four o'clock, the ford was under water.

When Lyle got back to the station, he found Hutton back at his desk, chewing raspberry-filled kolaches and filling in a crossword puzzle.

"Keeping busy?" said Hutton. He was older than Lyle.

"I've been doing your job all afternoon."

"Good of you," said Hutt, swallowing a last bite of pastry. He dusted his hands off, one against another.

Hutt was in good shape for a man three days past this sixty-seventh birthday. Lean gut. Fat savings account over at the bank. And, in spite of his age, no slouch at his job. He'd been a cop since his time in the Marine Corps, when he'd moved to Meadows Ford from Wisconsin ten years before. He planned to retire someplace close to a lake where there was plenty of fishing.

It was one of the reasons Lyle liked him.

"By the way," said Hutt. "Couldn't help but notice the tackle box. Is it yours?"

"Jen thought I needed something from Nora Willard's estate sale this morning."

"What's inside?"

Lyle shrugged. "Pick the lock and find out. Nora didn't have a key. Said she didn't even remember Herb having a box like it."

"How much she charge you for it?"

"Free," said Lyle.

"If I pick the lock, can I have first pick of what's inside?"

"I'm not so sure."

"C'mon," said Hutt. "Let a pro have a go at it."

Lyle poured himself a cup of coffee and fell back into his office chair. "After the afternoon I've had," he said, "You go ahead."

"First pick of the contents?"

"Sure. First pick."

It took Hutt fifteen minutes and three bent paper clips to pop the stubborn old lock. Its U-shaped bolt finally let go with a world-weary click.

When Hutt pried open the lid, the hinges wailed in protest.

"This thing hasn't been opened in years," said Hutt.

"Probably decades," said Lyle, coming around the edge of the desk to join him.

Sure enough, right on top of the stacked series of hinged trays was a square section of newsprint, its edges yellow and chipped, with the date prominently displayed.

Forty-two years ago this month.

Not a good day in Meadows Ford's history.

Lyle read the headline as much from memory as from the clipping he held.

Third Girl Found—Gruesome Murders Continue

"Weird thing to keep in a tackle box," said Hutt.

"Isn't it?" said Lyle, a creeping cold moving up from the small of his back.

He laid the piece of paper aside. The top tray was empty.

"Open it up," said Lyle.

"This thing's got an odd smell," said Hutt.

The icy hand moved.

"Open it."

Hutt grasped the trays and they accordioned up, creaking, sticking, a set of three tiered steps opening up to reveal long-hidden secrets.

The middle set of trays held five medical scalpels, three with blades, two without. They were rusty and crusted on the edges with flaking brown and black.

A separate compartment was filled with unused razor blades.

The bottom tray was a grab bag of sharp edges and picks, needles, and clamps. Again, coated with a dry, dark crust.

Underneath it all was more newspaper, crumpled, yellow, crackling from the disturbance after so many years.

Hutt reached in and pulled one ball of paper free. Unwrapped it to read the headline.

Lyle's heart froze, and for a second he was eleven years old again.

Like he was during that endless, horrific summer.

Inside the paper were the mummified remains of a ring finger.

And Lyle knew who it belonged to.

"I take it back," said Hutt. "I don't want first pick."

"Call Jennifer," said Lyle. "Do it now."

———

"THE MEDIA WASN'T AS hyperbolic back then," said Lyle. "Especially in rural Nebraska."

He sipped coffee from his mug and set it down on his desk-sized calendar, leaving a ring around Tuesday's EMS seminar and smearing Wednesday's dentist appointment. "I was eleven years old, and even though the authorities never had an official name for the bad guy, us kids called him the Tea Man. The papers called him the Willow Creek Killer."

Lyle walked around his desk and perched on the front corner near Jen, who sat in a nearby metal office chair with her feet flat on the floor.

Feet adequately encased in black Converse sneakers.

Hutt was back at his desk, the tackle box closed in front of him.

The three of them had convened over a fresh pot of coffee so Lyle could brief them on what had been—

until today—the frozen granddaddy of Nebraska cold cases.

"Three months of summer. Three teenaged girls dead. Each of them found on Willow Creek Road, a gravel stretch only a couple miles out of town. Each with their throats cut and their ring fingers severed."

"Why did you call him the Tea Man?" said Jen.

"Do we want to know?" said Hutt.

"Each girl was found with a tea bag in her mouth."

"That's horrible," said Jen.

"The fingers belonging to Amanda Ware and Kathy Allen were mailed to the Meadows Ford Chronicle. Annie Beck was the third victim, the one mentioned in the clipping we just saw. Her finger was never recovered."

"Until today," said Hutt.

"Until today," agreed Lyle. "However, won't know for sure without testing."

"Three victims? That's all?"

"That's it," said Lyle. "Three murders. Never resolved. Several different branches of law enforcement were involved in the investigation. Two or three private detectives. And a whole raft of conspiracy nuts. The furor died down after a few years without uncovering even one decent suspect."

"You're thinking the tackle box we got at the Willard sale belonged to the Tea Man," said Jen.

"I can't see it any other way," Lyle said. He reached for his mug and took another drink. "We'll need to CSI the box—blood, DNA, everything."

"We can send it to the state lab in Lincoln," said Hutt.

Jen shook her head. "Once State gets involved—a story this big—our little department will be brushed aside like so much wheat straw in the wind"

"Is that what you're thinking, Chief?" Hutt asked.

"I'm thinking this is our town," said Lyle. "We know the people here better than any state investigator. The people know us. I'd like to get as much solid information as we can before we start involving strangers." Lyle finished his coffee. "Tomorrow is Sunday, so we have maybe thirty-six hours."

"What do we do first?" said Jen.

"You and me are gonna go back to Herb Willard's estate sale," said Lyle. "Monday, after the sale, we'll need a warrant, but today the place is wide open."

"If she hasn't closed yet. The sign said she'd be there until six."

Lyle looked at his watch. "Ten minutes," he said. Then he turned to Hutt. "You hold the fort here and handle your regular Saturday shift."

"Ten-four," said Hutt. He shook his head. "Tea Man. See that's something you wouldn't hear about where I come from. Coffee Man, maybe. Not tea."

"I was thinking," said Jen. "Nora Willard drinks a variety of tea."

"Along with four or five billion other people on the planet," said Lyle. "Let's just do our job. One step at a time."

On State Street, they saw two cars and the Miller kid riding a bike down the wrong side of the road.

It looked like every quiet Saturday night in Meadows Ford.

Back in his patrol car, maybe Hutt could finish his crossword puzzle.

They turned into the Willard driveway with four minutes to spare.

The friendly garage doors were still open, and they found Nora puttering beside Herb's workbench.

"Welcome back," said Nora. "I was just getting ready to close."

"That tackle box was such a treasure," said Lyle. "I thought I'd better make sure there wasn't anything else I might need."

"I can't imagine where that box came from, Chief. Like I told you before, I don't remember Dad having one. I can't recall ever seeing it until you brought it up to the table."

"It's easy to forget things," said Jen.

"But I organized everything out there for the sale. I must've seen it." She shook her head. "I just don't remember."

"Mind if I walk around one more time?" said Lyle.

"Please, go right ahead. Who knows what else I might have forgot? Maybe you'll find the key to Fort Knox!"

Lyle smiled. "A key is just what I'm looking for," he said.

But after a half hour combing through Herb's workbench area and two bedroom storage closets, they turned up nothing.

While Nora made a fresh pot of green tea, Lyle and Jen convened back where they started, in the garage.

Somebody in the neighborhood was grilling burgers, and the cicadas were in fine tune. The moon hung above the brick house across the street like a soccer ball kicked into the air from one of the fine trimmed lawns.

"Not the kind of place to find a serial killer," said Jen.

"Or precisely the place," said Lyle, taking in the evening breeze.

"I mean this house. There's nothing here."

"Doesn't seem to be."

"No, Lyle. I mean it. You know my background. I'm trained to *see* things. *There's nothing here.*"

"So, Herb's not our man?"

"I don't think so."

"How do we explain the tackle box?"

"What if Nora is telling the truth? What if the tackle box doesn't belong here?" said Jen.

"Are you saying somebody carried it in?" said Lyle.

"Maybe during the sale," said Jen. "Maybe somebody wanted to get rid of it."

"Half the town was through here today," said Lyle.

"But half the town wasn't here before lunch. And the box arrived before lunch. That narrows it down somewhat."

They were quite a while.

"What do we know about Mariah Dale?" said Jen.

"Why her?"

Jen shrugged. "Just a weird feeling. We know Mariah was here, but she claims to have been waiting in her car while Brittney came in. It's a bit odd."

"You're still mad about losing your shoes."

"Damn straight," said Jen. "What about Brittney's father?"

"Guy from Omaha," said Lyle. "Mariah and her daughter moved here after the divorce and mom got the superintendent job. The father doesn't have any ties to Meadows Ford that I know about."

"What about—"

The side door to the garage opened, and Nora carried in two steaming mugs from her kitchen table, "Here's a cup of hot tea for each of you," she said, handing them out. "You're welcome to come inside and sit. It's a bit of a mess."

"No, thank you," said Lyle. "We need to be going."

"You must be exhausted," Jen told the older woman. "You had quite a day."

"I did indeed," said Nora. Then, with an impish grin, "Santa Fe, here I come."

"Good tea," said Jen after her first sip.

"You didn't find anything else to take home?" said Nora.

"I guess not," said Jen.

"I have a question," said Lyle.

Nora nodded for him to continue.

"I wonder if anybody might have carried in that tackle box we purchased."

Jen's phone buzzed.

She put her teacup down on the workbench and looked at her phone screen. "Gotta take this," she said, excusing herself to walk outside.

"I can't imagine who or why somebody would bring that box in here," said Nora.

"Here's another question," said Lyle. "Did any of your customers act in any way out of the ordinary?"

Nora narrowed her eyes. "You can't kid an old kidder, Chief. You didn't come back here tonight to shop for fishing gear."

Lyle pushed back his cap to scratch his head. "No, I guess we didn't."

Nora chuckled under her breath and held up the index finger of her right hand. "You came back here to fish, yes. But not to shop."

"If I'm honest with you, will you be honest with me?" said Lyle.

"Most certainly."

"One of your customers may have knowingly or unknowingly committed a crime. I'm looking into it with as much discretion as possible."

Nora winked at him. "I understand completely. And since you asked, I do remember one customer in partic-ular that made me think twice—Edna Larkin."

"Edna's a regular at garage sales," said Lyle.

"I didn't mention her name because of what she bought. It's because she kept asking about that Dale girl—the poor thing who ran off with my jewelry." Nora held up her open palm fingers spread. "Edna came back five times today. Literally, five times. I counted on my fingers.

She asked about Brittney Dale each time. I thought it strange."

"I agree," said Lyle.

"And then, of course, there were the knives."

Lyle nearly choked on his tea. "Knives?"

"Knives," Nora said. "Saws. Sharp-edged objects. Every single time she was here. And each time she wanted me to wrap them in old newspaper. Isn't that odd? What would she need them for?"

"Gotta go, Chief."

Lyle turned at the sound of Jen's voice. Urgent. Demanding

"What is it?"

"Tell you in the car," she said, holding up her phone. "I'll drive."

———

JEN RACED down State Street without lights or siren. She flew through the four-way stop, then past the Lutheran church to hook a quick right onto Edgewood where she floored it in anticipation of Highway 5.

Her heart kept time with the Chevy Tahoe's piston engine, fast as during her morning run—faster. But she worked to keep her voice calm and under control.

She needed Lyle to understand the big picture.

"That was Mariah Dale on the phone," she said. "Calling from Lincoln. Brittney never showed up at her friend's pool party. She's not answering phone calls or texts. Mariah is frantic."

"Why call us?"

"Like a lot of parents, Mariah believes in *trust but verify*. She's got a tracker on Brittney's phone."

"And where is Miss Brittney now?"

Jen swallowed hard.

"Her phone's been pinging from a gravel road two miles outside town for the past hour. Willow Creek Road," she said.

"I've got news too," said Lyle.

He told her about Edna Larkin.

Jen thought it was like one of those little plastic dexterity puzzles with the sliding plastic squares that make a complete picture once everything's arranged correctly.

She thought she saw it all clearly.

"Did Edna Larkin live in Meadow's Ford forty years ago?" said Jen.

"Sure. Edna and her husband, Ralph, were community-minded people. The family's an institution. Chamber of Commerce, volunteer groups."

"What happened to Ralph?"

"Heart attack. Or maybe a stroke."

"When? Look it up on your phone."

Lyle pulled out his phone.

"Type in *Ralph Larkin Obituary*," said Jen.

When the information came up, Lyle slapped the dashboard. "Ralph died exactly forty-two years ago this month."

"Same time as the killings stopped."

"Before he could mail Annie Beck's finger."

"And now Edna's taking up where Ralph left off. With Brittney Dale," said Jen.

"Hell, what are you lollygaggin' around for?" said Lyle. "Give it all you've got."

Jen pushed the Chevy hard, ran the stop sign at Edgewood, hit Highway 5, and drifted into the gravel corner at Willow Creek, lights flashing now, the siren wailing.

Through the storm of dust the Chevy raised, Jen followed Lyle's outstretched finger and saw the white Buick parked at the side of the road near a chain link fence bordering the city's brush and lawn waste dump.

She braked sharply, stopping within two feet of the Buick and taking up the middle of the road.

Lyle had his door open before they stopped rolling.

Jen stepped onto the road two seconds later, watching Lyle approach the Buick.

Neither of them drew their firearms.

Lyle knocked on the passenger side window of the Buick. Stepped back as the door opened from the inside.

Jen stood between the two vehicles. Alert. Ready for anything.

"Brittney Dale?" said Lyle. "Mrs. Larkin?"

"You people, again," said Brittney. "Why the hell can't you leave me be?"

The girl was dressed as she had been earlier in the day—sweatshirt, shorts, and sneakers. She crawled from the car with a world-weary sigh.

Lyle looked past her.

"Step out of the car, please, Mrs. Larkin," he said.

The driver's side door opened, and Edna Larkin popped her white-haired head out.

Jen moved around to help her, glancing inside the car.

The front seat was covered with dozens of Polaroid snapshots, fading color images of nude female cadavers.

Jen saw several close up shots on hands with missing fingers.

Taking Jen's proffered arm, Edna said, "Thank you, dear. This gravel gets so tricky underfoot. It's something I always try to remember. Willow Creek is tricky underfoot."

"We didn't do nothing wrong," said Brittney.

"I was just showing the girl around town," said Edna. "Sharing precious memories."

"Be careful coming around the car, Edna," said Jen, guiding the old woman to where Lyle and Brittney waited.

"She's a fast study, this one," said Edna, shaking her finger at Brittney. "I knew she would be the first time I saw her. I knew right away. She's got the talent for the job. The passion too."

"What job might that be?" said Jen.

Edna's eyes sparkled. "Murder of course. But more than that."

"It's like an art," said Brittney.

"And to think," Edna continued, "when I woke up this morning and decided to drop my old box at the garage sale, I thought I was putting it all away." Edna reached out for Brittney's hand. "Turns out, I found my heiress apparent."

"*Your* box, ma'am?" said Lyle.

"After my Ralph died, I couldn't go on without him."

Jen looked back inside the Buick. A new box sat on the back seat, full of knives, some wrapped in newspapers.

"Heiress apparent?" said Lyle.

"She's a future All-American," said Jen.

"Screw Harvard," said Brittney.

"Call Mrs. Dale," said Lyle. "Let her know her daughter's okay."

"I wouldn't say that," said Jen. "But I'll call her."

Lyle nodded and led Brittney and Edna back to the Tahoe.

"Be careful," said Edna. "This road has always been tricky."

Jen looked up the most recent conversation on her phone and hit the call-back number.

The moon was a somber bronze flame against the deepening black.

It was gonna be a long night.

Dinosaur
Nicholas Cain

I'm delighted to have snagged a story for this anthology from one of my writing heroes, Nicholas Cain. During the 80s and 90s, Cain created and wrote some of the best men's adventure series on the market, all with a deep connection to the Vietnam War and the brave men who served there—*Saigon Commandos*, *War Dogs*, *Chopper-1*, *Little Saigon*, as well as other novels under various pseudonyms. Cain's twelve-book *Saigon Commands* series is my particular favorite because of its unusual focus on the Military Police units serving in Saigon. Cyber meeting Cain last year explained a lot. His personal experiences as an MP in Saigon and his years in law enforcement on the home front are what gave the strong patina of realism to his work. The man knows of what he writes. I once stated, "If Joseph Wambaugh had served as an MP in Vietnam, he'd be Nicholas Cain." That's how much I respect his writing. Fortunately, I was able to get Cain to support a *brother in blue* and return to his fiction roots to share this unusual cop tale...

DINOSAUR

DEC. 7, 2017, Denver News Now: *Officials from the City of Thornton in North Metro Denver report they have been forced to halt construction of the new police substation at 132nd & Quebec after workers unearthed what can only be described as the fossilized bones of a prehistoric creature known as Triceratops. This particular dinosaur grew to thirty feet in length, stood nine feet tall, weighed up to twelve tons, and is famous for the two massive horns that protruded from the protective frill rising along the top of its massive skull. Every schoolboy has seen paintings of a Triceratops doing battle with the "king of the tyrant lizards," better known as T-Rex, both of which are believed to have gone extinct some sixty-six million years ago when, scientists theorize, a giant comet struck earth near the Yucatan peninsula, bringing an end to most life on the planet for many eons after that. Adding to the mystery, a human skeleton was also found lying atop the monster's carcass and appears to have been the victim of foul play. Officials have not revealed its age or whether they believe it was also doing battle with the Triceratops at the time of its violent demise.*

A BLIZZARD HAD BEEN FORECAST for Colorado's Front Range. I could sense the change in the weather by the throbbing in my left knee. It was the one that had stopped a sliver of lead in Saigon, 1972, courtesy of a rooftop sniper with an AK-47. His bullet had missed the squad of scrambling MPs in front of me. The bullet exploded across the blacktop of Le Loi Street, splintering into slivers of hot lead, one of which nearly ripped out my kneecap. It had been a typical humid, sticky night in the tropics. The sniper turned out to be a disgruntled whore —tired of being rousted by the American army coppers— and not a hardcore communist. This meant no Purple Heart, just a wicked scar, memories to last a lifetime, and a dull ache any time the weather changed, especially in winter.

I started to turn left across busy 84th Avenue at Fox Street but hit my brakes at the center median. Two blue and white police cars suddenly appeared in oncoming traffic, their multi-colored, rooftop strobes flashing bright as flares against the blackness of midnight. The first roared by, siren yelping. The two patrolmen inside were grim-faced and determined. A less urgent, mournful electronic wail emanated from the second cruiser twenty yards behind. Its occupants were seemingly unconcerned, laughing about something or other. Their carefree expressions instantly reminded me of my training officer forty years ago. Sipping at a paper cup of 7/11 coffee with one hand as he steered with the other, he maneuvered expertly through slower traffic as we raced to the scene of a head-on crash with fatalities. The Code-3 high-speed run was always fun. The ten or twelve hours of paperwork that followed, not so much.

The coast clear, flashing reds and yellows growing distant in my rearview mirror, I completed my left turn and pulled into the almost empty parking lot of a coffee shop. From outside, through the big picture windows, I scanned the interior for anything suspicious. Seeing nothing, I slipped my dark blue Dakota into Park and killed the Magnum V-6 under the hood. Opening the door, I got out, adjusted the holstered Sig under my jacket, and shook off the pain in my left knee.

I glanced at my bulky black wristwatch. It was 3:00 AM. The watch had been a gift from my nephew, who thought it was cool to have an uncle who had been a Saigon Commando—military police—back in the day. On the face of the watch, the words Vietnam Vetcran glowed an elephant-grass green.

Earlier, I'd cruised up busy I-25 in North Metro Denver. When I crossed into the working class suburb cops called Big T, my stomach started churning. It was a placed I'd avoided since I'd traded in my Thornton PD badge for a gig as a security consultant in Singapore in 1981. The gig had promptly gone sour, but I'd tried to learn from that regrettable mistake. It was why I was back here again.

As light snow began to fall, I figured the rest of the night should be peaceful. However, I was startled by the yelping of another siren. I turned to see an unmarked car, red and blues flashing from behind its front engine grille, sliding on some invisible black ice. It was chasing two intoxicated punks on a blacked-out snowmobile. They were speeding down the middle of the roadway, swerving back and forth on their stainless steel skis. The passenger threw an obscene gesture back at the pursuing officer.

Shaking my head, I walked into the welcome warmth of the coffee shop. Through the glass doors closing behind me, I heard another engine roaring into overdrive. I turned my head to see a four-wheel-drive police SUV appear from a side street. I watched as it passed the unmarked unit and began gaining on the snowmobile. *If only we'd had those babies back in the day*, I thought, but I didn't watch to see what happened. The more things changed in the Big T, the more they remained the same.

I vaguely heard what sounded like a distant crash as I moved toward the rear of the coffee shop. But whatever happened down the road was out of sight and no concern to me. I was retired, a certifiable old fart. I'd been summoned to my old battlegrounds "for a little surprise." The cryptic invitation had been left on my voicemail by a man I'd trained to survive on the night beat over forty years ago. He was now a Deputy Chief.

The coffee shop had changed dramatically from the graveyard shift refuge I remembered. The plate glass windows still afforded an unobstructed view of the streets outside, illuminated by the bright lights of the mall on the other side of I-25. However, the long, curving counter was mostly gone. Once the domain of the Thornton Thumpers—the cops who had policed this rowdy suburb of the Mile-High City—the counter had now been chopped off by someone with no imagination. The alteration made room for a booth and tables, but I felt oddly violated. A dark force had screwed with my sacred memories.

A heavyset black waitress emerged from the bakery in the back room. She was spilling out of a too tight, pink outfit that stretched obscenely whenever she moved. Holding a half-full coffee pot in one hand and a soiled dishrag in the other, she wiped sweat from her brow with a meaty forearm and narrowed her gaze in my direction.

"Can I help you?" she said as if I was trespassing. I instantly missed the slim waitress with blonde locks who had cooed, "Coffee, tea or me?" every time she greeted the Blues of First Watch as they came in for their first caffeine break of the midnight shift.

"Coffee," I said, then slid across the protesting plastic cover of a swiveling stool, positioning my back against an interior wall. Cream and sugar were on the counter in front of me. "Got any Buttermilks?"

"We don't make those anymore." She frowned and aggressively plopped a porcelain mug down in front of me. I paused, surprised it had not shattered.

Glancing up, I locked eyes with her, remembering all the stare-down contests I'd won with young, anti-cop waitresses during the seventies. "How 'bout a bear claw?" I tilted my head slightly. "You still make those, don't you?"

"You look like a bear," she said. The slightest trace of a smile cracked her grimace. She leaned forward, slipped one of her curved, inch-long fingernails under the slightly visible ribbon protruding along the edge of my blue calico shirt. She pulled free the good luck St. Michael's scapular that was usually tucked out of sight, worn for protection like a Viking's sacred talisman. Her tone was accusatory, a challenge when she added, "A *smoky*-da-bear."

Headlights pulling into the parking lot outside stopped any clever retort. It was a police car. The officers stopped their unit but did not get out. Instead, I felt they were staring directly at me. I knew one had to be consulting the BOLO Hot Sheet on the clipboard attached to his dash. It held passport-sized photographs of a dozen local fugitives.

"Friends of yours?" The waitress asked.

I ignored her. I turned, watching for movement in the reflection of a long mirror running the length of the wall. A second patrol car pulled up, and the headlights of both units went out simultaneously. Four haggard-looking patrolmen in their twenties dismounted in unison. One paused to lean back into the car and balance a riot helmet atop the front seat's headrest.

Their uniforms were dark blue, appearing almost black. The badges over their hearts sparkled beneath the street lights as one officer zipped up his leather jacket and another unzipped his own. The stormtrooper-style hats we'd worn back in the seventies were nowhere to be seen.

The officers had beautiful metallic-blue police patches on their shoulders. Forty years ago, we'd gone slick-sleeved, like our Denver PD brothers to the south. The officers were now standing between the two marked patrol cars, straightening their tucked-in ties and aligning their gig lines out of habit.

A third sedan cruised in off the street, its headlights already off. It was an unmarked muscle car, last of the Crown Vic Interceptors. It was driven by my old buddy, the once-young rookie I'd trained in 1979 before there were such titles as Field Training Officers. Now a watch commander, his hair was a bit thinner and graying, but his belly was still flat. He had a dozen white hash marks sewn above the cuff on the left arm of his long-sleeved uniform shirt. They glowed as bright as the teeth he flashed when he spotted me sitting inside.

I stood, approached the doorway, and dramatically held my arms out as if anticipating a romantic embrace— typical cop humor.

"This must be him," the nearest officer to me said. Held out an open hand to shake. "The living legend, we've heard so much about."

I felt my face flushing, even in the half light of red neon advertising *We Never Close*. I shook his hand without making solid eye contact.

The older lawman chuckled. "Only believe half of what you've heard about this old dinosaur." Roy was a stocky sixty-year-old with wire-rim glasses and a crew cut. He elbowed his way through the cluster of gun-belts and tactical boots.

"He still looks like a cop," one of the younger officers said.

Once inside the coffee shop, Roy held out a scarred and calloused hand that felt like old leather when I clasped it. "How the hell you been, Jonathan?" he asked.

"It's been a long time, brother!" I said, enjoying the warmth and sincerity of the handshake. "Are those *stars* on your collar, Roy?" I asked. "Does the Big T have generals supervising the line troops now?"

My old friend smirked, avoiding the question. "Anyone run this guy for warrants yet?"

"So what's one of the big chiefs doin' workin' graves?" I asked.

"*Deputy* Chief," he corrected me with a wink. "I like to get out with my troops. Keeps 'em honest."

Roy quickly introduced me to the four patrolmen, "Larry, Moe, and Curly—I forgot the last guy's name on the end," he joked.

"Just don't call me Shirley." The odd man out gave a poor imitation of the actor, Leslie Nielsen.

"He's the reason I asked you to come up to the Big T." Roy could not mask his pride. "My son, Joey. He's number one on the sergeant's promotion list."

As I said, "Congratulations," to Joey, Roy began to mock frisk me. He ignored my top-of-the-line, Swiss-made Sig in its concealed hip holster, but seemed surprised when he found and retrieved a pair of well-worn but intact leather sap gloves half tucked in under my belt. My wife always wondered why they were so heavy. I did not tell her they were lined with powdered lead, designed to take down even the biggest bad boy with one punch.

"These are illegal now," Roy said. He grinned, handing them back anyway.

"They were prohibited by department policy back when *we* worked the streets," I reminded Roy. I enjoyed his apparent unease at this revelation in front of his men. "Old habits die hard," I said.

Roy's eyes fell from the sap gloves in my hands to my black cargo pants, which hid most of my high-topped leather boots. He then looked up at my tactical mustache and the close-cropped thinning hair on my head.

"What happened to that full head of pitch black Dago hair I remember?" Roy feigned a disapproving snort. "What I'm seein' here is sun-bleached, like you been hidin' down in the tropics again,. Have you been playing pirate with Maggie Q or Michelle Yeoh?"

"My wife prefers the Doc Savage bronze skullcap look," I said, playing along.

"At least you still got those bedroom blue eyes that always got you into trouble." Roy rose on his tiptoes until our noses almost touched. He produced a mini-flashlight and shined it into my eyes without warning. "Pupils are a bit dilated."

"Glaucoma meds," I said. "Cataracts from retirement in red rock country, but on my worst day, I can still Roy Rogers your ass on any range of your choice."

He was unfazed. "Still married to that refugee-turned-interpreter who could out-shoot both of us even on a bad day?"

"Guilty, Chief," I assumed the position of attention, still mocking him somewhat.

Without warning, Roy slugged my gut hard, but not hard enough to double me over. Instead, I backed away into a mock karate stance, hands raised defensively. We engaged in the obligatory five-second shadow boxing, then slapped each other on the shoulder again. With the back of his hand, Roy tapped my gut a second time. "You're looking...*svelte*," he said.

"It's the morning workouts," I told him. "Keeps my back from going out."

"Service!" One of the officers pounded a fist lightly on the counter in mock impatience, yet with enough weight behind it to make some nearby silverware rattle.

The waitress, still standing in the distant archway to the dough ovens, appeared agitated. She started to say something snide, but thought better of it and began biting at her thick lower lip. She grabbed a pot of hot coffee and sauntered over.

I recalled how some of my fellow officers refused to take breaks at this particular coffee shop, claiming the floor to ceiling windows made it a sniper's delight. I did not mention the Code-3 incidents I'd witnessed outside upon my arrival.

I glanced out the plate glass windows at the three police cars. "Slow night?" I asked Roy.

"Been babysitting a bunch of politicians and back-stabbing wannabe's at a city council meeting that went until two a.m." Roy sighed loudly as he poured powdered cream into the cup of steaming coffee the waitress had placed in front of him. He glanced up at her. "Snort some snot into it for me, Kaneesha?" Two of the officers snickered while the other two appeared aghast. "You know I like my coffee strong and snotty."

"Been savin' up a big hack all night just for you, Rowdy Roy," she turned away, giving her ample derriere an exaggerated swish as she headed toward the back room. Roy grimaced and feigned a shudder.

He turned to me and muttered under his breath, "She don't like cops."

I nodded. "Kinda got that impression."

Outside, through the grimy plate glass, we all watched in silence as the powerful beam from a low-flying police helicopter swept back and forth through the industrial park across the street.

"Denver PD's Air One?" I asked. "Or Adams County's airship?"

"She's one of *ours*," Roy said proudly. "We call it 'Night Sun' and actually have *two* up on weekends, budget and parts permitting. The city's really expanded, Jonathan—more than doubled in size since you were here. We're on course to break two hundred thousand Thorntonoids this year."

"Sixth largest city in Colorado," One of his men added, beaming. "We're even building a fancy, new, top-of-the-line police sub-station way up at a hundred-and-thirty-second and Quebec."

Hearing that intersection spoken of so matter-of-factly was like an unexpected slap in the face. However, no one seemed to notice my spasm-like reaction.

Roy frowned. "Building was going fine until workers digging the foundation found some friggin' Triceratops. It brought everything to a halt until they could fully excavate the site under the supervision of the state geologist."

"It was a Torosaurus," I corrected him, and chuckled at the number of raised eyebrows. I shrugged. "I wanted to be a paleontologist before I wanted to be a cop."

"And now you is an old dinosaur yourself," Roy said. "Like me." He seemed uncomfortable with the subject, rubbing the back of his neck.

"They found human remains among the dinosaur bones," another officer said.

I glanced at Roy to find he was already staring at me. "Human, huh?" I said, my eyes locked with Roy's. He raised an eyebrow and nodded slightly as if acknowledging an old secret rising to the surface—sins of the Blue Templars, come back to haunt us.

"Probably an old caveman," Roy said. He took a long sip of brew, then tugged at one end of his drooping mustache. He looked grim but straightened his posture as if he'd remembered something important. "You heard Dante retired after forty years?"

"Great copper—a real stand-up guy," I said. "What about Glenn?" I'd heard rumors through the wait-a-minute-vine but decided to ask anyway.

"Suicide," Roy said matter-of-factly.

Everyone at the counter stared down into the depths of their coffee cups.

"Twenty years ago," Roy said. He smiled sadly.

A deep sigh escaped me, then I heard myself saying, "That would explain why he never answered my letters."

Roy's voice was flat, not responding to my dark

humor. "Danny-Boy and Keith-Two-Guns also suck started their guns. A couple years apart. God rest their tortured souls."

The voice of one of the officers cracked slightly as he said, "We lost more police officers in this country last year to suicide than to hostile gunfire from suspects."

Everyone nodded, but no one said anything.

The waitress reappeared noisily, like a janitor interrupting communion at a Catholic mass. She began refilling coffee mugs. "Seems I got the whole damn police force sittin' right here in my little ol' coffee shop." She glanced at her oversized wrist watch. It had a stylized fist outlined on the crystal. "If I was a criminal, dis 'ould be the perfect time fo' me to be out there commitin' my crimes." She stopped in front of Roy. "Another Long John, Chief? I just fried up a batch the ways you likes 'em —dark chocolate." She leaned on the counter, the tops of her ponderous breasts straining against her low-cut blouse. Roy made a point of ignoring her.

The waitress's watch crystal gnawed at me. The fist etched on the crystal was a symbol of the BLA radicals responsible for the ambush murders of dozens of police officers across the country during the 1970s. I resisted the intense urge to reach out and grab her by the throat.

Five pak-sets began crackling as their portable radios emitted a three-toned scrambler alert, followed by a woman's out of breath voice saying, "Officer Needs Help..." Static overwhelmed the radio net, then her voice returned, a bit more powerfully. "Hundred and sixty-third and Washington...Shots fired...One suspect down...One fleeing northbound on Washington toward the Costco parking lot..."

The officers beside me were already on their feet, jamming through the doorway as they raced out of the coffee shop. Roy and I sat calmly watching as the cruisers fired up and nearly side-swiped each other backing out onto 84th Avenue. Tires spun and sirens yelped—a metallic cat fight. Roof strobes momentarily blinded us as they flashed on with brilliant rays of red and blue, then a pulsating white star blazed out in the middle, twice as bright as all the others.

"Impressive," I said, trying not to sound sarcastic. "A brighter light show than we had on our old Novas and Malibus back in '81."

Roy shook his head. He'd seen it all a hundred times. "I tell 'em and I tell 'em, but nobody listens—*back* your patrol car in so you can split like Batman if you get a hot call."

He slowly rose from his stool, adjusting the squelch on his own pak-set as he slipped it into its leather holder. "I better get up there and see who shot who." He curled his fingers, glanced at his fingernails as if deciding if he needed a manicure.

I remembered how he used to do the same thing forty years ago, after a knock-down-drag-out fight at the Ghetto Bar or M-80s or the crazy cowboy juke joint boasting the longest bar counter west of the Mississippi. It was called The Wild Wild West, and bull riders from all over the country came to get drunk and ride the mechanical bull. They also ended up challenging the Thornton Thumpers to a round of fisticuffs so they could return to Dallas or Helena, Las Vegas, or Queens and boast they'd fought with Colorado's finest.

Roy had always checked his fingernails at end-of-shift for dried blood or bits of flesh because he didn't like to bring the filth home to the childhood sweetheart who'd been his dedicated, supportive wife for the past forty-some years.

"So, they found a body in the field up at hundred-and-thirty-second and Quebec?" I asked calmly.

Roy massaged the back of his neck again then rubbed at the stubble on his throat. It was a bad sign.

"No comment, brother," Roy said. He then lapsed into a bad Marlon Brando accent, "Fo'getta 'bout it. Forty years is forty years. Nobody cares anymore about the past 'cept them damn dinosaur hunters."

I thought about one of our *problem children* from back then. He was a homeless character who always wore a dark, threadbare suit. No one could figure out where he lived, but people were always calling the police on him. He had a habit of lurking in the back alleys behind the shops of District Two, and he always fought any cop who encountered him. Legend had it he was some sort of black belt and had killed a man with his bare hands. He supposedly served a couple years for manslaughter before returning to his old stomping grounds in the Big T. He got off stomping on cops, so two units were always dispatched to any call involving him.

Until one night when Roy and I were dispatched...

"What was that Adam Henry's name?" I asked.

Roy instinctively knew who I was talking about. He had an almost photographic memory, but he didn't answer me directly. Instead, he said, "It's all roadkill to me, brother. Good riddance."

"I heard he had a kid," I pushed. "Must be thirty or forty now."

"I don't know, and I seriously don't care, brother—and neither should you. Let sleeping mutts lie. No reason to stir up the coprolites. There's already some lowlife reporter from the *Sentinel* snooping around the dig site. It's the same long-haired bastard who gave you such a hard time in the press when you were writing stories for *Soldier of Fortune* magazine back in the seventies. Don't give him a bone to start gnawing at unless you wanna open up the whole can o' maggots."

Roy waved toward his city crate while turning off the squelch on his portable radio. "Better see if I can catch up with 'em. Of course, I just switched my rear-wheel studs to all-season radials 'cause I thought winter was 'bout over. Wanna come along—for old time's sake?"

"Not sure the old ticker could take it, Chief—you drivin' Code 3 up I-25 on the black ice buildin' up out there." I tried to appear sad at the missed opportunity.

Roy finished off the last of his Long John and washed it down with a gulp of lukewarm coffee. He set the mug on the counter and curled lips. I'd seen him do the same thing after he killed a last Viet Cong for laughs from atop the U.S. Embassy in Saigon in 1975. He'd been the Marine Corps' top sniper in-country during the Fall and had seemed in no hurry to leave.

"Suit yourself, Slick." There it was again, the word I'd first heard—that all new military recruits heard—at Boot Camp, just a couple of months shy of high school graduation. Even at age sixty-five, it still sent a weird chill down my aching spine.

"But before I go," Roy said, "I've got a little something for you in memory of the good ol' 70s." Roy produced an object the size of his backup Derringer. It was wrapped in blue silk. With a flourish, he pulled the silk cover back, revealing my old badge from forty years earlier, its menacing eagle sparkling up at me.

"The Chief said to just give it to you with his blessing." Roy showed some teeth in an odd version of a smile. "They were just gonna melt these old ones down," he said. "The design is obsolete. They did away with the eagle tops on the new ones. They stuck Marijuana Hill on instead."

He tapped the silver oval on his own chest, recited the private little joke. "We chopped off the top of the mountain and built police headquarters where we used to run off the potheads and bang the groupies."

I fought back something I hadn't felt in decades—a sentimental tear. I closed the silk folds over the badge, tucked it precariously under my belt, and changed the subject.

"163rd Avenue?" I was impressed. "I remember when the northern city limits was ass-backward to that at 136th. Whoever thought they'd build anything but cattle fences or pig farms up there?"

"We're *big* city now." Roy shook his head then patted

me on the shoulder as he headed for the door. "Take care, my brother."

"Stay safe," I replied. I put a lone dollar bill on the counter. From her expression of defiant disapproval, the waitress obviously felt the tip was beneath her.

"What did youse mean by *black* ice?" she asked accusingly after Roy had left.

I thought about punching her in the face for old time's sake, but I'd spotted the three closed-circuit TV cameras in the ceiling. Instead, I snatched up the dollar bill and slowly and clearly said, "I'm sorry you are so miserable and full of hate."

I took a last sip of my coffee and headed for the door. Roy's taillights were growing smaller down 84th Avenue. Then he activated his lights and siren, sending blue and red beams pulsing from one side of the Interceptor's rear window, like a fallen angel's halo.

I regretted not accepting the ride-along offer, but I was no longer driven by my old, personal motto—*Seek danger and adventure each new day*. These days, I just wanted to be left alone with my out-of-print books.

"I spitted in your coffee," the waitress called after me.

"You 'spat,'" I corrected her English. "And no, you didn't. I was watching you the whole time. Closely."

While still in the doorway, I bumped into what could only be described as a ghost from my past—a skinhead of large stature, in his thirties, wearing a black and gray Raiders hoodie and sporting a Fu Manchu prison goatee. Behind the facial hair, however, was the spitting image of the man who legend said could kill with his bare hands, albeit thirty years younger.

I hesitated, but he ignored me. Instead, he lunged in to confront the waitress, a blue-steel revolver with an eight-inch barrel in one hand. He pressed her flaring nostrils flat with it as her wide eyes bulged in terror. "Gimme your twenties," he demanded. He pulled a Capri pillowcase from inside his waistband, tossing it on the counter between them. "No small bills—do you understand? Only twenties." He paused. The waitress' oversized watch caught his eye. He ripped it off her wrist, glanced at it for a second then threw it back at her.

He saw her hands drop to her waist, out of sight.

"Lemme see your hands!" he shouted. "Get 'em up here! No alarm buttons! If you tripped the alarm, you are dead, bitch. You understand me?" His words slowed, each one coated with determination. "You want to *die* here tonight? You get paid enough to make it worth it?"

She glanced in my direction, but I was already out the door, standing beside an ancient oak coated in white and wider than me. I started to unholster my Sig-Sauer semi-automatic. "*One of the most expensive handguns in the world.*" Clint Eastwood's Dirty Harry voice echoed in my brain, which was already operating in fast forward due to three cups of coffee. However, I thought better of my knee-jerk reaction. I slid the .45 back into its customized holster, which was decorated with a subdued combat patch of the 18th MP Brigade, Vietnam.

I pulled out my cell phone. **No service** appeared on the screen. "You've *got* to be kidding," I muttered, replacing the Android in its waterproof sheath. I could feel my heart racing, pounding to get out of my chest. As cops called it, I was drunk on adrenaline. I mentally warded off the stress-induced tunnel vision trying to cloud the dangerous scene before me.

Hand resting on the butt of my holstered pistol, I assessed the situation. Everything was happening fast. With all the Code-3 Action up north, it was doubtful any local LEO would show up. There was a chance a state trooper or Adams County deputy would stop for a coffee break, but the odds weren't good.

My choices were simple. I could draw my Sig and blast the gunman between the eyes as he exited the coffee shop. Or I could remain unseen behind the tree then follow him. I might get a license plate number if he went to a hidden vehicle, or get an address if he disappeared into the many apartment complexes nearby. It was probably best to simply be a good observer, a solid witness. My days and nights of crime fighting had been over for a while. It just didn't seem worth it anymore.

I was no longer a twenty-five-year-old single street cop living in an apartment with no assets a civil attorney could go after regardless of my actions being right or wrong.

I was now married to a woman who worked hard seven days a week so I could remain retired. I owned multiple homes and had responsibility for a lot of people. With all the ambulance-chasing attorneys out there, even a righteous shooting would put it all in jeopardy. I was too old to start over.

"Come on!" I could hear the robber yelling at the waitress as he scooped up the large denomination bills she'd dropped and scattered across the countertop before tipping over the coffee pot on them. He kept glancing back over his shoulder but was having a difficult time seeing the dark streets outside through the semi-reflective sheets of plate glass.

Frustrated, he raised his revolver and fired a shot into the ceiling. Even from where I stood, the Magnum's discharge was deafening. My ears started ringing. This dip-wad definitely meant business and was loaded for bear.

The discharge was louder than even *he'd* anticipated, and he was thrown into panic mode. He scooped up the half-filled pillowcase, ignoring the scattered five- and ten-dollar bills, and dashed for the door.

I was hoping he'd exit to his right, which would take him away from where I stood beside the tree. He, of course, ducked to his left, bent over as if expecting a fusillade of bullets to greet him.

It had been a couple decades since I'd employed it, but I still remembered how to use my brand name Mark of Cain Elbow Smack. When thrown properly—with the weight of my entire body propelling the blinding thrust of bone and muscle—even a big man stood little chance against the devastating impact.

As he moved past me, my elbow slammed into the unsuspecting suspect's right temple. The impact caused instant disorientation for the suspect while darn near fracturing my arm in two places. When he stumbled right into me head down, my right knee broke his nose and snapped his head back with a sickening crack. He crumpled at my feet. It was over that quick.

He was moaning, not quite unconscious, but definitely out of the fight. He still clutched his revolver in an iron-tight grip. When I tried to pull it free, his trigger finger functioned as God intended and the pistol discharged, ripping the pretty biker buckle off the side of my Engineer's boot. I twisted his hand with as much strength as I could muster, heard two fingers break, and the Colt was mine.

The suspect remained semi-conscious, groaning nonstop in pain. Blood trickled from his right ear. It also dripped more liberally from both his nose and mouth. This concerned me because shards of nasal cavity bone can penetrate the frontal lobes of the brain if struck with too much force. Not a lot of people know this, but all cops do.

I flipped open his pistol's cylinder, noted four.357 cartridges intact, slammed the cylinder shut again. I tucked the revolver under my belt until it was seated firmly against my crotch. The long barrel fought for space with the odd erection this whole confrontation had unexpectedly given me.

I made some adjustments to be sure the barrel was pointing safely away from my family jewels. Murphy's Law was no stranger to me—I'd butted heads with it numerous times in my various careers. I was resolved to the fact that whatever could go wrong in my professional life usually did.

Out of habit, I reached for the handcuffs case that wasn't there. I considered removing my civilian belt and tying the suspect's hands behind his back. Dip-wads like this guy always recovered consciousness before help arrived, and this bastard was six inches taller than me. He also outweighed me by fifty pounds, most of it muscle laced with meth, PCP, or something equally dangerous.

However, removing my belt would result in gravity-prone pants, and I was smart enough to know I didn't have a gangbanger's ability at keeping loose trousers from falling to their knees. I left the belt on.

I was kneeling on one knee by the suspect, mentally considering my options, when a three-wheeled contraption skidded up the wet pavement into my peripheral vision. Its lone headlight came to a stop inches from my face. The cutest little rent-a-cop jumped out, her nightstick at the ready.

"I heard a shot," she shouted. "I was patrolling across the street at the strip mall and heard two shots. Can I assist you, sir?"

"Loan me your handcuffs," I said. I glanced at the web belt straining to pop forth from beneath her rain slicker. There was no handgun visible, but it had everything else imaginable hanging from it.

I expected a protest, but she produced a set of pink designer cuffs before I'd even finished my sentence. I sensed cars pulling up behind me, but their headlights were on high beam so I couldn't tell who they were.

"Help me search him for more weapons," I said after the security guard helped me force the gunman's steroid-swollen arms close enough together for the handcuffs to secure both vein-popping wrists.

A husky male's voice erupted above and behind me. "Do you have this situation under control?"

I glanced back to discover an Adam's County Sheriff's unit had pulled up to the scene. Neither deputy had bothered to draw their service weapons, but stood with hands on hips, trying to assess the bizarre situation.

Snowflakes the size of silver dollars began to fall from the sky in force. The lack of wind and the eerie red beams of the patrol car swishing lazily back and forth gave the parking lot around the coffee shop a distinct fairytale feeling.

"This guy just robbed the coffee shop," I told the deputies. "An easy collar, if you want it. I can write-up a Supp' for you in five minutes if you scribe the Face Sheet. I think the PD is busy up north with a shooting. Some female officer was calling for help."

"Yeah," came a chuckle from one of the deputies. "One of their Affirmative Action hires tripped over her training bra or something. Accidental discharge. *Roy Roger-That* is on top of it. But, yeah, we'll take the arrest if you don't want it."

"You off duty?" the other deputy placed the slightest bit of command authority in the tone of his voice.

"Retired," I coughed a bit, out of breath and feeling my age. I took in a deep breath, held it, exhaled slowly, took another deep breath. My heartbeat slowed a bit. I hoped I didn't drop dead then and there. I did not want to die of a heart attack or stroke in the town that had black-balled me forty years earlier—even if success was the best revenge and now a lot of coppers seemed to welcome me back as a semi-celebrity, which was mind-blowing.

"Where's the perp's gun?" The first deputy lost the humor in his voice.

"Stuffed down the front of my pants against my crotch," I kept my hands away from my torso, but not dramatically. "I've also got a.45 holstered on my right hip. My CCW permit is in my wallet."

The cop challenged me. "Why do you have a license to carry concealed if you're retired?"

"Because I've been one sort of cop or another for forty-two years but never stayed any one place long enough to qualify for a Leosa Card." I used the slang term for the Law Enforcement Officers Safety Act, which regulated the ability of retired coppers to carry their concealed firearms anywhere in the country.

After they secured both weapons, one of the deputies took my ID's over to his patrol car to run verification checks. The other officer allowed me to go back into the coffee shop when I noticed I was missing the blue silk packet containing the obsolete badge Roy had given me.

The waitress was holding it toward me with both hands in a sort of peace gesture. "You shoulda *shot* that sum'bitch," she said decisively. She made it a pouting pronouncement as she touched the trickle of blood smeared across her upper lip from having a pistol barrel jammed her nose, nearly breaking it. "He 'bout walked right into you—I saw da whole thing!"

"Hold that thought," I said, raising a finger in the air for emphasis as I felt my cell phone vibrating. Service had apparently been magically restored.

There was a text from my wife—**Are you still lollygaggin' around, having fun with your pals up at the Big T?**

Just 'bout done, I texted back, despite fingers that wouldn't stop shaking. **They're getting busy up here. We're saying our goodbyes.**

Her reply came back quickly—**Don't forget you have a date with Dr. Andrews at the museum in Morrison first thing tomorrow. Don't stay out too late.**

I glanced at my watch. I'd no doubt I'd be here writing a witness statement until well after dawn.

Roger your Last, I texted. **Looking forward to helping Dr. Andrews clean strata from that Brontosaurus skull using dental picks.**

I'd spent the summer accompanying the famed pale-ontologist on a dinosaur dig just west of the Red Rocks amphitheater. Currently, a Pink Floyd tribute band was booked there for the entire month. Pink Floyd's *Dark Side of the Moon* album had been a favorite during my entire tour of duty with the 281st MPs in Thailand, circa 1974-75. I still kept a CD of it in my truck.

My phone vibrated again with another text from my wife—**That buddy you were worried about down in Trinidad. Ex-cop type. It's on the news: he killed himself. Some kind of barri-**

cade situation. Sorry, baby-san. Another one bites the dust. Soon you won't have any friends left except ME.

I replaced the cell phone in its holder without responding. She could be ice cold at times, but it had been just her and me through thick and thin, and she was all I had to fall back on.

"How much you want for your groovy wristwatch?" I asked the waitress, motioning toward the BLA commemorative. She quickly slipped it off and handed it to me.

"Honey, after the way you cold-cocked that loony-tunes tonight, you can have whatever you want. Coffee, tea, or ME, baby!"

"Thanks," I set it back on the counter and smashed my fist down onto it—destroying most of the crystal and watch face beneath it. I enjoyed the sight of her jaw dropping. I slid off my own black, quarter-inch-wide rubber wristband with its neon blue letters proclaiming Blue Lives Matter. I handed it to her and was happy when she accepted it. "You don't have to wear it."

"Don't plan to," she said, her defiant bluster returning.

"Just keep it someplace safe," I said. "Remember what went down here tonight and *think* about it."

"Only if *you* promise to watch some Denzel." She grabbed her purse and produced a banged-up DVD disc without the protective container of the black actor's greatest movies.

I glanced at the DVD. It was one of my Top Ten

favorite cop flicks of all time *"Training Day,"* I said. "Denzel was the bad guy."

I detected a bit of a smile as a truce seemed in effect, but she remained silent. I turned away, slipped the DVD in my shirt pocket, buttoned the flap, and exited the coffee shop.

I was stopped by one of the deputies.

"Change of plans," he said. His demeanor was unsmiling, all business.

A white van slowed to a stop on 84th Avenue and began backing into the coffee shop's parking lot. Stenciled across the double back doors was the word CORONER.

"Aw, shit," I felt my body temperature plummet, my heart starting to palpitate once again.

The deputy motioned at the robbery suspect's unmoving body lying at our feet. "Bastard had the gall to go and die on us." He stifled a laugh. "I'll need to hold onto your Sig a while longer. You're gonna have to accompany us to headquarters in Brighton. Maybe Commerce City, if there's not anyone at the station house this late. Detectives are gonna wanna interview you formally, draw a blood-alcohol sample, you know the gig. I'm gonna have to advise you of your Miranda Rights—nothing personal."

"I already know them by heart," I said. I could taste blood from chewing my lower lip, the way I used to back in the day when I was in uniform—like the night Roy put out a back-up call from behind a deserted collection of dilapidated shops and vacant restaurants in the narrow, unlit alleys of District 2.

I was the only other unit available for twenty miles, and I jumped on the call. An eternity passed in less than a minute before I skidded into the alley. In the light from the beams of blue and red fired from my rotating over-heads, I saw the Boogey Man—the man whose son was currently growing cold on the ground in front of me.

He was the man said to be a legendary black belt who knew the secret Chinese death grip, and he had Roy in a vise-like chokehold. Siren echoing off the back walls of dark stores rising all around, I tried to brake but slid side-ways, nearly running them both over. As I finally rocked to a stop, I was already pulling on my weighted sap gloves.

Adrenaline pumping, I jumped from my squad car, half-falling and twisting an ankle on a sheet of frozen sewer runoff, the stench curling my nose. Limping franti-cally forward, I saw Roy's eyes were bulging from lack of oxygen. I entered the fray in a fury, slamming my sap-gloved fist into the Boogey Man's left temple again, and again, and again...

Even after the layer of powdered lead sewn into the gloves cracked two of my right-hand knuckles—which swelled so badly we had to cut the glove away later with a switchblade—I kept punching.

The Boogey Man, the dysfunctional, degenerate, larger-than-life alley monster, finally went limp, the arm he had around Roy's neck loosening slightly. I saw the silent rage in his bulging eyes, and then I saw the life go out of them.

Roy pulled himself free from the standing corpse, which seemed to melt to the ground. Gasping for air, Roy started going ballistic with his nightstick on the thug's uncaring body until the hickory stick finally snapped with an ear-splitting *crack!*

There came the *whop!-whop!-whop!* of a helicopter, and my heart started to race as if it might explode in an ironic end to a real-life horror movie. Then I spotted DPD's Air One far to the south. Its blinding thirty-thou-sand-candle-power spotlight was turning solitary shafts of night into day, but it was circling a different Officer Needs Help call, this one in the high crime area near 52nd and Washington.

I had forced myself to resume breathing, to concen-trate on the matter at hand, which could go sideways on us in a nanosecond if we got careless. Standing next to Roy, I stared down at our handiwork. I sighed long and hard.

"You know this is gonna mean a *ton* of paperwork," I said, simply to be saying something, anything. "No doubt the Chief will have our badges this time, brother."

Roy said nothing, just popped the trunk of his patrol car.

Then he broke his eerie silence asking, "Know a good dump site for this kind of trash?"

I glanced around, but the strip mall was empty, the streets deserted—no one else had answered his call for assistance. Back then, in the seventies, on graves, we only had four cars to handle the entire city. There was a roving sergeant, but he was always drowning in paperwork at the station.

Even at the moment, I was disappointed in myself for hesitating only a second or two before volunteering, "There's that sinkhole up near 132nd and Quebec. A pack of mean coyotes hangs out there. Legend says it's where Pat Garrett dumped Billy the Kid before Hollywood got it all wrong."

Roy stared at me in silence, probably not sure if I was pulling his leg about Pat Garrett. He was maybe wondering if I'd fallen into the mental sinkhole some coppers step into and never return. I certainly didn't sound worried about anything or even our current predicament in particular.

Roy spat a wad of bloody phlegm onto the black ice. He wiped his mouth with the back of his bruised and battered fist, and said, "Quit pontificating and help me lift this Adam Henry into the trunk. Watch his feet—might throw one of them fancy Bruce Lee high kicks like a dead rattlesnake that'll still strike."

"Better leave this chapter out of your autobiography," I said. Then, unbelievably, I started laughing despite the dark and dire circumstances.

"You're the writer, Wambaugh, not me," Roy said. "I never write anything down unless the Colorado Revised Statutes require it." He started laughing too. "The sinkhole it is," he said.

"Works for me." I grabbed the Karate Kid's shoulders, heaved, and felt a twinge of protest in my lower back. I sent a silent prayer up to St. Michael, protector of police-men, having a vision of Roy also throwing me into the sinkhole if I collapsed on the ground in pain. The moment passed. My back relaxed, but I was breathing hard. The stiff seemed to weigh a ton.

"Let's do it," Roy said, his confident order clearing my head.

———

AFTER THE INCIDENT, I often volunteered to work graveyards in District 1, which covered the intersection of 132nd and Quebec. Nobody wanted the assignment, because it was too quiet with mostly upscale houses belonging to the rich residents who lived on the city's outer perimeter. There was no action except the occa-sional family disturbance or request for a welfare check. There was nothing but coyotes and rattlesnakes beyond the blue haze of suburbia—and a hidden secret.

I'd park my patrol car on the edge of the sinkhole. I'd sit there and sip hot coffee from the thermos my dear, loyal, trusting wife always prepared for me. I'd watch the orange crescent moon setting along the southwest hori-zon, and think about the madman who'd burst from the darkness of a deserted back alley at the witching hour and drop-kicked Roy to the filthy blacktop, then coldly tried to kill my best friend with a vicious chokehold.

I'd say a silent prayer for all the lost souls out there in Never Never Land, those the police had killed and those who had killed the police. Then I'd walk to the edge of the sinkhole and peer down into the abyss, careful not to slip in. I'd pull down my zipper and relieve my bladder, aiming for the center of the bottomless pit, proud to be a Seventies copper—pistol on my hip, badge over my heart, upholding the tradition of American lawmen since the days of the Wild, Wild West, when they charged toward the sound of gunfire aboard Appaloosas instead of Interceptors. I knew sometimes they were also forced to take the law into their own hands for the salvation of humanity.

"The only thing necessary for the triumph of evil is for good men to do nothing," Edmund Burke, the author and philosopher, had said two hundred years before I was born. His were words I tried to live by. We were the Thin Blue Line that held back anarchy. We were the righteous.

———

BACK IN THE PRESENT, the crystal-clear memory of forty years earlier fragmented like a bad dream at dawn, when you awake unable to recall what so terrified you in the dark. The deputy who was standing next to me now got down on one knee and unfolded a shiny tinfoil survival blanket. He draped it over the gunman's facial features, which were frozen in an ugly, accusing grimace.

"Congratulations, champ," he said to me. "Another victory for the good guys. Looks like you killed him with your bare hands."

Gentle Insanities
Christine Matthews

Christine Matthews' terrific short stories have been praised by such writing icons as Ed Gorman, Martin H. Greenberg, John Lutz, and others. I've long enjoyed her Gil & Claire Hunt mystery series (written with Robert Randisi) and was excited to have her contribute one of her patented twisted crime tales to his anthology...

GENTLE INSANITIES

"THEY HIRED me because I'm a crazy lady." I squinted into the camera. Was my eye shadow smeared? *Please don't let me sweat through this new blouse—it's silk.* God, I was enjoying my fifteen minutes of fame.

"A crazy lady? Is that what it takes to be a private investigator in Omaha?"

"It can't hurt."

The audience laughed.

The topic of today's *Oprah* was *Daring People—Exciting Occupations*. I admit I'm more exciting than the fire-eater sitting stage left. What does it take to douse a flame? Lots of practice and some sort of protective coating gargled inside your mouth. But I don't think I'm as daring as the eighty-seven-year-old skydiving great-grandmother. Now that takes real guts.

"Have you ever had to use that?" He pointed to the .32. I didn't have the heart to tell him I'd worn it because the leather shoulder holster matched my skirt.

"Once." I hung my head, as though the memory was too sad to discuss.

Questions from the audience were coming in spurts: "I've read that being a private investigator is boring, lots of routine, paperwork, photographs of cracks in sidewalks...you know."

"The agency I work for specializes in people, not pavement. We track down deadbeats who owe child support, runaway kids...that kind of thing. And I've only been licensed a year. Guess I haven't had enough time to get bored."

The next question dealt with the great-grandmother's sex life and I zoned off, wondering if it was true the camera would add an additional ten pounds to my hips.

———

WHEN I GOT to the office the day after the show ran on TV, Jan and Ken stood beside their desks and applauded.

I smiled, took a slow bow, and blew them each a kiss. "Please, be seated. I'll walk among you common folk and sign autographs later."

"Roberta," Harry called from his office.

"Robbie," I shouted. I hate the name Roberta, especially the way my boss, Harry Winsted, says it.

I sat across from Harry in a leather chair, crossed my legs, and waited for him to tell me how lousy I was on *Donahue*. The more shit Harry gives me, the better I know I'm doing.

"Saw you on *Donahue*. That number about your pipsqueak .32 was great stuff. Makes us look big time."

"Just doin' my job, boss."

"Well, it's back to the real world, kid. I got a job needs your special touch." He picked up a folder from the table behind him. "Name's James Tanner. Seems the bastard skipped town with his three-year-old son, and the wife's not getting enough help from the police to suit her." He tossed the file at me.

I reached out, caught it without looking away from Harry's beady little eyes. "Anything else?"

"Yeah. You look fat on TV."

"Love you, too." I made a point to slam the glass door as I exited Harry's office. The glass rumbles, and he always flinches. With my back turned, I waved over my shoulder.

After reading through the file, I found James Lucias Tanner was all of twenty years old. He'd got married when he was seventeen, to a pregnant sixteen-year-old from the right side of the tracks. It was her family money paying for this investigation. After a series of bad career moves, James finally landed work as a manager at the Touchless Car Wash over on Dodge.

I made a note to check out Kevin Tanner's preschool.

———

THE NEXT DAY I drove to La Petite Academy, in Millard. I expected to see rows of toddlers dressed in red uniforms. Good soldiers with teeny, tiny swords tucked inside their Pampers and baggy coveralls. Instead, I found a neat room full of partitioned activities. The smell of paste and warm milk reminded me of my own kindergarten class. I'd called ahead for an appointment with Kevin's teacher. I made my way to her office, which was located in the back of the main room.

"Ms. Kelly?" I extended my hand.

"Ms. Stanton. I saw you yesterday on *Donahue*."

A fan. "It was taped weeks ago." I assumed a modest smile.

"I enjoyed it a lot. Is being a private investigator really exciting?"

I shrugged, surveyed the room cluttered with Nerf balls and blocks. "I do get to go to some very exotic locales."

She laughed. However, her smile curved downward into a sad pout when I asked about Kevin Tanner.

"Kevin's such a sweetie. All the children and teachers miss him. But his father—what a creep. Always came in here dirty and mean. Such a mouth on him. Tattoos all over, including a green and black snake on one hand, which spelled out the name Donna. Kevin's mother is Lynn. The man's a pig."

Good, she was a real talker. All I had to do was sit back, nod, and wait for recess.

Ms. Kelly told me, down to the rip in his seams, what James Tanner had been wearing the day he kidnapped Kevin. She described how the backseat of Tanner's car was littered with Burger King and Taco Bell wrappers. But best of all, Ms. Kelly's anal-retentive memory recalled a bumper sticker—a Mary Kay pink design telling every tailgater that inside was a representative. And the pink coffee mug Ms. Kelly saw stuck to the dashboard was stenciled with the name Amy.

––––––

BY THE TIME I got back to my apartment, it was eight o'clock. The red light winked at me from the answering machine. I punched the gray button. The tape rewound, then replayed. My father's voice shouted from inside the machine, frantic.

"It's your mother. Jesus, she almost died! We're at the hospital. What am I going to do..." His sobs were cut off by the infernal beep.

The next message started. It was Dad again. "For God's sake, it's five. Your mother's in radiation. I'm at Christ Community. They've assigned a specialist. I don't know what..."

The beep disconnected his agony, but before I could call information for the number in Chicago, the phone rang.

I grabbed the receiver, startled. "Hello?"

"Where the hell have you been? I've called twice."

"Dad, I just got home."

"We were having lunch. All of a sudden she couldn't breathe, grabbed her chest, turned an awful color, and just crumpled. I got her in the car and rushed to the Emergency Room. She almost died." He choked on his fear. "I can't lose her."

I maintained an artificial calm, not even allowing the idea of my mother's death to seep into my brain. "Could it be pneumonia?"

"Haven't you understood a word I've said? She's in radiation. The X-rays show there's a spot on her lung. But the technician said we caught it in time and your mother's so strong. You know how strong she is. Robbie?"

Cancer.

"Yes, Dad. I know." Thirty-five years had taught me well. Agree and listen. That's all Dad ever required. Nod, smile, be Daddy's little girl. I played the part so well, I sometimes lost my adult self in the charade.

"What am I going to do?"

"I'll come up and—"

"No, we'll be fine. We're fine."

"Have you called Delia?"

"I'll do it now, while I'm waiting. Talk to you later." The connection broke.

Tears welled behind my eyes, refusing to roll down my cheeks. Mother always said she'd live to be one hundred.

"I'm holding you to your promise," I whispered to her from five hundred miles away.

———

AFTER STARING at my scuffed floor tiles for half an hour, I couldn't wait any longer. I called my sister.

She sniffed. "Dad just called."

"What should we do?"

"I couldn't go up there even if I wanted to. The shop's busy. With Halloween coming, I'm swamped with fittings and special orders. Then there's Homecoming gowns."

"And I just started a new case. If I can wrap it up, I'll go see what's happening."

"Thanks. You know how Daddy gets. He blows everything out of proportion. Maybe it's not that bad."

"Maybe." I hoped, but deep inside I knew the truth.

———

THE LEAVES SEEMED PARTICULARLY vivid as I walked to my car. The apartment complex I live in offered covered parking, for an additional fee, of course. While my car is protected from the rain and ice, birds love to poop on it as they huddle above on steel beams supporting the ceiling. I cursed the black and white blobs covering my blue paint job. The morning was mild, and I could smell burning leaves. Someone dared defy the law, and I applauded them. What was autumn without that toasty aroma clinging to orange and yellow leaves?

Ken was using the computer when I entered the office. He glanced up and grinned. "Get any last night?"

"Why do you ask me that stupid question every single morning?"

"Because I want to know if you got any."

"Sleazeball." I punched his arm as I walked to my desk.

"If you call me names, I won't show you a new program we just got in."

I admit it—I'm computer-unfriendly. I admit, too, I've depended upon the knowledge of others when accessing or exiting a screen. I still needed to pick Ken's brain.

"I'm sorry. You're not a sleazeball. You're just scum. Better?"

"I knew you'd come around. Take a look. This is great."

Reluctantly, I stood behind him as he pushed keys with the artistry of Liberace. "All we have to do is punch in a last name and we practically get a pint of blood."

"Could you try Tanner and see what comes up?"

Before I could turn for the file, the screen displayed twelve Tanners in the Omaha metropolitan area.

"First name?" Ken asked.

"James L."

"Bingo! We got your credit ratings, places of employment, marital status, number of children, pets, even a ring size from a recent purchase at Zales."

"Can you print it out for me?"

"No," he scolded. "I showed you how to print something. Do it yourself."

"Kenny." I pulled his ear. He loves it when I pull his ear. "Kenny, sweetheart, you're right there, in front of the thing. Please?"

"This is the last time." He pushed some more keys and the printer started to life.

"Thank you very much," I said in my best Shirley Temple voice. He also loves it when I talk like a little girl.

Hell, if it'll get the computer work done, I'll talk like Donald Duck.

I sat up straight behind my cheap desk and studied the printout. In between reviewing blue and white lines of tedious, boring statistics, I suddenly remembered Amy and let my feet do the walking to the yellow pages. I flipped to Cosmetics. There were four Independent Sales Directors listed. One of them was named Amy Schaefer. I jotted down her number and address and stood to return the book to its shelf. Passing Ken's desk, I poked his shoulder. "I bet I crack this case and don't even have to use a computer. Brains, ole bean. Human brains beat your computer friend any day."

"You're the most bullheaded—"

"Careful," I warned.

"—woman I've ever known. You belong back in the dark age."

"When men were men..."

"Careful," he warned right back.

———

OMAHA HAS a small-town feel to it. Tractors frequent busy streets, cowboys visit from out West when there's a cattle auction or rodeo. People are friendly and move in second gear instead of third. But with a population of half a million, a symphony, a ballet company, museums, and great shopping, it also has a big-city mix.

I turned onto L Street and took it to Seventy-second. Making a right onto Grover, I found the apartment complex where Amy Schaefer lived. I backtracked to the Holiday Inn and dialed her number from a phone in the lobby.

After three rings, a timid voice answered.

"Amy Schaefer?"

"Yes. Who's calling?" She was a regular church mouse.

"Let's just say James is a special friend of mine."

"Where do you know Jimmy from?"

"We've been friends a long time. We met at…" Think, think. I looked across the street and saw a sign for a lounge named Jodhpurs. "Jodhpurs," I said. "It was twofer night, ladies were free. You know how cheap he is." Was she buying any of this? From all the fast-food wrappers in his car, I figured the guy was not a big spender.

"Why are you telling me all this?"

"Jimmy's been begging me to come back to him, but after he told me about you, no way."

"You know so much about me, and I don't even know your name." She waited.

"It's Donna."

Suddenly her schoolmarm act exploded across the phone. "That son of a bitch!"

"Calm down," I said. "The way I figure it, us women…broads…should stick together."

When she slammed down the receiver, my head felt as though it had been shot at from close range. She was mad! Hell hath no fury and all that jazz.

I dashed to my car and swung back onto Grover.

Parking across from the Grover Square Apartments, I saw a woman come stamping across the lot toward a pink Cadillac.

As she screeched into traffic and across an intersection. I floored the accelerator as the light turned yellow, and chased her. Then a Trailways bus pulled out of the McDonald's parking lot.

Amy swerved, the car between us rammed into her rear bumper. I jerked my steering wheel to the right, hoping no cars were in that lane or riding my tail. The last thing I saw as I passed the accident was one screaming woman, a busload of Japanese tourists snapping pictures, and a salesman-type male calling the police from his car phone. I hate those things.

"Damn," I hissed, rubbernecking as I passed the scene. I was hungry, frustrated, and had a headache that wouldn't quit.

––––––

WHILE I HATE the plastic trappings of twentieth-century life, I do love the simple pleasures. Like mail, for instance. And as I poked through my mailbox and found only an ad for a new beauty salon, I felt cheated.

The apartment seemed cold. I hiked up the heat. Rummaging through the refrigerator, I looked for the chili left over from last night. The bowl had worked itself to the back of the middle shelf. I scooped a heaping portion into a smaller bowl and put my lunch into the microwave.

The microwave is another simple pleasure. It also fits under the category of twentieth-century conveniences. I use it, each time giving thanks I don't get contaminated from the radiation or whatever flies around in there to produce heat. If I should one day wake up to find all microwaves have disappeared, I'd survive. I don't depend on the convenience. That's the difference—the mindset. I enjoy the convenience while knowing one power outage will not upset my life. Dad taught us don't depend on anything or anyone and you'll never be disappointed.

Dad.

I looked across the room. The answering machine was blinking. As I programmed the time into the oven, I realized my headache was fierce and went for some aspirin before listening to messages.

After gulping a last swig of water, I reluctantly pressed the gray button.

Beep.

"This is Mrs. Calhoun from American Express. Your account is now two months past due, and we were wondering if a payment had been made. Please call me at 800-555-9100."

Beep.

"Ro-ber-ta," Harry whined. "Some guy called. Says he's your father. He's been calling every fifteen minutes. Sounds weird. Give me a call, okay? Roberta?"

Beep.

"Just got a frantic call from Dad." It was Delia. "He's kidnapping Mother from the hospital. Call me!"

Beep. Rewind.

I pulled the phone over to the table, set my place for lunch, then poured a Coke over lots of ice. I dialed Delia's number. She answered on the first ring.

"Are you okay?" I asked.

"No. I don't know what's going on. I talked with Mother's nurse—the doctor wasn't available. She said when Dad brought Mother in, she was barely breathing. They thought they'd lose her right there. What the hell have they been doing all this time? I've called and called and no one's home. I'm scared."

"Calm down," I advised with my mouth full. "If the doctor let her go home, she wasn't kidnapped. I'll talk to him and call you back."

"I think one of us should go up there." She was suddenly the frightened little sister. I knew which one of us would be going to Chicago.

———

"YOUR FATHER NEEDS HELP, MISS STANTON." It was the first thing Dr. Blair said after I identified myself.

"I've known that for a long time." I bet he thought I was kidding. "But right now, I'm more concerned about my mother."

"I can appreciate your position. Your mother's a heavy smoker. Maybe if she'd come in sooner." He took a breath then dove right in. "Your mother has lung cancer."

"Should she be home now?"

"She responded very well to treatment, and your

father understands how important it is she come in twice a week for it. When she regains some of her strength, we can start her on chemotherapy."

"And then? After the chemo?" I really didn't want to hear his answer.

"Six months, a year. A year and a half—tops."

I had to hang up, quickly. "Thank you."

I ran to the bathroom, unsure if I was going to cry or collapse, but feeling the bathroom was the direction to head. I ended up sitting on the edge of the tub, holding my head in my hands, rocking back and forth until the panic passed. I thought I was going to die.

Delia took the news better than I had, or maybe she just pretended. It's hard to figure her out sometimes. While she stands five feet seven, I barely reach five feet four inches. She has dark hair—I'm light. She explodes over situations I find amusing and laughs when I want to scream.

We had agreed I would fly to Chicago. I'd have to be the eyes and ears for both of us now.

I called Harry and told him about my near-miss with Amy Schaefer. He grumbled until I added in the news about my mother.

"Geez, kid," he sighed. "You do what has to be done. Family comes first. I'll sit on this Tanner case until you get back."

"Thanks, Harry. Thanks a lot."

"Hey, no skin off my ass."

————

I COULDN'T TELL if Dad was happy to see me. He'd always made me feel as though I was intruding. Most times he looked annoyed.

"What are you doing here?" He stood behind the storm door talking through the screen.

"Can I come in?"

"Sure." He held the door open. "It's just this is such a surprise."

I set my suitcase down and wrapped my arms around him. He felt thinner, bony. I whispered into his ear, "How's Mother?"

Tears welled in his eyes. "Not too good today."

I held him at arm's length, surprised at how old he looked.

"Let me go tell her you're here."

He walked away from me, went down the hall, and I stood waiting, feeling like a salesman calling on the lady of the house. Then I followed.

"Hi," I said softly. She lay on her side on top of the bedspread. She was wearing a pink sweat suit, her feet tucked inside a pair of white cotton socks. She didn't turn to look at me. I walked to her side of the bed and knelt.

And then she whimpered.

I threw myself on top of her, and we hugged.

When my eyes adjusted to the light, I saw how swollen and misshapen her face was. She reminded me of one of those Betty Boop dolls.

"Why didn't you call me? Or Delia."

"What could *you* do?" she asked, puzzled.

"What could I do? Love you. Comfort you. What

does a family do for one another?" I knew then she hadn't the slightest idea.

I couldn't get any information out of them. For two days, I watched my father dole out vitamins, steroids, and antibiotics. He cooked, he helped her up, he helped her down. I was in the way most of the time.

When I asked about Dr. Blair, I received mixed reviews. I decided to check out Blair for myself. Telling my folks I was going shopping, I headed for Christ Community Hospital and the two o'clock meeting I'd set up the day before.

He looked like Elton John. Dark hair cut in bangs across his forehead, a toothy grin, and oversized glasses. I agreed with Mother. I liked him.

"Her mental attitude is wonderful, and your father takes excellent care of her." His compassion assured me he wanted Mother to be well as much as I did. But doctors can't guarantee miracles.

I called Delia from a pay phone in the hospital lobby. She seemed relieved and encouraged. I felt better about the relieved part, but cautious about the encouragement.

———

I PACKED my suitcase as my father trailed behind me. He walked in a clipped step and waved his arms as his voice rose. "How dare you?"

I folded a blouse, keeping my back to him. "I'm her daughter. I have the right."

Words came in slow, deliberate syllables. "You're

trying to turn your mother against me. We were doing fine until you came."

Hot, angry tears dripped down my face. I bent over the suitcase, quickly fastened the clasps, and turned to get my coat.

"Now what are you crying about? I can't say two words to you without you bawling. You're too goddamned sensitive, Robbie. Always have been. We're just having a conversation, and you get hysterical."

"I gotta go." My eyes scanned the carpet as I walked toward Mother's room. I crept in and kissed her cheek. She breathed slowly, never acknowledging my presence. Confrontations were not her forte.

My father followed me to the front door, all the time telling me how I didn't understand, how selfish I'd always been.

I called a cab from the store across the street and waited, staring out the window.

———

IT WAS worth one more try. I dialed Amy Schaefer's number. Timid as ever, she asked, "Hello?"

"Amy. Just thought you'd like to know we're taking Kevin and going to Disneyland for Christmas." That seemed like the kind of thing Tanner would do. At least I hoped it was. "Sorry if it screws up your holiday, doll."

"You're full of shit! Jimmy ain't going nowhere."

"Jingle bells, jingle bells, jingle all the..."

Slam.

I dashed out of the Holiday Inn and got in my car. Sure enough, after a ten-minute wait, Amy Schaefer came out of her apartment. This time she carried two shirt boxes wrapped in Christmas paper and tied with red ribbons.

I giggled. "Someone's gonna get their Christmas presents early."

Once again we headed up 72nd Street. Turning west on Dodge, we passed the Touchless Car Wash. She made a right on 120th and turned into an apartment complex. Amy got out of her pink car and opened the door of apartment number forty-nine with her own key.

I knew I'd have to sit and wait. And I admit, okay, it would have been nice to have a phone in the car.

I checked my watch against the bank's huge read-out. My watch showed two-ten; the bank displayed two-twenty. I decided to compromise. It was two-fifteen.

Around three o'clock, the door of number forty-nine burst open, and I saw those two Christmas packages come flying across the parking lot. Amy Schaefer dashed for her car, followed by a short guy with dirty hair. I'd seen his driver's license photo and recognized James Tanner.

I called the police from the Taco Bell across the street, identified myself, and gave them the address where they could pick up James Tanner.

Within ten minutes a squad car pulled in behind me. They'd kept the siren off as I'd advised, but Tanner spotted the car just the same. He ran for the apartment while Amy stood screaming after him, "Run! You lying son of a bitch. I wish I would have called the cops myself. Coward!"

The police knocked at number forty-nine until Tanner answered. By that time, several neighbors had gathered, and traffic slowed to catch a glimpse of the action. I waited while an officer escorted James out. A female officer went inside and after a few minutes came out holding a frightened little boy in her arms. She patted his back, talking softly into his ear. The boy clung to her.

I opened my car door. I just couldn't resist.

"Amy?"

She spun around, relieved to see I wasn't wearing a uniform. "What? How'd you know my name?"

"Santa told me. Said you'd been a really good girl. *Jingle bells, jingle bells, jingle all the way.*" I kept singing as I returned to my car. "Thanks for all your help. We couldn't have done it without you."

"You bitch!" the timid church mouse screamed. "You fuckin' bitch!"

Some days are like that. You get no appreciation.

————

"HERE YOU GO." I dropped the papers onto Harry's desk. "All wrapped up neat and tidy. Tanner's in custody, Kevin's being reunited with his mother as we speak, and Amy Schaefer is selling Passionate Pink blusher with a heavy yet cheerful heart. Life just keeps—"

"Your mother died this morning."

It took me a minute. "What did you say?"

He stood as I fell into the chair. Coming around his desk, he bent to touch my shoulder. "Roberta…Robbie, I'm so sorry."

"But I just saw her." I was angry. No, I was upset. I was going to cry. No, I was going to faint. Don't let go. Hang on.

"Your sister's been trying to get you all day. She broke down, couldn't say another word after she told me. I offered to break the news. I didn't want you to feel, you know…alone."

My grief started slowly and built into deep gulping sobs. Harry knelt in front of me, hugging me against his chest.

———

AS THE FUNERAL procession wove down the street my parents had lived on for the past eighteen years, I noticed the Christmas decorations. A brick house at the end of the block had a life-sized wooden Santa, painted a hideous red and white. I hated it. The tree lights twinkling around doorways and windows seemed to accentuate our sadness.

Dad stood by himself at the cemetery. Bitter. He told anyone who would listen that now he had no family. Friends reminded him he had two lovely daughters, but he didn't hear. He repeatedly told Delia and me that he was alone and no one had ever loved him but my mother. I was too empty to fill him with reassurance.

———

"WE'VE GOT THROUGH EASTER, Mother's Day, Father's Day. I really don't think he should be alone for his birthday," Delia was worried. "We'll make a cake, bring some presents."

It was August, and once again, I found myself back in Chicago. The birthday party had been a good idea. But the pressure of having a normal celebration had tired us all. Delia had gone to bed early. I sat in the living room, rocking and watched a *Fawlty Towers* rerun. John Cleese always made me laugh.

Dad walked into the room, grunting.

"What's so funny?" Before I could answer, he attacked. "How can you laugh? Your mother's dead! You know, come to think of it, I haven't seen you or your sister cry."

"We've cried a lot." My agony was all that would comfort him now.

"I've never seen it."

I stared at the TV.

When he realized he wasn't going to get me to play, he changed tactics. Reclining in his chair, he sighed. I glanced sideways at him and he smiled. When I turned to look him full on, he smirked.

"I've got to tell you something." He leaned forward. "This is just between us."

"What?"

"I hired someone to kill the doctor."

This had to be one of his lies. The kind he took back later claiming he had only been kidding.

"Your mother's doctor. That cocksucker, Blair."

"A hitman?"

"Yes." He sat back, satisfied his announcement had knocked the laughter out of me. "Money can buy anything, Robbie. That bastard is to die on the anniversary of your mother's death at exactly eleven-ten in the morning. And if he's not alone, his wife or children, whoever's with him, are gonna die, too. Slowly, in agony. I want them to suffer like I have—like your mother did."

"Mother told me she was never in any pain."

"That's beside the point," he almost shouted.

"But what about Delia? And me? You could ruin our lives—our futures. There'd be headlines, reporters, we'd be humiliated. You'd end up in prison."

"It'll be done right."

"Don't you care about any of us?"

"He killed your mother. You expect me to let him get away with that?"

I walked over to him. Softly I tried to reason. "No one killed Mother. She had cancer, and she died."

"She didn't have cancer. She was getting better. You heard what they said. It was that doctor, he killed her. And I'm going to kill him."

"I can't talk to you now." I walked down the hall and went to the room I shared with Delia. In the morning I'd tell my sister that our father was crazy. She'd laugh and say, "Tell me something I don't already know."

BY THE TIME I returned to Omaha, it was late. The nine-hour car ride had allowed time for lots of thinking. I called Delia.

"I really think we should take Dad's threat seriously."

"Me too." She offered no resistance.

"Before we do anything, I've got to be sure. I'll try to trip him up or get him to admit he lied."

"Do it now. Please," Delia said. "I can't sleep until you do."

"Right now."

I made a cup of tea to warm my hands, spirit, and mood. All the time wondering when things would get back to normal. But as Delia said at the funeral, "Normal will never be normal again."

Finally, I placed the call.

Dad spoke in a calm and serious tone. "I meant every word. Everything's been taken care of, there's nothing you can do now."

Then I lost it. All of it—my composure, my logic, my last shred of loyalty. "How can you do this?" I screamed hysterically. "How can you do this to us?"

Slowly, he explained, "Nothing will go wrong. No one will ever know. Just forget about it; it doesn't concern you."

"Please." I was crying now. "Please..."

"You don't owe this man anything. He's a murderer."

"No." I stopped. And that proverbial straw, the one

that broke the camel's back, had finally been hoisted upon my own. I hung up the phone.

"From here on out," I later told Delia, "we're taking care of ourselves because no one else will. I'll go see a guy I know—a criminal lawyer. I'll pick his brain."

"You're the mother now," she said. "Please, don't let Daddy hurt us."

"I won't," I said, and swore silently to protect us both. Our lives had suddenly taken on a soap opera quality, and I did not like being cast in the role of victim.

———

BRADLEY JOHNSON HAS this great office located in the Old Market area. A bricked passageway flanked on one side by restaurants and on the other by shops, illuminated by large skylights. Bradley's office is at the top of four flights of wooden stairs.

His secretary, Lucy, sits behind a small desk and greets clients with a cup of coffee.

"I heard your mother died. Harry told me. I'm so sorry." She buzzed Bradley.

"Thanks."

Brad escorted me into the large room that serves as his office, meeting room, and lounge. We sat next to the tall windows he prefers to keep free from draperies. He shifted his legs and leaned back in an overstuffed chair.

I confided everything. Bradley reacted with a raised eyebrow.

"Legally, there isn't a thing you can do, Robbie. It's your word against his."

"What I wanted, I guess, was more of a favor. I thought maybe you could contact my father, tell him we've talked. That might scare him enough to call everything off—if there really is a hitman. This way I'd be covered, the doctor would be safe, and my father would have to forget about all this."

"My advice is to call Dr. Blair yourself. Explain the situation, see what he suggests. That's the best you can do. But, Robbie?"

"Yeah?"

"None of this is your fault. You know that, don't you?"

"I guess. It's just that I feel so dirty. It's hard to explain."

———

THE HOSPITAL RECEPTIONIST said Dr. Blair was with a patient and would get back to me. I knew he kept late hours and told her I'd wait up for his call, no matter what the time.

Around ten o'clock, he called.

He was kind, and my hands immediately started to shake. I finally worked the conversation around to where it should have started.

"My father told me he holds you responsible for my mother's death."

"Your father has been through a lot. He and your

mother were married forty-some years. It's only natural he misses her."

"I know." Nothing would ever be as difficult as this moment. "But my father told me he's hired someone to have you killed."

Silence.

"Let me take this call on my private line, Ms. Stanton. Hold on a minute."

When he came back, his tone was hushed. "You don't really think he's serious?"

"Yes, I do. It's to be done in four months, on the anniversary of my mother's death." My voice trembled. I felt sorrier for all of us having to go through this than I ever could for my father.

Dr. Blair said he wanted to think about things. He'd get back to me.

———

SERGEANT DANTA of the Oak Lawn Police Department contacted me two days later. Dr. Blair had filed a complaint.

I'd talked with police before. Lots of times. But this was about me, about my life. I repeated my story for what seemed like the hundredth time and for the hundredth time, I didn't believe it myself.

"We'll have to proceed with this as if it were the truth. But tell me, Ms. Stanton, would you be willing to testify against your father in a court of law?"

I thought about all the years I'd worked for Dad's

approval. I thought about all the agony Delia and I were going through so soon after losing our mother and I answered.

"No."

———

"CALL ON LINE TWO. Pick it up, Roberta," Harry barked.

"Miss Stanton? I'm Detective Carter with the Chicago Police Department. A report has been filed with us concerning your father."

"I've already been through this with Sergeant Danta."

"Danta's out of Oak Lawn, where the hospital is located. We need something filed in your father's precinct."

I repeated my story from the day before.

"I have to tell you, Miss Stanton, when he first opened the door—"

"Wait a minute. You spoke to my father? You confronted him? In person? What did he say about Dr. Blair?"

"We had to get his statement. He said he thought the doctor killed your mother."

I suddenly felt as though I'd been strapped into a roller-coaster and was slowly being hauled up to the top of Anxiety Mountain. I could hear the gears clicking and I prayed I wouldn't crack before Christmas reared its holy head.

"Your father's in bad shape."

"We all are."

"There's nothing else we can do."

"I know."

Detective Carter apologized and promised there would be no need to disturb my father again.

———

"GET ANY LAST NIGHT?" Ken asked as I walked through the door.

I punched him on the shoulder. "Scum."

"You may think I like it when you call me that, but I don't," he complained.

"Sorry. I had an awful night, didn't sleep at all."

He waited for the punchline, and when none came, he shrugged and sat down at the computer.

Harry came banging in from outside, and a frigid gust slammed the door. "Roberta. In my office. Now."

I followed behind, like a little spaniel, and watched as his boots tracked wet black prints along the dirty carpet.

"Close the door." Harry pulled his gloves off and stuffed them into his pockets. Without removing the snowflaked overcoat, he abruptly turned.

"The body of one Dr. Blair, practicing out of Christ Community Hospital in Oak Lawn, Illinois, was found this morning in the trunk of his car. The car was parked in the doctor's reserved space in the hospital lot. He had been beaten to death. They think it was one of those aluminum baseball bats. Very sloppy. I spoke with

Sergeant Danta. He said it definitely was not a professional hit."

Click. Click. Hang on.

"Your father's in custody."

"Was anyone else with the doctor?"

"No."

I turned, and we just looked at each other for a minute.

"What do I do?"

"Go home. The police will be calling you."

"Don't tell anyone. I feel so ashamed."

"It'll be all over the news soon enough." Harry shook his head in disbelief. "Go on, get your butt out of here."

After talking with the police, I booked a flight into St. Louis.

Delia was in shock when I told her. "Oh God, oh God, oh God," she repeated. "He really did it. Oh, God."

"Will you meet me at the St. Louis airport at ten-thirty tonight?" Springfield was only a few hours away, and I knew the distraction would be good for her.

"I guess. But why St. Louis?"

I didn't want to scare her, to tell her that soon reporters and television crews would be camped out on her front lawn. "We need to be together now," I said.

———

WHEN MY FLIGHT FINALLY LANDED, I spotted Delia standing by a fat man in a blue sweat suit. I could tell she'd been crying. I smiled hello.

We walked silently to the baggage claim, then she said, "I almost forgot. Your office called. Ken somebody. He wants you to call him tonight. Here's his number."

After we registered and fought over who got which bed, I called Ken from the hotel.

"You lose our bet."

"What bet? What are you talking about?"

"Computers versus brains," He sounded so sad.

"That was months ago," I said. "The Tanner case."

"Now it's the Stanton case."

"I'm tired and…"

"I was playing around with the computer today and punched in your name. It showed all your credit card charges for the past year."

"And?"

"There was this code number that looked familiar. When I cross-referenced with the police computer, we came up with Freedom, Inc. They offer a very unique personal service. Geez, you can buy anything with a Visa card. It's really disgusting."

Click. Click. Click.

"We plugged into the airline computer, so we know you're in St. Louis. Even the phone number you're calling from is being recorded. Why'd you do it, Robbie? Your own father?"

"Kenny." I know he loves it when I talk in my little girl voice. Daddy always did. "I had to protect all of us. Delia and I don't want Daddy to bully us anymore. This way, he won't be alone. Maybe the doctors can help him now."

It's those gentle insanities that bring such clear insight. The huge problems only come once in a while. They're easy to fix. But the small, every day, constant, infuriating irritations drop you over the edge.

Click. Click. Click.

So Beautiful, So Dead
Robert J. Randisi

Robert Randisi and I have been friends for more years than I'm going to share in public, but I have long admired Bob as a legendarily prolific wordsmith, an icon in the mystery and western genres, and the keystone to the longevity and popularity of the private eye novel. He's also an all-around nice guy and a mentor to many beginning writers. This anthology would not have been complete without his presence...

SO BEAUTIFUL, SO DEAD

VAL O'FARRELL LOOKED DOWN at the dead girl with gut-wrenching sadness. So beautiful, so dead.

"What a body, huh? Why would anyone want to cancel the ticket of a babe like her? And pluggin' her in the head, too. Jeez, how you gonna figure that?"

O'Farrell turned to look at Detective Sam McKeever.

"What?" McKeever asked. "She's a babe. Hey, she's lyin' there naked under a sheet. What am I supposed to do, not look?"

"No," O'Farrell said, "she's used to bein' looked at."

"Like most beautiful young dames, huh?"

"This one more than some," O'Farrell said. "She's supposed to be one of the contestants at that new beauty pageant out in Jersey."

"Yeah? No kiddin'?" McKeever said. "I heard they was gonna let them wear these new skin-tight bathing suit things."

"Tight and skimpy."

"You seen 'em?"

"Not yet."

The previous year during the beauty pageant in Washington, D.C., the contestants had worn long stockings and tunic bathing suits. However, Atlantic City's first contest was going to be something really different and special because the censors had seen fit to lift their bans on bare knees and skin-tight suits. It remained to be seen if the idea would fly.

"Hey," McKeever said. "You better get out of here before the boss shows up. You ain't a cop no more, you know."

"I know."

O'Farrell had retired from the force two years earlier in 1919 and had opened his own detective agency. He'd been on the inside so often while on the job that he catered to a pretty high-class clientele these days. He'd gone from being the best-dressed cop in town to the best-dressed shamus.

"How'd you know to come up here, anyway?" McKeever asked.

"I was supposed to pick her up and take her out to Jersey."

"You knew her?"

"Yeah."

"Maybe you better tell me about it, Val," McKeever said, folding his arms.

O'Farrell laid it out for the detective just as it had happened.

Vincent Balducci had come to his office two days

before with flash and confidence bordering on arrogance. Most of the flash came from the sparks he was wearing in a couple of rings.

"I've got a job for you, Mr. O'Farrell," he'd said, after introducing himself. He'd pronounced his name like O'Farrell was supposed to know who he was. O'Farrell did, but he didn't tip his hand.

"How did you get my name, Mr. Balducci?"

"You were referred to me by a mutual acquaintance," Balducci said. "His name is not important. He said you used to be a cop, an honest cop—or as honest as they get around here. He said you were thorough, and you wouldn't gouge me on your fee just because I'm rich." Balducci looked around O'Farrell's well-furnished office. "I'm thinkin' the last part is probably right."

"All the parts are right, Mr. Balducci," O'Farrell said. "Why don't we get to the point of the visit?" O'Farrell motioned his visitor to a chair.

"All right." Vincent Balducci sat down. He laid his coat over his lap. It had a velvet collar. He laid a matching hat atop it. His hair was dark—too dark to be natural— and shiny, combed straight back. "Yes, why don't we. Do you know who I am?"

"I read the newspaper," O'Farrell said. The *New York Times* regularly carried stories about Vincent Balducci, a millionaire philanthropist. What that generally meant to O'Farrell was the man had a lot of money and didn't know what to do with it.

"That will save time, then," Balducci said.

Balducci then told O'Farrell about Georgie Taylor.

Balducci was married but said it was a loveless, sexless marriage entered into for convenience. Naturally, he needed a friend outside his marriage. When he met Georgie, he knew she was the one.

"She's younger, right?" O'Farrell asked.

"Quite a bit younger," Balducci said. "I'm sixty-five and she's, uh, twenty-five."

"You look good," O'Farrell said. "I had you pegged for fifty-five."

"Thank you," Balducci said, "I try to keep in shape."

And he did a fine job. Except for his obviously dyed hair and some lines on his face, he did look younger than he was. He was tall, fit, and moved like a younger man. O'Farrell sneaked a look at his own growing paunch. He was more than fifteen years younger than the millionaire, but they probably looked the same age. He decided not to think about it.

"Lots of married men have dames on the side, Mr. Balducci," he said. "Where do I come in?"

"Have you heard about this beauty pageant in Atlantic City this weekend?"

"I heard something about it," O'Farrell said. "Is that the one with the new bathing suits?"

"Yes," Balducci said. "One of the major sponsors is the Atlantic City Businessman's League, of which I am a member."

O'Farrell was starting to get the drift, but he let the man go on.

"I've entered Georgie in the pageant."

"You didn't guarantee she'd win, did you?" O'Farrell asked. "You're not going to tell me the fix is in, are you?"

"No," Balducci said. "That part is not your concern."

So maybe the fix *was* in. But okay, the client is always right. That wasn't his concern.

"Fine."

"Georgie is very beautiful and talented. She has a big career ahead of her."

O'Farrell almost asked, "As what?" but bit his tongue.

"But I think she might be in danger."

"From who?"

"An old boyfriend, other contestants, even my wife."

"Does your wife know about Georgie?"

"Not exactly. She knows I have friends on the side, but she doesn't know about Georgie specifically."

"All right," O'Farrell said, "go on."

"The contest kicks off with a gala event at the Atlantic City Yacht Club on Friday. Among others, my wife will be there. I want you to escort Georgie."

"Be her date?"

"As it were, yes—and protect her."

"We've never met—"

"I will take you to her apartment on Beekman Place for an introduction," Balducci said. "After that, it will be up to the two of you to plan your Friday evening."

"Mr. Balducci," O'Farrell said, "today is already Wednesday, and I haven't got a thing to wear."

"On top of a thousand dollar fee," Balducci said, taking the comment completely serious, "I will buy you a new wardrobe and pay all other expenses for the night. I would send you to my tailor, but there's no time, so you can simply shop in the best men's stores available."

O'Farrell was a man who enjoyed good clothes. He knew where to shop. Even while still in the employ of the New York City Police Department, he dressed better than any other detective—regardless of rank—leading to speculation he was on the take. It was only the fact that everyone knew how scrupulously honest he was that undercut the speculation.

"All right," O'Farrell said. "When and where do I meet the young lady?"

"Tonight, if you're free," Balducci said. He leaned forward and placed a slip of paper on the desk. "Come to that address at eight pm. I'll make the introductions."

O'Farrell picked up the paper, glanced at it, then put it in his shirt pocket.

"I'll need an advance."

"Of course," Balducci said. He took a wad of cash out of his pocket. No checks, no paper trail.

"Five hundred now? And a hundred for clothes?"

"Better make it two for clothes," O'Farrell said.

Balducci didn't hesitate. He peeled off seven hundred-dollar bills and placed them on O'Farrell's desk.

"Will that do?"

"That's fine." O'Farrell left the cash where it was.

"I'll see you tonight, then."

"I have some more questions."

Balducci stood up. He shot his cuffs and looked at his watch. "I'll answer the rest of your questions tonight. Right now, I have another appointment."

O'Farrell walked his new client to the door.

"Eight o'clock," Balducci said and left.

After Balducci was gone O'Farrell picked up the hundred-dollar bills and rubbed them together. He turned and looked out his second-floor window down to Fifth Avenue, where a chauffeur was holding the back door of a Rolls Royce open for Vincent Balducci. He probably should have asked for more money. A guy who rides in a Rolls and is dizzy for a young dame probably wouldn't have squawked about it.

O'Farrell presented himself at the Beekman Place address at 7:55. He paused out front to look up at the building. It was only five stories, but Beekman Place was not an inexpensive address. Each apartment was occupied by money—or, as in this case, paid for by someone with money.

He was wearing one of the new suits he'd bought that afternoon. It was September and the weather was still mild, so he'd bought one brown linen and one blue pin-striped. He was wearing the linen. The pin-striped was for the night at the Yacht Club.

The young doorman announced him, and he was allowed up to the third floor. When he rang the bell, the door was opened by Balducci himself. O'Farrell had expected a butler or a maid.

"Come in," the man said. "Georgie is still getting dressed."

O'Farrell entered and closed the door behind him. He followed Balducci down a short hall until they entered a plushly furnished living room.

"I've made a pitcher of martinis," his host said. "Would you like one?"

"Sure."

"Olive or onion?"

"Olive, please."

Balducci poured out two martinis, put olives in both, and handed one to O'Farrell.

"I was expecting a servant to answer the door," the detective said. "Maid's night off?"

"No servants," Balducci said. "It's bad enough the doorman knows me and sees me coming here."

O'Farrell understood.

"Ah," Balducci said, looking past him. "Here's Georgie now."

O'Farrell turned. He didn't know what he'd expected, but Georgie took his breath away. She was tall and slender with a proud thrust of breasts. Her dark hair was piled high atop her head. Her powder-blue gown was high-necked but left her pale shoulders bare. Since 1919, hems had been rising. Currently, it was not unheard of for them to be six inches from the floor—affording a nice view of ankle—but Georgie's gown was full length. It was her eyes that really got O'Farrell. They were violet, the most amazing color he'd ever seen, and they were great-big-eyes. When she blinked, he thought he could feel it inside.

She was pretty enough to be a Ziegfeld girl. O'Farrell wondered why Balducci didn't use his pull to get her that job rather than put her in some silly pageant?

"Georgie, this is Val O'Farrell, the private detective I hired to protect you."

"To hide me, you mean," she said tightly. She was smoking a cigarette, took a moment to remove a bit of tobacco from her tongue with her thumb and pinky while appraising O'Farrell. Flashes of light on her fingers attested to the fact Balducci didn't mind sharing his love of diamonds. "Well, he's big enough for me to hide behind."

"I just want him to protect you, darling," Balducci said.

O'Farrell suddenly realized how dressed up the two of them were and what it meant. Balducci's suit easily cost five times what his own new suit had cost.

"Are you folks going out to dinner?" he asked.

"We all are," Balducci said. "I thought it would be a good opportunity for us to get acquainted."

"Don't let him fool you, Mr. Detective," Georgie said. "He just wants to use you as a beard. That way if anyone sees us together, he can say I was your date. He's become an expert at hiding me."

"Georgie..."

"All right," she said, "I'll be a nice girl. Mr. O'Farrell, would you care to join us for dinner?"

"I don't know—"

"Please," she said. "Vincent will be paying the bill."

"Well," O'Farrell agreed, "when you put it that way..."

THE ONLY CHINK in Georgie Taylor's beautiful armor was her voice. It was high-pitched, almost a whine, and marred what was otherwise a perfect picture. O'Farrell knew nothing about how this beauty pageant was supposed to be run. He wondered if it called for the girls to actually speak.

Dinner was a tense affair at a nearby restaurant that O'Farrell suspected was below Balducci's usual dining standards. Even Georgie had lifted one side of her lips and sniffed when they entered. For his part, O'Farrell found his steak delicious.

For a dinner where he and Georgie were supposed to be getting acquainted, Vincent Balducci did most of the talking. O'Farrell spent more time looking at Georgie than listening to his client.

Later, when they returned to the apartment house on Beekman Place, Balducci stopped in the lobby and said, "I'm not coming up."

"Why not?" Georgie asked.

"Because you two need to talk," Balducci said. "I want you to spend some time together and really talk, this time." He turned to face O'Farrell. "Georgie has all the details about the party at the Yacht Club Friday night. I won't see you again until then. I'll have my wife with me, so if we come face to face, we will just be meeting. Do you understand?"

"Perfectly."

"My dear," Balducci said. He leaned over to kiss Georgie, but she presented him with nothing but a cheek. "I'll see you soon."

"Yes," she said, quietly. Then she looked at O'Farrell. "Come on, then."

The building had an elevator, but Georgie preferred to walk, which O'Farrell had discovered on their way down. He, in fact, had a distrust of elevators and had walked up when he first arrived.

This was something he had shared with his friend, the great Bat Masterson. Masterson, a legend of the Old West, lived in New York, and not only had a column in *the Morning Telegraph* but was a vice president of the newspaper. In his mid-sixties, the old lawman still had more faith in a horse than an elevator, and almost never used a telephone if he didn't have to. O'Farrell liked to think of himself as someone who had been born too late. He should have been with Bat on the streets of Dodge City, with a gun on his hip.

Georgie opened her door with her key and marched right to the sideboard. She was dragging her mink stole behind her and let it drop to the floor. O'Farrell bent, picked it up, and deposited it on a chair.

"I need a drink," she said. "Join me?"

"Why not, but if you don't mind, I'll have bourbon."

"A man after my own heart," she said. She poured bourbon over some ice cubes in two glasses and handed him one. She sipped hers, clunked the glass against her teeth and eyed him over the rim.

"After this, we could go to the bedroom and fuck our brains out," she offered. "Or we could take the drinks with us and go now."

"Somehow," O'Farrell said, "I don't think that's what

your boyfriend had in mind when he said he wanted us to get better acquainted."

"You don't think so?" she asked, raising her eyebrows. "Why else do you think he sent us up here alone? Come on, I saw the way you were lookin' at me in the restaurant."

"We're supposed to talk about Friday night," he said. "About the beauty pageant."

"Beauty pageant," she said. She held her glass tightly and let her other arm swing loosely about. He didn't remember how many drinks she'd had at dinner, but she certainly seemed drunk now. "What a crock! What a stupid idea. Marching around in bathing suits while a bunch of lecherous old men decides who the winner will be."

"I wasn't aware the contest would be judged by a panel of old men?"

"It's not, but you know what I mean." She finished her drink and poured herself another.

"You don't think you can win?"

She turned around quickly, sloshing some bourbon onto her wrist. She took a moment to lick it off. It was a move O'Farrell found particularly erotic, especially since she kept those violet eyes on him the whole time. He shifted his legs, rearranging his position in his chair, but it didn't help.

"Of course I can win," she said. "I've got the looks, don't you think?"

"Definitely."

"I just don't have the voice," she said candidly. "I'm

no dummy, I just sound like one. I know that when the contestants start to speak—to answer questions—my voice is going to be a liability."

O'Farrell was impressed. The girl had no illusions about herself or, apparently, her situation.

"And Vincent doesn't love me," she said. She wiggled the fingers of one hand at him, the light playing off the sparks. "He owns me, like one of these diamonds. It sounds odd. He just wants to have me on his arm to show me off, but then he never takes me out. I can't explain it. All I know is he's not here tonight, and I really want it. Whattaya say?"

"Look, Georgie—"

She did something with the top of her dress, and it fell to her waist. Her breasts were beautiful round orbs with tight pink nipples. She would not have made a good Ziegfeld girl, after all. Too big. She stared at him with those big violet eyes and poured the rest of her bourbon over her bare chest. One ice cube fell to the floor while another disappeared into her dress.

Why not? he thought, coming to his feet. When would he ever get a chance like this again? He had to find out where that second ice cube had gone.

———

THEY SPENT the next morning getting acquainted over breakfast because they really didn't do much talking during the night. When O'Farrell asked her about the doorman, she told him not to worry. The doorman liked her and wouldn't say a word to Balducci about O'Farrell staying the entire night.

"So, who would want to hurt you?" he asked her over steak and eggs at a diner around the corner. He was wearing his linen suit again but had left the silk tie off this morning, stowing it in his jacket pocket. Georgie was wearing an angora sweater with a pin in the shape of the letter G and a skirt with a fashionable six-inch hem. The sweater molded itself to her breasts. Her hair was pulled back in a ponytail. She wasn't wearing as much makeup as the night before and looked much younger. But those eyes… Made up or not, they popped.

"That's another one of Vincent's fantasies," she said. "Nobody wants to hurt me. I don't need a bodyguard— although I certainly needed you last night, didn't I?" She ran her toe up his leg.

"Just answer the question and stop playing footsie, young lady."

"Ooh, Daddy," she purred, "scold me some more."

Somehow, after spending the night with her, her voice didn't seem quite as whiney or annoying. She certainly had more than enough other qualities to make up for it—although some of those qualities certainly would not be seen by the judges.

"Georgie," O'Farrell said, moving his leg, "be serious."

"I am serious," she said. "Nobody wants to hurt me. Vincent thinks everyone wants what he's got. Well, if no one knows he's got me, what's the problem?"

"Someone must know," O'Farrell said. "Somebody

who works for him and knows when to make excuses for him."

"Sure, they know he's got *someone*," she said, "but not who."

"Look," O'Farrell said, "Balducci is paying me to protect you, and that's what I'm going to do."

"And more, I think," she said.

———

AFTER BREAKFAST, O'Farrell walked Georgie back to her building then said he had to go home to change.

"Aren't you afraid someone's gonna attack me?"

"I think what Vincent wants is for me to escort you to the beauty pageant, and protect you," O'Farrell said. "Starting with the party at the Yacht Club. So, I'll pick you up here. What time is the party?"

"The festivities start at three," she said. "I'm supposed to be there at noon, though."

"Noon?"

"I'm part of the show, after all," she said.

"How many contestants are there?"

"There were supposed to be a lot, but we ended up with just twelve. Some folks—sponsors—are really upset about it."

"Twelve beautiful girls, huh?" O'Farrell said. "All right, then I'll pick you up here at ten. I assume Balducci will supply transportation?"

"He'll have an automobile here to take us over to New Jersey. Probably a Rolls."

O'Farrell made a face. He still preferred horses, but it was a long way to Atlantic City.

"Okay," he said. "I'll see you then."

"What about tomorrow?" she asked. "Don't you want to see me tomorrow?"

"I don't think—"

She came closer to him.

"After everything we did to each other last night, you can wait two days to see me?"

"Hey, Georgie," O'Farrell said, "you're the one who said what we did last night was just sex."

"Well, yes," she said, touching his lapel. "But it was good sex, wasn't it?"

"It was great," he said. "Fabulous. You're a wonderful gal, but you belong to my client."

"That didn't seem to bother you last night."

"Last night, I gave in to bourbon and a pair of gorgeous…eyes."

She smiled. "You think my…eyes are gorgeous?" she asked.

"You know they are." Behind Georgie, O'Farrell could see the doorman watching him. A different one than the night before, but another young man, this one eyeing Georgie appreciatively—not that O'Farrell could blame him.

"You sure this doorman is not on Balducci's payroll?"

"I'm this sure," she said. She slid her hands around his neck and gave him a kiss that could have melted the soles of his shoes. Her tongue fluttered in his mouth and she bit his bottom lip lightly before stepping back and smiling at him.

She wiggled her fingers at him, smiling mischievously. "See you the day after tomorrow, lover."

———

BUT FRIDAY, when he went to pick her up, there was no answer at the door. He went down to ask the doorman if he'd seen Georgie Taylor that morning. This was the same doorman who had watched her kiss him goodbye the other day.

"No, sir," the man said. "I haven't seen her today at all."

O'Farrell studied the man for a moment, then took a ten out of his wallet.

"What's your name?"

"Henry, sir." Henry was a young man in his late twenties. He was eyeing the ten in O'Farrell's hand hungrily.

"Tell me, Henry, has Miss Taylor had any visitors since I was here?"

"No, sir."

"Not Mr. Balducci?"

"Well, yes, sir," Henry said. "He came by last night. I didn't know you meant him."

"Did he stay the night?"

"No, sir," Henry said, "He left after a few hours."

"Anyone else?"

"No, sir," the doorman said. "She hasn't had anyone

else upstairs since you left the other morning except for Mr. Balducci."

"Did she go out at all?"

"Yes, sir," Henry said. "I saw her go out yesterday. She did some shopping and came home with a few bags. She stayed in after that—at least, as long as I was on duty."

"How many doormen are there, Henry?"

"Three, sir, but only one other—Leslie," he said the name with a wry grin, "has been on duty since you were here. He worked yesterday afternoon and evening, as well as the evening you arrived."

"I'd like to find out what he knows, Henry," O'Farrell said.

"I could ask him when I see him."

"No," O'Farrell said, "I'd like to find out as soon as possible. Could you call him? There'd be ten in it for him, and a second ten for you."

The promise of twenty bucks sent Henry to the phone to call Leslie. He asked the second doorman the same questions O'Farrell had asked him and hung up shaking his head.

"Leslie says he never saw anyone go up to Miss Taylor's apartment, and he never saw her leave."

O'Farrell went over it in his head. So she'd only been out once all day Thursday, didn't go out Wednesday after he left her, or any time Friday morning until now. Balducci was the only person seen going up.

"Is there a back door, Henry?"

"Yes, sir," the doorman said. "It's kept locked.

Tenants don't use it and don't have a key. It's access to an alley where we throw out the trash, or sometimes take deliveries."

"You have a key, in case of deliveries?"

"Yes, sir."

"Any deliveries since I left here Wednesday morning?" O'Farrell asked.

"No, sir."

O'Farrell gave Henry the twenty dollars and then took out another twenty.

"Henry, have you got a key to Miss Taylor's apartment?"

"Yes, sir. Do you think something's happened to her?"

"Let's just say I have a bad feeling."

Henry waved away the second twenty and got the key.

———

"WE FOUND HER LIKE THIS," he told McKeever.

"You've got each other to vouch for that," the detective said. "Is there anything you haven't told me?"

There was. He'd left out the part about having sex with his client's girl and spending the night. He only hoped Henry had left that part out, too.

"No, that's it."

"That pretty much jibes with what the doorman told us. You better scram, Val. The lieutenant is gonna show up soon and he ain't gonna like it if—"

"Too late," the police officer on the door said.

O'Farrell and McKeever both turned to see Lieutenant Mike Turico enter the room.

"Well, well," Turico said when he saw O'Farrell. "Guess you musta forgot you ain't a cop no more, O'Farrell."

"Hello, Mike."

Turico approached O'Farrell and felt the texture of the wide lapel of the private detective's blue pin-striped suit.

"Turnin' private musta really paid off for you, Val," he said. He looked down at the matching fedora O'Farrell was holding.

"I'm doin' okay, Mike," O'Farrell said. "Thanks for askin'."

"Bet the swells really like you in this outfit." He touched O'Farrell's red silk tie, straightening it. Without looking at McKeever, he asked, "Who let him in here?"

"He just walked in, boss," the detective said. "You know how Val is."

"I do," Turico said. He stepped back from O'Farrell, jerked his thumb at the door and said, "Blow."

"Nice to see you again, too, Mike," O'Farrell said. The two had not got along when they were both police detectives, and it was no different now. Turico had always resented how O'Farrell got the high profile cases, but O'Farrell had a reputation for getting results, and Turico didn't. Turico had risen to the rank of lieutenant since rank had more to do with who you knew than results.

Turico moved to inspect the body. McKeever followed O'Farrell to the door.

"Sorry to bust in on you like this, Sam."

McKeever waved his apology off.

"Forget it. If the boss is gonna chew me out it's gonna be over this or somethin' else. But just between you and me, Val, you got a personal interest in this?"

"My client pays the bills for this place," O'Farrell said. "I met the girl. I liked her."

"Ah," McKeever said, "the sugar daddy. You got an idea where I can find him?"

"You can get his address from the manager of the building," O'Farrell said. "I don't have it on me. And he's got an office downtown somewhere. If the manager can't help you, let me know."

"McKeever," Lieutenant Turico yelled, "get your ass over here."

"Gotta go, Val. You gonna look into this?"

"I'm not sure, Sam."

"Well, let me know, huh?" McKeever said. "Turico might be here, but this is my case."

"I'll stay in touch." As he went out past the uniformed policeman, he patted his arm and said, "See you, Ed."

Did he have a personal interest? Goddamn right, he did.

———

O'FARRELL WAS STILL DRESSED for the Yacht

Club party when he approached Bat Masterson at his desk at the *Morning Telegraph*. The old lawman turned newspaperman made a show of covering his eyes.

"I'm blind! I'm blind!" he cried, then dropped his hands. "Damned if you ain't the prettiest man I ever did see, O'Farrell."

"Cut it, Bat," O'Farrell said. "You're not the only one who can get all duded up."

"'All duded up?'" Bat asked. "I don't think I've heard anyone say that since Wyatt Earp back in ninety-nine."

O'Farrell rushed on, afraid his friend would start telling one of his stories, which would end with him taking a replica of his old gun out of his desk drawer. O'Farrell usually enjoyed Bat's stories, but he had no time for them today.

"Bat," O'Farrell said, sitting down across from his friend, "what's the skinny on the beauty pageant out in Atlantic City?"

Bat sat back and smiled broadly. Approaching his late sixties, both his waist and his face had filled out, but when he smiled, it took years off him.

"I know I'm one of the judges," he said.

"How'd you get that job?"

"Hell, they just up and asked me," the old gunman said. "Who am I to say no to judging a bevy of beauties?"

"Who asked you?"

"Some fella from the—what's it called—Atlantic City something—"

"—Businessman's League?"

"That's it. Said they needed artists to judge and I

qualified 'cause I'm a writer. You believe that? I've never been called an artist before."

"Or a writer."

"You want me to shoot you?"

"Sorry."

"What's your interest?"

"I'll tell you," O'Farrell said. "But you've got to keep it under your hat for a while."

"That's a hard thing to ask a newspaperman to do, Val, but okay. For you, I'll do it."

O'Farrell fed him the whole story, and Bat listened in complete silence.

"What do you want me to do?" Bat asked when O'Farrell finished.

"I want to find out what you know about Balducci, and about the pageant."

"Like what?"

"Like are they on the up and up, both of them?"

"As far as I know, the pageant is," Bat said.

"Does that mean Balducci isn't?"

"There's been talk that Balducci is in bed with a certain criminal element."

"Like what?"

"Some of the crime reporters have been wondering if he's in with this new Mafia," Bat said. "They wonder if he's not involved with the giggle juice trade and other illegal activities."

"You sound like you're being real careful with your language. Why would a rich man like him want to run liquor with the mob?"

"Well," Bat said, "this new breed of—what do they call 'em—gangsters is a lot different from the bad guys of my day. You can't tell by white hats and black hats anymore, Val. And who knows why rich men do what rich men do?"

"So Balducci might be in bed with the Mafia," O'Farrell said. "But the pageant is on the level?"

"As far as I can tell," Bat said. "I wouldn't have agreed to be a judge if I thought different."

"How are you getting out there?"

"They're sending a car for me."

"What time?"

"Around five, I think. Do you want to ride with me?" Bat asked.

"Yes, I would," O'Farrell said. "I think if I walk in with you, I'll be able to get around easier."

"Fine," Bat said. "Meet me here around quarter to five and we'll go look at some girls. What will you be doing until then?"

O'Farrell stood up. "Trying to find my client before the police do."

———

O'FARRELL KNEW MORE about the Mafia and Johnny Torrio—which were natural offshoots of Paul Kelly and his Five Points Gang—than he wanted to let on to Bat Masterson. Friend or no friend, it wasn't wise to let a newspaperman know all that you knew. However, he'd met Vincent Balducci and didn't see him as a gangster. It was more likely he had some connections—crooked and lucrative—to Tammany Hall.

O'Farrell was unable to locate Balducci that morning and into the afternoon. He wondered if the police were having the same problem. At least he knew the man was supposed to be at the Yacht Club in Jersey that evening.

He decided to make one more stop before meeting Bat Masterson to go to New Jersey. There were still things he needed to know, and his buddy Sam McKeever would have the answers.

———

O'FARRELL HAD DECIDED NOT to change his clothes after leaving Bat Masterson, so when he returned to the offices of the *Morning Telegraph,* he was still dressed for the Yacht Club party.

He met Bat in front of the building as a boxy yellow Pierce Arrow Roadster pulled up. He and Bat got in, and the driver pulled away and headed for New Jersey.

"Find your man?" Bat asked.

"No."

"Think he's in hidin'?"

"I doubt it," O'Farrell said. "Men with his money—and his connections—rarely go into hiding, even if they are suspected of murder."

"And is he?"

"He's on the list," the detective said. "He was paying the bills for the girl."

"What's your interest in this, Val, other than him bein' your client?"

"I met the girl and liked her," O'Farrell said. "She shouldn't have died like that."

"Like what?" Bat asked.

"She was shot, once, in the temple."

"Any chance of suicide?"

"The word I got from the cops is she was shot from close range, but there was no gun at the scene."

"That rules out suicide—unless someone removed the gun."

"Too complicated," O'Farrell said. "In my experience, the simplest answer is usually the right one. Once you start factoring in *what-ifs*, you just muddy the waters."

"What about the gangster angle?"

"That muddies the waters," O'Farrell said as if it was a perfect example of what he'd been talking about. "I'm looking for a clean, simple solution."

"You're gonna solve this thing?"

"Bat," O'Farrell said, "I think I already have."

———

WHEN THEY PULLED up in front of the Yacht Club there were many vehicles already there—Pierce Arrows, Rolls Royces, even some sporty Stutz Roadsters.

O'Farrell and Bat were dropped in front of the club. A tent had been erected to accommodate all the guests for the party. Festivities seemed to have already begun. A man dressed as King Neptune arrived at the docks on a barge surrounded by twenty women in costumes and twenty black men dressed as Nubian slaves. A second barge brought the beauty contestants in. There were eleven of them, O'Farrell knew, because Georgie Taylor would have been the twelfth.

The contestants were allowed to wear their new risqué bathing suits on the barge, showing lots of skin, but were then whisked away to don something more appropriate for the party.

"It won't be easy judging the most beautiful out of that lot, tomorrow night," Bat said, when the girls had gone. "I'd better find the officials and ask what they want me to do."

"I'll see you inside the tent, then," Val O'Farrell said.

"Better stick with me, Val," Bat said. "At least until I get you introduced to someone in the know."

That was wise, O'Farrell knew. On his own, he might end up being kicked out before he could find Vincent Balducci.

The pageant officials pinned a button on Bat's lapel identifying him as a judge and agreed to give O'Farrell a guest button. So armed, both O'Farrell and Bat joined the party in the tent.

There was a stage with a big band on it, playing their hearts out while a male and female singer alternated songs. Guests filled a dance floor or milled about holding champagne glasses or martinis or wine, all of which were being circulated by uniformed waiters. Money had been paid, whether it was for a license or just a bribe, and the giggle juice was flowing freely.

The men were wearing expensive suits and in some cases tuxedos. The women flaunted jewelry—rings, bracelets, even tiaras—and the fashions of the day, some with six-inch hems flying higher while they danced the Charleston, the Shimmy, the Fox Trot, or the Black Bottom. It seemed as if many of the women who were young enough to care thought they had to do something to compete with the bathing beauties, some of whom were on the dance floor. He could imagine Georgie out there, and it made him angry—angrier than he'd been since he first discovered her body.

A male singer started to sing *My Time Is Your Time* and couples moved in to dance closer together.

"See him?" Bat asked.

"Who?"

"Your client?"

"Not yet."

"I see somebody you know," Bat said, pointing to Detective Sam McKeever of the New York Police Department, who was fast approaching with another man in a suit and some uniformed New Jersey police in tow. Right on time.

"Val," McKeever said, "this is Detective Willoughby of the Atlantic City Police."

"What did you find out?" O'Farrell asked McKeever after tossing Willoughby a nod.

"She was killed sometime Thursday night. Both

doormen have alibis," McKeever said. "They were both seen on duty by other tenants."

"They could have slipped away long enough to kill her," Bat offered.

"You're muddying the waters again, Bat," O'Farrell said. "There are three logical suspects for this crime."

"And you've cleared the doormen?" Bat asked, looking at McKeever.

"Yeah," McKeever said, then, "Hey, you're Bat Masterson."

"At your service," Bat said.

One of the uniformed policemen said to the others, "That's Bat Masterson."

O'Farrell saw Bat's chest inflate until another officer said, "Who's he?" and a third said, "Newspaperman, I think.'

"Did you manage to keep this from Lieutenant Turico?" O'Farrell asked.

"Yeah, but he ain't gonna like it."

"I wanted you to get the collar," O'Farrell said.

"Wait a minute," Bat said. "You said there were three logical suspects."

"Actually four," McKeever said. "But I'm clearin' Val, here."

"If you've cleared Val and the two doormen," Bat said, "that leaves—"

"There he is," O'Farrell said, cutting Bat off. He started to push through the crowd, causing several people to spill their drinks.

"Follow 'im," McKeever said to the other cops, and Bat followed them.

O'Farrell was faster than they were and was not being careful about who he bumped. As he got closer, Vincent Balducci turned and saw him coming toward him. The millionaire was impeccably turned out in a black tuxedo and was holding a champagne glass. He was chatting with some people—one of whom was a matronly lady covered in jewels that did nothing to hide the fact that she was *not* one of the contestants. He frowned when he saw O'Farrell coming toward him, then saw something in the detective's face he didn't like. He turned and started pushing through the crowd. O'Farrell increased his speed, leaving McKeever and Bat and the other police to struggle through the crowd behind him.

The band started playing an up-tempo number, and people started doing the Charleston again. Balducci was trying to run now, and as he burst out onto the dance floor, a heavyset woman trying to keep up with the music slammed into him with her hip and sent him flying across the floor. He bumped into a man whose arms and legs were flailing about in an obscene caricature of the dance, and they both fell to the floor. The man shouted, but Balducci—in excellent physical condition—jumped up and began running again. He got a few steps when a slender but energetic girl in a flapper's dress banged into him with a sharp-boned hip and knocked him off balance. He managed to stay on his feet, and finally made his way across the dance floor to the exit next to the bandstand.

O'Farrell, following in his wake, managed to avoid all

the traffic Balducci had encountered and was right behind him.

It was dark out, and Balducci headed for the marina. O'Farrell wasn't even sure why the man was running, but he took his 45 from his shoulder holster just the same.

The millionaire ran to the end of a dock, then turned to face O'Farrell.

"You can't shoot me!" he cried out, waving his hands. "I'm not armed."

"Why would I want to shoot you, Vincent?" O'Farrell asked. He holstered his gun. "In fact, why are you running from me?"

Balducci was sweating so much some of the dye from his hair was running down his forehead.

"Why were you chasing me?"

"Was I?" O'Farrell asked.

"You came at me. From the look on your face, I thought..."

The man was too fit to be winded from running. He was out of breath for another reason.

Suddenly, there was a small automatic in his hand. O'Farrell cursed himself for holstering his gun.

"I didn't mean to," Balducci said. "She told me about the sex and I just went crazy. It wasn't my fault."

"Is that the gun?" Georgie had been shot at close range with a small caliber gun. "Where'd you get it?"

"It was hers," he said. "I gave it to her for protection. I-I never thought she'd try to use it against me."

"You must have frightened her."

"She...she was mine! She wasn't supposed to be with anyone else."

O'Farrell felt bad about that. Maybe if he hadn't slept with Georgie, she'd still be alive now. Or maybe it would have happened later, with someone else.

"Come on, Vincent," O'Farrell said. "If you shot her by accident, you're not going to shoot me deliberately."

"You know," Balducci said, "I knew it when I saw your face. I can't let you tell anyone."

O'Farrell wondered where the damned police were. And where was Bat Masterson? He was wondering how close he'd get to his gun if he tried to draw it now.

"Vincent—"

"I'm sorry," Balducci said. "I had no idea it would come to this when I hired you. I'm so sorry."

Balducci tensed in anticipation of firing his gun, but before he could, there was a shot from behind O'Farrell. A bullet struck Balducci in his right shoulder. He cried out and dropped his gun into the water, then fell to his knees and clutched his arm. O'Farrell turned to see Bat Masterson standing at the end of the dock with an old Colt 45 in his hand. He turned to check Balducci was neutralized, then walked over to Bat.

"Thanks, Bat."

"I still got it," Bat said.

"Where'd you get that?"

"All the guns in my desk aren't harmless replicas, you know."

Behind Bat, Sam McKeever came running up with the other policeman.

"Damned Charleston," he said. "How'd you get across that dance floor without slamming into somebody?"

"I'm graceful."

"Did he do it?"

"He did it," O'Farrell said. "He confessed. I'll testify, but I don't think I'll have to."

The other detective, Willoughby, waved at his men and said, "Go get him."

"You'll need divers," O'Farrell told both detectives. "The gun fell in the water when Bat shot him."

"The same gun?" McKeever asked, surprised.

"Yeah," O'Farrell said. "For some reason, he was carrying it around. He said he gave it to her for protection."

The uniformed police helped Balducci to his feet and started walking him off the dock. When they reached O'Farrell and the two detectives, they stopped.

"I'm sorry I slept with her, Balducci," O'Farrell said. "It just happened, but she shouldn't have died for it."

Balducci's mouth flopped open and he said, "*You* slept with her, too?"

As they marched him away, McKeever said, "One of the doormen. Apparently, he went up there when Balducci wasn't around."

"He didn't know about her and me?" O'Farrell said.

"He does now," McKeever said.

"And so do we," Bat said.

"You dog," McKeever said.

"I wonder if his money will be able to buy him out of this?" Bat asked.

"Don't matter to me," McKeever said. "My job's just to bring 'im in."

Bat and McKeever started after the other policemen. Let them rib him, O'Farrell thought, bringing up the rear. It wasn't his fault she was dead. That's what counted. Now he could be sad for her and not feel any guilt.

The Last Ride

Brian Drake

Brian Drake has a wicked sense of humor. He makes me laugh every day, except if he's gone too far yet again and been virtually grounded and sent to his room by Facebook or Twitter. I keep expecting his next book to be titled *Anarchy For Dummies*. However, he seems far too busy writing his Scott Stiletto thrillers or another entry in the fast action *Team Reaper* series. On his way to breaking into the big time, Brian wrote an entry (*Copper Mountain Champ*) in the *Fight Card* series I created and edited. It has been inspiring to see him keep punching at the keyboard as his writing has gone from strength to strength. He was a natural choice for inclusion in this anthology...

THE LAST RIDE

THE BULLETS DROPPED into the revolver's chambers with sharp clicks. Eddie Milano liked the clicks so much, he took the cartridges out and slipped them back in again one by one. In the silence of the messy living room that followed, Milano rolled the cylinder slowly left, right, then snapped it closed. It made a louder click this time, but he didn't like it as much.

He swallowed another gulp of whiskey. It burned down his throat, with some of the liquid dripping down his chin. They joined the larger wet spots already covering the front of his thin t-shirt. He wiped his chin with the back of his hand, winced as he touched the still-raw cut caused by his gun. He'd gone out to the lake to practice a few shots with the shiny Dan Wesson .44 Magnum the morning before, holding the gun at the waist like John Wayne always did. When he fired, the gun had snapped back and struck his chin, nearly knocked him over. His dog had been watching, and Eddie could have sworn the animal laughed. His three-day stubble irritated the cut as well, but he had more on his mind than taking care of himself.

He sat back on the stained couch with the .44 in one hand, the whiskey bottle in the other, and stared at the digital clock on top of the dusty TV. He drank some more whiskey but didn't dribble any this time. He felt much calmer now. No turning back.

A framed picture of a sandy-haired woman sat on top of the television. She stood in a small boat in the middle of the lake, holding up a fishing line with two freshly caught trout dangling from the end. Big grin, wide fore-head. She was short, thick in the middle, with wide hips. Milano's bowling buddies always said you could show a movie on her forehead. Milano always said her forehead wasn't where he focused his attention.

He drank the rest of the whiskey and flung the bottle across the room. It tumbled end-over-end until it smacked the picture right off the television. The bottle cracked the picture's glass cover, and both clunked onto the carpet. He laughed, stood up, jammed the gun into his pants, and grabbed the keys to his truck.

If he'd bothered to look at the cracked picture, he'd have seen that one of the cracks cut right across the woman's neck.

———

THE WEATHERMAN on the radio said it would be cloudy, cold, with snow in the mountains. As he lay in bed, Dean Rowe was listening with one ear, the other was tuned to his wife knocking around in the bathroom. It always snowed in the mountains. He decided the weatherman was either a rookie—or stupid. He'd had enough of both lately and hoped the bad weather would bring a better day. He could use a break from the robberies, traffic violators, DUI stops, and domestic disturbances he had to deal with as a patrol officer. His trainee could also use a break, especially after their misadventure the day before.

"I'm done, sweetie," Steffie said, returning to the bedroom. She tossed her bathrobe on a chair. Rowe watched her dress. She pretended to ignore him. He waited until she'd wiggled her hips into a skirt that was too small a year ago but she was too stubborn to get rid of before rolling out of bed.

He stifled a groan as he stood up. His left leg wouldn't cooperate. The bullet that had smacked through bone and muscle five years ago had been removed and the damage repaired, but the leg was always stiff when he awoke. It really bothered him when it was cold out. He hoped it wouldn't be so cold today as to cause a problem.

Steffie had his toast and eggs ready when he finished his shower and shave. However, she left before he did, telling him to make sure he washed up and wiped down the counter because the ants were coming back. He lingered over a second cup of coffee while thinking about his trainee and what the two of them would face once they hit the street. He didn't want a repeat of yesterday.

POLICE TRAINEE TONY FALLON didn't want a repeat of the day before, either. As he laced up his boots, he was glad he learned not to strap on his bulletproof vest before he put on his boots. You couldn't reach the boots with the vest on, sitting or standing, because of the vest's bulk. Rowe had supplied the correct formula after Tony had made the mistake his first day—*boots first.* That was assuming, of course, Tony had already put on his uniform pants and shirt. But Rowe had given him credit for doing *that* much.

Tony wasn't the only officer in the locker room. The area was buzzing with conversation, slamming locker doors, steam and running water from the showers. There was also an odd odor, which grew throughout the day despite air fresheners and air conditioning. Gray walls and concrete floors with drains here and there contained the smell, making the place interchangeable with a pile of manure. Tony could never get his uniform on fast enough.

There were several other officers dressing in his aisle. None said a word to him. However, when Tony heard the booming voice of Sergeant Harrison the hassles would begin.

"I guess I lost the bet," Harrison said to Tony, opening a locker two spaces down. "Some of us weren't sure you'd show up for work today."

Tony forced a smile, didn't look at the bulky, bald-and-goateed Harrison. Tony pulled a leather pistol belt from his locker then checked the compartment for his pepper spray, handcuffs, extra magazines, and cell phone.

"Did everybody hear?" Harrison said over the noise. "Trainee Fallon locked his pistol in the jail gun locker when he and Rowe booked a bad guy yesterday but forgot it when they left. When he needed it to chase another bad guy, he realized he was about to get into a gunfight without a gun!"

The young rookie mashed his teeth as he strapped on the belt, but noted nobody seemed to be laughing—except Harrison, who brayed his usual animal screech of a laugh. The sergeant said, "How did you handle your screw-up, trainee?"

Tony kept his eyes on the ground, took a breath, and said, "I grabbed the automatic rifle from the trunk."

Harrison laughed. "Then after the chase, some citizen called to complain about a certain cop running around with a machine gun."

Officers nearby slammed their lockers and headed for the exit.

Harrison seemed oblivious to the lack of response to his humor. "Thus began the captain's latest lecture about the appropriate use of the automatic rifle. I'm sure trainee Fallon will enjoy the inevitable memo since the captain is always thorough when ripping somebody a new one." Harrison ended with a final, satisfied exhale and started undressing.

Tony pushed a magazine into his .40-caliber Beretta pistol, snapped back the slide extra hard. Holstering the gun, he walked away. Harrison said to his back: "Be careful today, trainee."

The young rookie let out a deep breath as he left the locker room, following the checker-tiled hallway to the briefing room. The department wasn't like the army, which was where he'd spent most of his twenties before an honorable discharge. He'd returned to town, reunited with the rock band he'd put together in high school. They played a few gigs a week, but he also took a job as a personal trainer at the local fitness club. The work was boring, so he joined the force.

However, there were a lot more rules to follow on the PD, and fitting in wasn't easy. Most of the officers had been around for fifteen to twenty years, and he was one of only three rookies. At least he was on day shift —for now.

Tony reached the briefing room, a dozen or so officers already there. He saw Rowe—his field-training-officer or FTO—seated at a rear table and joined him. The watch commander stepped up to the podium, called roll, and began the morning run-down of overnight incidents, stolen car reports, and robbery suspects at large. Tony took careful notes, but noticed Rowe only scribbled a few.

The briefing ended quickly, and the officers filed out. Outside in the parking lot, Tony ignored the sharp morning chill and spent ten minutes reviewing the contents of their patrol car's trunk—DUI kit, first aid kit, rifle and shotgun, extra ammunition, fire extinguisher, spare tire, ponchos, and rubber boots. He triple-checked everything while Rowe waited in the car. He stopped when he realized he couldn't spend all day checking gear.

Tony shut the trunk, went around to the passenger side, and stopped when he saw Rowe already sitting there. The older officer had his face in his notes and didn't look up. Tony swallowed, pivoted, walked around the back of the car, and slid behind the wheel. He let out a breath. The weight of his equipment made him sink into the vinyl seat. Space was tight, taken up by the computer screen, radio, and other electronics. The plastic dashboard, warped and cracked in places, had a layer of dust on it. Odds and ends of extra pens and ticket books decorated the rest of the interior.

Rowe handed him the keys and said, "Let's go."

Tony steered into the street. The city wasn't much—about half a million people and more country than residential with tall, rocky mountains—granite sentinels—casting a shadow over everything.

"Don't worry about Harrison," Rowe said.

"Trying not to, sir."

"He once screwed up worse than you. He and I were partners when we arrested a couple of the Red Tigers. We had a tip about a rumble and wanted to get as many of them off the streets as we could. Harrison had been using the shotgun. When he went to put it back in the rack—we kept them inside the cars at the time—his finger touched the trigger, and he blasted a hole in the roof." Rowe chuckled.

Tony remained quiet.

Rowe said, "So, forget about him."

"Yes, sir."

"You'll have a chance to make up for yesterday soon enough, and everybody will forget the blunders."

Tony hoped so but didn't say anything more.

———

BETTY GAVILAN SWORE LOUDLY as she swung her thick legs onto the street, struggling out of her car. Tight skirts, itchy nylons, and high-heeled pumps that squeezed her toes didn't mix with her low-slung blue Camaro. She caught a reproachful glare from a woman on the sidewalk who had a baby in her arms. The woman turned away as Betty slammed the door. Betty narrowed her eyes at the mother's back, then tap-tap-tapped her way up the sidewalk to Joe's Donuts. She was glad the door was already open.

Smilin' Joe greeted her with his usual toothy grin, saying, "Beautiful mornin', miss." Betty almost told him to get tied. Instead, she said, "Two dozen assorted." She waited for him to turn his back before jamming a bright red manicured fingernail under the waistband of her skirt and scratching.

She caught her reflection in the mirror behind the counter. At least her hair, which was a color resembling sand, looked good, flowing just past her shoulders. She wondered if she should dye it black and put in some highlights like her hairdresser had suggested. It would be a nice change. She wanted a change. She checked her watch and cursed inwardly, because if Smilin' Joe didn't hurry up and fill those two pink boxes, she'd be late. He finished the first, set it on the counter, grabbed the next, and whistled as he began filling.

Betty tapped a finger against her thigh and wished she could kick her heels off. Anything that hurt as much as they did couldn't be good. Maybe her feet were too big. And why did she have to be the office gofer? Her grinning witch of a boss had told her the morning donut run would be part of the job. But they did give her a dealership credit card to pay the bill. Still, after two months of the duty, she was ready to tell the sing-song-voiced slut to jam the donuts.

"Here go, miss," Smilin' Joe said, placing the two pink boxes on the counter. Betty handed him the credit card. She didn't want to go into work and be around all the salespeople pushing new and used cars. When the guys weren't chasing customers, they chased her. While sometimes the flirting was fun and helped to pass the time, she wasn't in the mood today.

Smilin' Joe gave her a receipt. She signed his copy and carried the boxes in both hands as she left the shop. Why couldn't she win the lotto, spend the rest of her life fishing? She hadn't been fishing in two weeks, since she'd left Eddie. He had the boat. Fishing off the shore wasn't the same, and renting a stupid boat was too expensive.

What in the world was Eddie doing standing by her car?

———

EDDIE MILANO FOUND Betty very easily. She'd complained about donut duty enough, so he knew her routine. He'd been parked in his high-wheeled truck, across the street for over an hour, watching the shop. He saw Betty pull up in the Camaro and struggle out. As soon as she went in, he hopped down from his truck and raced across the street. He stopped by the Camaro's bumper. He couldn't see her through the shop's front window. Moving carefully along the passenger side, he stopped again by the hood, took the heavy .44 revolver from under his shirt, and placed it behind his leg like the cops on the TV. A chill raced up his arms and neck. He wore no coat, and his head was dizzy from too much whiskey. His pulse, though, felt normal.

Betty emerged from the donut shop with the two pink boxes in her arms. She froze when she saw him. "Eddie," she said quietly.

"Get in the car." He kept the gun behind his leg.

"Go away," she said.

He stepped toward her, she stepped back. As she turned to run, he grabbed a handful of her collar and yanked. She yelped, the boxes crashing to the ground. He wrapped his left arm around her neck, jamming the muzzle of the .44 just under her ear. She screamed. Onlookers stopped, some grabbing for cell phones. Eddie pulled her toward the Camaro, wrapped his right arm, gun and all, around her neck, and reached back with his now-free left to open the passenger door.

Betty brought a foot up and slammed it down, the heel digging through his shoe. He yelled and hammered the butt of the .44 on the side of her head. She went all doughy, Eddie letting her sagging weight help him shove her into the car. He slammed the door, slid across the hood to the other side, and jumped behind the wheel. Betty moaned and shifted in the other seat as he buckled up, like his mother always said. He ripped her purse from her shoulder and batted her hands away when she tried to grab it back. He found the keys and started the engine. As he pulled away, he saw a police car in the rearview mirror. Betty took a deep breath to scream but wound up face-first in the back of the seat as Eddie hit the gas.

DISPATCH BROADCAST THE ALERT, calling it a fight, and Rowe radioed they were nearby. As Tony steered around the corner, scanning for the donut shop, they saw the Camaro screech away. Onlookers gestured wildly.

Rowe said, "Hit it!"

He radioed dispatch, saying they were in pursuit of a blue Camaro with the victim of a possible kidnapping inside.

"Time for the blink-blinks and wee-wees," Rowe said, flipping the console switches to activated their lights and siren.

Tony saw the Camaro a few blocks ahead and wove through traffic, catching up fast. The sports car picked up speed. Tony pressed the gas harder, dodging a minivan to keep the other car in sight.

Rowe rattled off their direction into the radio. His request for additional units was met with a 10-4.

Tony kept his hands tight on the wheel, his eyes locked on the Camaro. He breathed deeply with his pulse and heartbeat racing.

"Don't stare," Rowe said. "Scan."

The Camaro took a sharp right. The tires of the patrol car screeched as Tony followed.

———

INSIDE THE CAMARO, Eddie Milano decided the best thing Betty had ever done was buy a muscle car with an automatic transmission. He wove around traffic and blew through an intersection, other cars screeching and swerving to avoid the speeding vehicle. The cops were six cars back.

Betty was crumpled up in the passenger seat. She finally sprang up to crawl between the front bucket seats to get in the back. She flapped her hands wildly, shouting for help.

Eddie swerved around another car, hitting the brakes as he approached a second intersection. Betty flew backward, her head striking the passenger seat. Dazed, she rocked side to side as Eddie maneuvered through the intersection, the engine growling as he again stomped the gas.

———

ROWE SAID, "Dispatch, where are those units?"

The reply sounded like static to Tony as he threaded along in the wake of the Camaro. Sweat trickled down his face, coating his forehead. He felt more sweat under his vest, the back of his neck. His breathing came faster and faster, his knuckles white.

The road began to twist and turn. Traffic eased as buildings gave way to forest. Rowe broadcast their new location and direction. Tony followed the road, crossing the median to stay on the pavement. Brake, gas, twist, turn, brake, gas. They were gaining on the Camaro, but Tony wasn't sure how that improved the situation. The fleeing driver obviously had no plans to stop.

"You're doing fine, Tony," Rowe said, but suddenly yelled, "Stop!"

Tony stomped the brakes.

———

BETTY SOBBED, wedged between the front and back, as Eddie followed the twisting road. Her bleary eyes saw one of her black pumps lying on the back seat. She grabbed the pump, rose, and began bashing Eddie's head.

Eddie hollered as the heel bit into the side of his head, then his neck, then dug into his shoulder. He batted away another blow with his right hand but couldn't stop the next. It scored dead-on with his temple.

Eddie's vision spun as he tried to follow another curve and he cursed as the tires left the road. He twisted the wheel too hard, the car screaming toward the trunk of a tree. A sudden violent jolt shook the car, screams cut off by shattering glass and grinding metal. The airbag exploded in Eddie's face.

Blood leaked from his cheeks and forehead, his vision fuzzy. He grabbed for the seatbelt, his fingers not responding. He had to unbuckle with both hands. He pushed the door open and hauled himself out of the car, unsteady on his feet. He frowned at the two policemen with drawn guns, covered by the patrol car doors, who were shouting at him. He raised the .44 and fired.

One of the officers went down.

EDDIE TOOK off stumbling into the trees as return fire nipped at his heels.

———

WHEN ROWE SHOUTED, "STOP!" Tony had pushed the brake pedal down with so much force he thought he'd bust through the floor. The car began to spin, stopping with Rowe's side closest to the Camaro. The two cops jumped out with drawn guns and began shouting instructions to the driver: "Hands up! Get down on the ground now!" The suspect was teetering on his feet.

Rowe saw the shiny revolver first, yelling, "Shoot!" But the bad guy brought up the .44 and let a round go, knocking the veteran officer off his feet.

Tony opened fire with shaking hands. The man made

the tree line and vanished into the woods. He ejected the empty mag from his automatic as another blast thundered from the suspect's weapon. The round buzzed overhead. Tony raced around to his partner, who lay moaning on his back. Tony tore at the opening in Rowe's uniform shirt where the suspect's bullet had struck. It had been stopped by his bulletproof vest.

"Get...the...bad guy," Rowe said, gasping.

Tony raced off as the veteran officer rolled over, pushed up to his knees, and leaned against the car for support. Hurt and sucking air, Rowe leaned against the car and relished the growing wail of sirens in the distance. Then he glanced at the wrecked Camaro and realized only the suspect had made it out.

———

A SHARP PAIN ran through Tony's stomach as he raced through the trees. He couldn't breathe right but he didn't dare stop. One of his academy instructors claimed pain only meant you were alive. *Doesn't it feel good to be alive?* he'd say.

Tony saw the suspect ahead as the ground began to slope upward. He shouted, but the word came out, "Ack!" even though he'd tried to yell, "Stop!"

Milano did stop, but only to turn and fire another round. It missed by a mile. Tony braced his arms against a tree, fired twice. Milano staggered back, blotches of red showing on his shirt. Tony kept the suspect in his sights.

The other man turned his back and took several long

strides forward, then began to stagger and bend at the waist.

Tony advanced. "Drop the weapon!" The words came out this time.

Milano turned and began to raise his gun.

Without hesitating, Tony fired again and again.

Milano's body rocked with each hit until he tumbled face first into the dirt. Tony ran up and kicked the .44 away and stepped back. He continued to hold his gun on the fallen man.

As he stood panting, lungs burning, the beat of his pulse loud inside his head, he tried to comprehend what had happened, but his mind couldn't grasp it.

A voice. "He's up here!"

And then, "Fallon!"

Tony turned. Sergeant Harrison and his patrol partner Scott had reached him.

Harrison said, "You okay?"

Tony nodded. He kept nodding until he realized he looked like an idiot and stopped. Scott knelt by the suspect. He put two fingers on the side of the man's neck. He then shook his head and stood. "Goner."

Harrison slapped Tony's back as the rookie stared, stunned, at the dead man.

"Nice shooting, trainee," Harrison said. "Feel good about yourself. You're one of us after all."

Tony slowly holstered his still-hot automatic. He tried to speak. Nothing came out. Everything around the edges of his eyes looked blurry, but he didn't know why. Then he remembered something about *tunnel vision*. He hadn't noticed it during the fight. He followed Harrison and Scott back to the road, reaching for Harrison's shoulder to steady himself.

Harrison didn't argue.

––––––––

TONY SHOOK as he sat in the cold metal chair, his arms on the table in front of him. The bare white walls of the interview room had nothing reassuring to cover up their drabness. The bright fluorescent lights above reflected off the walls and created a glare that made Tony squint. It was in a room like this where suspects were interviewed by department detectives.

The homicide team investigating the shooting had brought him here. They were looking over his statement, he knew, but wished they hadn't put him in this room. His mind began filling with doubts over what he'd done. Should he have fired those last two shots or waited for the suspect to fall on his own? He wondered if the man would have been able to get off another shot like he'd tried. Would they use that against him?

He jumped in the seat as the door squeaked open and the two detectives, Holt and Savage, entered. Holt sat on his left, Savage his right. Savage, his eyeglasses on the edge of his nose, looked through a file folder while Holt just looked at Tony. Tony stared at the center of the table.

"This is a good shoot," Savage said, and Tony looked up at him. "I think the district attorney will agree when she sees our report. Good driving, too. No civilians were hurt. You may get a medal."

Tony tried to swallow the lump in his throat, but it stayed where it was.

"It's okay," Holt told him. "Your reactions are normal."

Savage said, "I don't think we have any further questions."

Holt nodded in agreement, asked if Tony had any for them.

The young patrolman looked at Holt for a moment, noticed the specks of gray in his mustache that didn't show in his hair. His question came out in a low whisper. "Is Rowe okay?"

"Bruised and banged up," Holt said. "But he'll be home in a few hours."

"The girl?"

"DOA," Savage said, removing his glasses. "When the car hit the tree, she flew over the passenger seat and crashed headfirst through the windshield."

Tony's face turned pale, his mouth hanging open. He choked, swallowed, said, "I don't under…I mean, what was it all about?"

"Her name was Betty Gavilan," Savage said, putting his glasses back on, flipping to the beginning of the folder. "Her family says she'd just dumped the prince you tangled with. He probably wanted her to change her mind."

Tony stared at his shaking hands, his stomach turning over. He felt sick.

"There's nothing more you could have done," Holt said. He gave Tony's shoulder a reassuring squeeze and patted his back. "Sometimes we have to settle for what we get, but it's always a win when we go home alive."

Tony nodded. "I guess so."

Black Cherry
Nicole Nelson-Hicks

I have always enjoyed the company of people who are funny, intelligent, and a bit perverted. My favorite whack-job writer, Nikki Nelson-Hicks, is a rock star in all three of those demographics. She has been pronounced the unholy lovechild of Flannery O'Connor and H.P. Lovecraft, a designation she wears with pride. Jake Isten-hegyi, the hero of her *Accidental Detective* series, is as one of a kind as she is. He'll make you laugh until you cry, then scare you half to death. I knew Nikki would bring her trademark fiendish twists to a story for this anthology, and she delivered a killer...

BLACK CHERRY

IT WAS AUGUST, the hottest damn summer on record for the past hundred years. I'm sure you remember it. Every day there was something in the news about a forgotten kid who got broiled in the backseat of a van, or Grandma in Texas baking in her recliner because the rolling blackouts cut off her air conditioner. That summer, civilization was melting around our ears.

Maybe it was the heat of that summer that spurred the idea. Maybe it was seeing Fontana at all my favorite haunts, dancing and laughing while her husband rotted in his grave. Or maybe it was like my momma always said, "Mick, I'll never have to worry about you. All a person has to do is look in your eyes and see that you don't give a shit."

It wasn't like that for Fontana's dead husband—Ronald, my younger brother. Where I was tough, he was soft. Where I was bold, he was meek. I was in and out of jail while he went to college and stayed clean. We fit each like yin and yang. I was also the bastard who introduced him to Fontana.

Looking back, I guess I should've known better. Ronald dropped dead in love with her as soon as he laid eyes on her. She had gallons of curly hair piled on top of her head, with ringlets falling down her back like a dirty blonde stream. She poured sparkly blue eye shadow on her eyelids, and painted her lips so red they stained her teeth. Her laughter bounced off the walls as she slapped the back of her latest mark while he poured her more beer.

I still don't know what Ronald saw in her. She ignored him at first, so he upped his game and started sending her roses. Finally, she relented, and he took her to a restaurant with linen napkins and crystal glasses. Before Ronald, the best Fontana had ever gotten on a date was french fries and a free beer before going down on somebody behind Dirty Dick's Bar & Grill. I know this to be true because I wasn't the only one to go through my share of fries with her, if you get my drift. They got married six weeks after that first date. I was the best man. It was as awkward as it sounds.

Ronald did something in computers—programming, writing software, or some damned technical thing. Whatever it was, he made a serious chunk of green. He needed every penny to keep the new Mrs. Fontana Montresor happy. When Fontana asked for a McMansion in Brentwood, she got it. When she asked for an Escalade with a special paint job to match the color of her favorite finger-nail polish, she got it. His money ran through those painted claws like water. Ronald near crippled himself working harder and harder to make sure the well never ran dry.

In the end, it didn't matter. Fontana was still a bar hag, no matter what her new mailing address read. She added new vices to her closet: cocaine, meth, and a little pot—hydro, the best on the market—all designed to take off the edge. Ronald never knew a thing. I'll believe that to the day I die. Two years into the marriage and his eyes were that closed.

To pay off her dealer, a nasty Spic known as Big Bird, Fontana started dealing. She did good business in Brent-wood and Belle Meade. All those socialite bitches liked to pretend they were still hip enough to play in the hood as long as they could stay inside the safety of their tree-lined cul-de-sacs.

Things might've gone fine except one of the stupid bitches' kids found mommy's special stash and overdosed. Mommy rolled on Fontana like a mutt scratching his back on hot asphalt.

Ronald took the punch. Mommy started a crusade, enlisted all her friends in high places, and they crucified him. They ran editorials in the paper, and the worthless vultures who call themselves news reporters played the brat's funeral over and over on TV. Ronald didn't have a chance. His company fired him. The IRS did a surprise audit and froze his bank accounts. The concerned parents of Brentwood picketed his house and threw eggs at his windows.

After being granted immunity, Fontana turned witness for the prosecution. She pulled the abused wife defense—*Ronald was so far in debt and, you know, he could get so angry sometimes.*

I nearly puked.

Ronald got sixty years. He served eighteen months before dying of a heart attack. He was thirty-nine years old, for shit's sake. How does a thirty-nine-year-old man have a heart attack? I'll fucking tell you in one word—Fontana. That bitch ripped his heart out and stomped on it.

At his funeral, I remember the look in my mother's eyes. She kept staring at her son, the good one, the one with a future, now lying stiff in a box. Then she'd look at me—the drug-dealing felon with more tattoos carved in his skin than real teeth left in his head. In a world where God sits in His Heaven with Baby Jesus on his knee, she couldn't understand why it was Ronald in that box instead of me.

When they put Ronald in the ground, I saw her eyes dim with each clump of dirt they shoveled into the hole. She never smiled again. Her box garden went untended and withered. Sometimes I would catch her staring at me with those dead headlights in her skull, and knew she hated me. Every day, my upright and breathing presence reminded her there was no God, or if He was there, he didn't give a rat's cold ass about what happened to the likes of us. I'm only telling you this so you can understand why I had to do what I did. Shit, that's not it. I want you to know why I *wanted* to do what I did.

———

I FOUND Fontana one night at the Rutherford County Fair.

Perhaps you are only familiar with fairgrounds during daylight hours. During the day, the sun bakes the asphalt, and the air smells of cotton candy, funnel cakes, and popcorn. Most of the people walking around are either Mommies and Daddies trying to reach some sort of Rockwellian high with their kids, or FHA kids looking to show off their prize heifer—the moon-eyed, shitting hunk of beef they've raised since it was a calf—and sell it to the highest bidder for hamburger.

At night, the fair takes on a new vibe. The heat from the day remains trapped in the tortured midway. There are screams from the rides that twist and meld with their swinging, turning, and churning lights as they toss the food in their bellies around and around. The smells filling your nose at night are a salad of grease, vomit, and the sweet undercurrent of ganja.

At night is when the throwaways, the rejects, and the stupid come out to play. That was when I found Fontana. She was puking into a trash can.

The years had not been so good on her. She was thin and wasted. The colored lights played up the hollow of her sunken cheeks. She was a shadow of the blonde who had married my brother. I almost turned away, I swear. I thought maybe God or whatever else the fuck is out there was doing the job for me. However slowly, justice was being served, right?

Then she saw me. She looked into my eyes and said, "Looky, looky here, it's Mickey Montresor." She stumbled over and wrapped her arms around my waist. I could smell the vomit on her breath. "Give your sister a hug!"

She cupped my balls. I swear to God, she grabbed my cock.

That was when something inside me broke. That last little piece of...I don't know what to call it. Compassion? Hope? Goodness? I felt it snap as soon as she squeezed my nut sack.

Fuck it. God works too slowly.

I pulled away from her. "Fontana! Hey, girl, can you do me a solid? You know where I can find Rhonda Zidanka?"

"Rhonda? What do you want her for?" She smiled with yellow-gray teeth and walked her fingers up my chest. "I'm here. I used to be enough for you."

"It's not that, girl." I pushed her hands down. "A certain, ya know, business opportunity has come my way. I heard she was the one with the game this side of town."

"What sort of game?"

I looked around and spoke softly. "I got a cone of hydro I want her to test before I fork over more money. Can't trust spics. They might've cut it with some home-grown shit. I hear she's got a nose for the good stuff."

Fontana laughed and snorted. "Rhonda? That bitch wouldn't know hydro from the shit her uncle grows behind his shed. Fuck, Mickey, why didn't you just come to me? You know I got links."

"I don't like to twist business with family, Fontana."

"You see a ring on this finger?" She wiggled her leathery, bony hands in my face. "I sold that piece of shit months ago. A girl has to live, ya know? Let it go and move on. We got no problem doing business. Let me see your shit."

"Not here."

She smiled and wrapped her arms around me, grabbing my ass. "Let's go to my car. I got some happy juice in the back." She raked my ass with her stiff fingernails. "We'll seal this deal in style."

We left the fairgrounds the back way, behind the tents with the screaming barkers and the lights of the swirling rides, staying to the dark routes known only by carnies and stray cats. She led me, laughing all the way, to her car. Please remember. I almost left.

———

"HERE IT IS, LOVER." She ran her hands over the hood of her Cadillac Escalade before giving it a sloppy kiss. "This is my pretty baby. I like to park her way out here in Bumfuck, Egypt so she won't get scratched. She's all I got left." She flashed her long fingernails. "See? It's the same color as my nails. Black cherry. It looks like regular old black here in the dark, but when the sun hits it, the cherry just smacks you in the face." She laughed so hard at her own joke, she almost fell.

I caught her and she patted my face. "Always a good boy, ain't you, Mickey? You always there to save a girl in distress."

I helped her to her feet. "Business first."

"Right, right." She pulled a fuzzy bunny keychain out of her purse and I heard two chirps as she unlocked the doors. "Get in the back," she said. "I sold the two middle seats for some blow. All I got back there now is the long bench seat." She smacked my ass as I climbed in. "Good for snuggling."

Beer cans, candy wrappers, and dirty laundry covered the floorboard. I kicked them aside as I found a place to sit. It had black leather seats. They had probably been very nice before all the pizza and booze and God only knows what else caked into them. Fontana climbed in behind me.

"Excuse the mess," she said, starting to throw trash out the open door. "It's Juanita's day off."

She closed the door and climbed into the driver's seat. "Let me find the button. Here it is." She pressed whatever she'd found, and the overhead console reading lamps came on. "And then there was light!" She giggled.

"It's kind of stuffy in here," I said. "How about you roll down the windows?"

"I love a man who knows what he wants," she said.

The windows came down with a whispered hush. I heard snippets of screams from people riding the roller coaster in chorus with the crickets. I leaned against the open window and breathed in the hot, heavy-air deeply, like a drowning man who had broken through the water's edge for the first time. I love the heat of summer in Tennessee. The entire state is like a sweat lodge. Stepping outside, your body begins to bleed sweat, cleansing you, bringing all that shit to the surface to either evaporate or cling to you like a stain.

Fontana crawled into the back with me and slowly squeezed my crotch. "Don't fall asleep on me, lover."

"Business first," I said. She smiled with those horrible grimy teeth as I pushed her hand away. I reached into my jacket pocket and pulled out a baggie. Inside was a cone of pure hydro, good shit, the best. I know because it's my own blend.

She took the baggie, opened it, and took a long sniff, as if she had any idea what she was doing. "Oh, shit, yes! Mickey, this is the shit! But can't know sure, you know, unless I...until we test it. Got some papers?"

"Way ahead of you, darling." I pulled out another baggie with two joints already rolled.

She clapped and squealed like a little girl finding a Shetland pony under the Christmas tree. "I got something to bring to the party, too!" She reached under my seat, her face nestling right into my junk. She pulled out a plastic carton filled with bottles of booze. There was vodka, gin, whiskey, a six-pack of Pabst, and some white lightning in a mason jar.

"Damn, girl," I said. "You know how to host!"

As she fired up the first joint, the fair's midnight fireworks show cracked open the sky with thunder and flashed the clouds with streaks of red and blue and green. Fontana took a deep toke and held it, her dull blue eyes staring up at the fireworks. She exhaled and fell over into my lap. "Good shit."

"As good as the stuff you used to sell?"

She smiled slyly. "I don't know what you're talking about."

"That's right. I keep forgetting it was my baby brother, a man who wouldn't know a hydro from oregano, who was the brains. It keeps slipping my fucking mind."

"Shit! Did you have to bring him up? Damn, buzz-kill." She took another toke and held it. "Damn!" her voice was high and squeaky as she fought not to exhale. "It's so freaking hot!" She took off her t-shirt. She had a fine rack, the best tits Belle Meade plastic surgery could offer. They hung like bloated melons on her wasted frame. Still, there was something odd about them, something new.

"Damn, girl! What are those things? Propellers?"

She exhaled and held up her tits and pinched the tiny rotary blades that pierced each nipple. "It's the newest thing. The guy at the tattoo studio called them Titty Twisters. Want a pull? First time is free."

I shook my head.

She leaned back and took another toke. "Your loss." She exhaled with a grimace. "You were never shy before. What happened? Didn't turn queer, did you?"

"No." I took a beer. It tasted like hot, foamy piss. "Just like to keep outside business separate from my personal business."

"Thank God." She took a deep drag and burned down the joint. She held it in, making sharp yipping sounds before letting the smoke roll out of her mouth like a white fog. "I always knew I married the wrong fucking brother."

In the next seven hours, Fontana consumed both bottles of vodka, half the whiskey, two swigs of white lightning, smoked both joints to the nubs, and popped two white pills she took from her back pocket. I confined myself to the piss-poor beer. She had her head in my lap, humming and smiling up into my face. Her eyes were closed. I doubt she even knew it. "Wanna me to blow you?" she slurred.

I stroked her hair. She'd had such pretty hair a long time ago. Now, it was stiff and dry, like corn husk. "No. I think I'm done here." I moved, letting her head fall onto the soft leather car seat. I got into the driver's seat, She had left the keys.

"Where you be...lover?" she mumbled from the back.

I took the keys out of the ignition. I heard her snoring. I closed the back windows first, and then the front. I used my shirt to wipe down the steering wheel. I wiped off the keys and dropped them on the floorboard. I took my beer cans and put them in a sack I found among the trash. I located my baggies and stuffed them in my front pocket. I thought about wiping down the seat but decided it would be pointless. How many other sets of prints were back there? Besides, by the time they found her, I doubt anybody was going to want to dust.

I closed the door, using my shirt as a mitt, and left her in the back seat. The sun's heat had already burned away the morning dew. I looked up into the cloudless azure-blue sky. It was going to be a hot one. Scorching.

I finally got to see the paint job she's been crowing about. She hadn't lied. When the sunlight hit it, the cherry color sparkled within the darkness. It was like a deep purple-red bruise. The color of a split over-ripe black cherry.

It suited her.

No Confession Required
L.J. Martin

The first time I met L.J. Martin, it was like reconnecting with a long-lost friend. L.J. is the consummate professional writer, a storyteller able to turn his hand to any genre. His novels are rife with action, but it is his characters and the moral dilemmas they face that stay with you long after the last page is turned. L.J. flexes his writing muscles again for the following story...

NO CONFESSION REQUIRED

I CHECK my iPhone for the time and activate the record feature. I doubt if I'll need proof of the conversation, but if the phone is found, some clever police forensics dude may be able to figure out how I was whacked and by whom.

I've given myself an absolute twenty-minute time limit. In and out, and back in the van with the goods.

"Mornin', Father," an old black gardener says, looking up from his knees in the flower bed, tipping his wide-brimmed straw hat. His hair and whisker stubble are pure white and soften a face lined deeply—a dusky bean-brown peach pit. He quickly cuts watery eyes down, going back to work with a short grub hoe. I wonder if real priests would presume, as I do, that he has a great deal to confess. But then again, maybe a couple of centuries of being at the bottom of the food chain in the Deep South keeps one's eyes lowered. Even if so, even if he carries the sins of the South on his drooping shoulders and has a list of sins longer than the hoe handle, don't we all?

"Bless you, my son," I say, pontifically, tipping the black porkpie. I've always wanted to say that to an older man. It has such a nice ring to it.

Priests have had the brunt of it the last few years, not that they haven't brought it upon themselves. I hope this ecumenical collar and black suit don't bring the wrath of God down upon me, or the wrath of the Vincinti family— by the way, I use "family" in the worst sense of the word —whose driveway I'm wandering down carrying nothing more than my thick black briefcase embossed with a cross. A nice touch, if I do say so.

It's amazing what one can pick up in a pawn shop. I was told by the pawnbroker that the black leather case was formerly owned by a cemetery plot salesman who thought the embossing lent a certain trustworthy ambiance to his efforts. I hope it does so for mine.

The briefcase is the least of the impediments of the outfit. Anyone who'd wear a black suit, black shirt, and white choker collar in August in Louisiana must be a few beads short on his rosary. Maybe that's what pushed the boys in black over the edge.

Then again, maybe what drove many members of the clergy to violating their vows, and too many of us laymen to equate "priest" with "pedophile," is this damn plastic-lined collar, tight, stiff, unforgiving, and unrelenting—like I must be for the next half hour, until I can happily get shed of it. Of course, having to swear to celibacy was likely far more responsible. Somehow the plastic choker reminds me of the white flea collar I force upon my ten-pound seal point Siamese, Futa. His is embossed Repels Fleas, mine is figuratively embossed, Repels Mafioso No-Neck Goombahs.

If I'm lucky and everything goes perfectly, it'll only be a half hour in and out. Twenty minutes is my limit, not that I expect to keep to it. But lofty goals seem appropriate at the moment.

This could be my last half-hour on Earth if I'm not so lucky, and I may face judgment for my terrestrial sins far faster than contemplated.

Thirty minutes could be worth over a quarter million, so the risk is well worth it.

One year and two months ago, one point five million was what the rap of the Los Angeles Superior Court judge's gavel confirmed as bail for Vinny. And I'm now in the mix for three hundred thousand gross, or twenty-percent, thanks to a half-hour negotiating with my good friend and number one client, L.A. bail bondsman Sol Goldman. My expenses will be in the neighborhood of fifty grand, a major risk for this middle-income bounty hunter. Two planes await me at the Louis Armstrong New Orleans International Airport; one to transport Vinny back to L.A., another to transport me to Nashville, where I'll connect with a commercial flight to Atlanta—and hopefully, another fat check to be collected from Sol's partner. It's common practice for bondsmen to partner up on huge bails.

St. Tammany Parish, where I've been for the last two days, is one of the classy areas of southern Louisiana, just north of decadent New Orleans. Moss hanging from giant live oaks, perfectly manicured lawns rolling down to Lake Pontchartrain, where the normal contingency of alligators and water moccasins are forbidden to roam. Not that they pay much attention. Here, the predators and varmints mostly live inside the stately old antebellum mansions.

Particularly in the column-fronted ivy-covered walls of the one I'm approaching at the moment.

Gambling brought a lot of good things to the Mississippi River state, and it also brought a few bad. The Vincinti family being head and shoulders above—or should I say below—that norm.

But I'm only interested in a nephew, Vinny; a bad boy of whom the family must want to be shed. If what Sol Goldman overheard in the hallway outside the courtroom is true, Vinny is lucky that old godfather Vincinti, known to associates as Fat Guido the Hammer, didn't ventilate Vinny's three-grand Armani suit right there. It seems Vinny was running his own operation in L.A.; the families are not organizations who encourage individual initiative. Had it not been for Vinny being a blood relative, he'd be wearing concrete boots in the bottom of the lake.

Sol's been known to exaggerate when he wants me to take a contract.

The front doors are carved from a log large enough to shame California's redwoods; tall and wide enough so that Shaq-attack could dribble through without ducking or turning sideways. The bell button is half the size of my palm, backlit and surrounded by a sconce that looks to be solid gold. High up under the eaves flanking the door, I hear the hum of a small servo and glance up into the single, bulbous, appraising eye of a video camera. I left my van half a block away, outside the high wrought iron gates of the compound, and I have already been scanned by a least three cameras as well as patted down by an apologetic gate guard. The old secondhand balloon-tire bike, purchased for forty bucks, added to my innocuous appearance. How could a priest on a bicycle be a threat? And I've shaved, my cheeks now smooth as a baby's lower ones.

The bell does a few notes of Beethoven's Fifth.

Yes, the riverboat gambling biz, a good chunk of the cocaine trade, and the majority of the numbers running in Louisiana's ghettos have done well by the former New Jersey family.

The door creaks open slowly.

It's Bela Lugosi, with brooding deep-set ebony eyes flanking a bent avocado nose, only thicker through the shoulders and neck—if you can call an appendage that begins at cauliflower earlobes, bulging with muscle and sloping almost to shoulder point, merely a neck. And speaking of bulges, the bulge under his butler's jacket is surely a Mac 10 or something that chatters with equal speed and fatality.

He speaks slowly and deliberately in New Jersey-ese as he surveys me slowly from black-felt porkpie to gleaming wingtips. "Good...uh...morning, sir. Are youse... uh... expected?"

"No, my son. However, I'm from St. Joseph's. There are things regarding the ceremony I must discuss with Mr. Vincinti."

"Father or…uh…junior?" he asks.

I'm rapidly coming to the conclusion this guy's not a Rhodes Scholar. Then again, maybe he is—ninety miles of bad road, so a roads' scholar, where he was run over by a semi several times.

"Vinny Vincinti." I don't use his street name, Vinny Slick.

"He's da nephew." Hopefully, the tone of voice and look on No-Neck's face reflects the family's disdain for Vinny.

"Aww," I say sagely.

"Do youse…uh…mind, padre?" he asks, reaching out with both hands.

"Mind?" I ask, as if I don't know what he means.

"I need…uh…to pat youse down. Mr. Vincinti… senior…has had some threats…uh…corporate problems… and we's careful at da moment."

"Aww, corporate problems. The gentleman at the gate…."

"Sorry, padre, but it's da rule."

I set the briefcase down on the polished marble and turn around; he pats away. He goes all the way to the ankles, not bashful about familiarity, then comes up with the briefcase; snapping it open on an entry side table by the time I get turned around.

"Mr. Vincinti is in the corporate world?" I ask, seemingly clueless. He ignores me while he does a thorough job, running corncob-size fingers through the briefcase.

It's full of papers, a medium-size Bible, my newly acquired rosary beads, and a can of Off, the mosquito haters' best friend.

He avoids the Bible as if it would spew out green stuff like a spinning-head Linda Blair in *The Exorcist*—the reaction I'd hoped for, since I've desecrated it by cutting out room for my little Ruger .380. I'll give a dozen Bibles to the homeless shelter when I'm back home to repent. Rather, he picks up the can of mosquito repellent and eyes it carefully.

"Mosquitoes bother youse?" he asks.

"I'm allergic to the little fellows, God bless them."

He smiles for the first time, showing a gold tooth. "God's wrath even for youse."

"Yes, my son—a small bump in the road of life. If all was roses and robins, we'd have no benchmark by which to judge their beauty." I like that. Maybe I missed my calling. "So," *speaking of lowlife bugs*, I'm thinking, "Mr. Vincinti?"

"Youse wait here, padre. Tony," he shouts into what appears to be a living room.

As he walks down the hall, another no-neck appears and leans against the door jamb. He folds his arms and watches me closely.

"Good morning, my son," I say.

He nods and continues to glare. I can hear a college football game on the TV in the background. I guess he's pissed, probably has a C-note on the game. I've picked

Saturday for my mission as it's the day the Vincintis are most likely in residence.

I smile and glance at my iPhone, deciding to ignore No-Neck Two. I'm inside, Vinny, hopefully, is on his way, and I've only used eleven minutes. God bless.

But the fellow who walks into the hallway down which No-Neck has disappeared is not Vinny Vincinti. He's much older, much fatter, yet far more ominous.

Guido Vincinti himself.

The good news is, as he approaches, his look is benevolent, and when he comes face to face, I feel like he's going to bend, take my hand, and kiss my ring.

Jesus, I think as I glance at my hand, I haven't removed my Marine Corps ring. I guess I can claim I was a chaplain. The M60 I carried sent plenty of Iraqis to heaven—or elsewhere—so I guess I did some priestly good.

"Father…" he says. His fat cheeks and wattled throat quivers as he speaks, but his eyes are penetrating—ice picks poised over your chest.

"MacCarthy. Father MacCarthy, and you're?"

"Guido Vincinti, father. Where's Father Pierucci?"

"Preparing for tonight's mass. He asked me…."

"Of course. Can I offer you a drink, Father?"

He doesn't wait for an answer, which doesn't surprise me as this man is not accustomed to waiting for approval from anyone. Instead, he turns and heads down the hall.

I snatch up my briefcase and follow.

Before he reaches the end of the hall, he speaks over his shoulder. "You shoot pool, Father?"

"Not as a habit," I reply, and he looks at me, or into me, with an icy glance. To my surprise, his speech is much more refined than his employees'. This old boy probably *was* a Rhodes Scholar or, at least, could have been had he not been busy busting kneecaps and plunging ice picks into ear canals.

"Vinny is in what we call the Saloon."

I too look over my shoulder, to see both no-necks following.

I track Guido into a spacious room with a bar seating a dozen, a pool table, a flat screen TV as big as a picture window, and Vinny Vincinti shooting a game of eight-ball by himself.

The no-necks take up positions flanking the doorway out.

"Vinny," Guido snaps. "Pay goddamn attention. This is Father..."

"McCartney," I say, then bite my tongue when I realize I've suddenly changed my name. Sometimes it doesn't pay, being a Beatle's fan.

"I thought you said MacCarthy?" He again poises the proverbial ice pick over my heart.

"McCartney," I correct convincingly, "Sorry, I bit my tongue and am mumbling a little. Father Ian McCartney."

He eyes me carefully but turns back to Vinny. "Put down the goddamn stick and come say hello to the Father. He's here to talk about the wedding." He turns to me. "Pardon my blaspheme."

I give him a condemning look, as a priest should.

Vinny, concentrating on the four-ball off the cushion into a corner pocket, glances up. Then he goes back to lining up the shot. Guido, with the quickness of a cobra, snatches up the cue ball and shakes it at Vinny, his knuckles so white I think for a moment he's going to powder it.

His tone is so low I can barely hear him. "You want this up your skinny ass, Vinny?"

Vinny blanches and cuts his eyes down. "Sorry, Uncle Guido."

"To the Father. Apologize to the Father."

Vinny sets the pool cue aside, walks over, and demurely extends a hand, glancing at his uncle apologetically as he does so. "Sorry, Father McCartney. I'm pleased to meet you, but I went over all this stuff with Father Pierucci."

"Just a few more details," I say.

"A priest as a bloody wedding director." He laughs and glances at his uncle, whose glare would melt lead.

"Sorry, Unc… I didn't mean…"

I clear my throat, then my tone is condescending. "The church will have a substantial role, will it not? Even though I understand your vows will be here on the grounds?"

Vinny actually blushes. "Of course, Father. But shouldn't Angela be here?"

Guido snarls, "Just sit down with the Father and give him what he needs."

"Yes, sir." He turns to me. "You want to sit at the bar, Father?"

"That's fine, my son."

Guido fits himself behind the bar and pours three glasses half-full of Black Bush, one of the fine Irish Whiskeys. "In honor of you, Father McCartney," he says, passing a glass to me.

"Are you going to stay, Mr. Vincinti?" I ask.

He shrugs.

So I press it. "Some of this will be very personal, sir. Only between God and Vinny here."

"And you, of course, Father MacCarthy?" he asks, but I won't trip up again.

"McCartney," I say, smiling.

"Sorry, McCartney."

He turns to Vinny. "I'll be in my study. Come get me when you're through. I'd like to walk the Father out to his car."

"Bicycle," I correct. "Exercise, you know."

He smiles and pats his generous stomach. "No, actually, I wouldn't." Then he laughs and walks out, waving the two no-necks to follow.

Now I can get on with the business at hand.

We talk for fifteen minutes, going over vows and flowers and more, and I'd presumed right—Vinny is quickly bored and eager to be rid of me, so I stand.

"Thank you for your time, son. I'm sorry to be in a bit of a rush."

"No problem, Father. Should I call Uncle Guido to walk you out?"

"Don't bother him, but I'd prefer you did so. We can talk on the way."

"Fine, let's go." He seems eager to send me on my way and not so eager to be reamed by his uncle.

We stroll casually out through the big doors, then to the gate. When passing through, the gate guard leans out of his little gatehouse window and says goodbye with a smile and nod. Vinny is six feet ahead of me, and I lean close to the guard. "Mr. Vincinti wants to see you."

The man blanches as if he's in trouble, and in seconds is out his little door and on his way to the house.

"What's up?" Vinny asks, watching the guard trot away.

"I forgot to give you something," I say, and walk far enough to the side of the gate where I can't be seen from the house and prop my briefcase on the seat of my bike.

He comes close, curious. Pulling out the can of bug spray, a label I made myself on my printer and am rather proud of, I hit Vinny between his squinty eyes with a shot of mace.

He yells and goes to his knees. I crack him a good right on the cheekbone, and he goes to his back. Leaving the bike and briefcase, I jerk him to his feet, and with him yelling like a cat with his tail slammed in the door, shove an arm up behind him. We move the fifty yards to my van.

His head is obviously swimming less as we reach the sliding door, so I give him another right hook to the side of his noggin and bounce his head off the van's doorjamb. I'm trying not to mark him up. He's goofy again as I shove him hard, and he goes to his back.

Bounty hunters, bail enforcement officers, have

eyebolts in the back of their vans, and I cuff his wrist to one and stretch out his ankle to another.

As I fire up my van, nicely remodeled and tricked out with a supercharged 6.2 Hemi, I smile as two guards run through the gate and stand looking up and down the road. I've had Alex, my two-hundred-seventy-pound employee, drive it all the way out from L.A.

Then the pair of guards' searching eyes center on me as the van roars to life.

I'll be long gone by the time they can get to Guido's eight-car garage.

I flip a U-turn and burn rubber as I head for the Louis Armstrong New Orleans International Airport. Satchmo is an old favorite of mine. I've made arrangements to stow the van in one of those rent-a-garage units, and the pilot of Vinny's ride should be waiting there with Alex, my helper. After Vinny is checked into the L.A. lockup, Alex will fly back with the pilot and drive my van back to Santa Barbara.

As we near the airport, Vinny yells, "I got two or three grand in my wallet. It's yours, you turn me loose."

"Thanks, Vinny. It's mine anyway if I wanted to be as lowlife a thief as you. Fact is, you're worth way more to me."

"You're going to hell for impersonating a priest."

"Doubt it, as it's already crowded with Vincintis. Now shut up. No confession required."

Split Decision
Eric Beetner

Eric Beetner has noir flowing through his veins instead of blood. He is a modern master of the art form where bad choices lead to worse choices, which lead to things inevitably getting far worse—and far more deadly. I first met Eric on the set of the ABC reality show *Take the Money and Run*. I was the dubious on-screen talent, while Eric was the genius editor behind the scenes. He was much more important to the success of the series, since all I had to do was show up and look pretty. While filming the first episode, I realized I'd recently read a cool novel, *One Too Many Blows To the Head,* by some guy named Eric Beetner. Once confronted, Eric confessed to his sins of authorship and a beautiful friendship was born. Since then, Eric has written a baker's gaggle of novels on the cutting edge of modern noir. He has the knack of making you care deeply about desperate characters facing impossible decisions, forcing you to hold your breath as you turn pages long past your bedtime. Some of the toughest noir novels are set in the world of boxing —*Fat City, The Professional, The Leather Pushers*. Noir and boxing are perfect matches. *Split Decision* is Eric's homage to these boxing noirs, and it punches as hard as any of them.

SPLIT DECISION ROUND 1

KANSAS CITY, KS. 1953

I KNEW I had Barker when he started to fight dirty. Most fighters start out on the up and up, only turning to the cheap shots when things weren't going their way. Round three though, the son of a gun tried to lace me.

Barker pivoted around so his back was to the referee, then came at me high with a left jab. He made like he was aiming for my right eye, then he let his glove drift wide. The idea was to get the laces on the inside wrist of your glove to rub alongside your opponent's face like a cheese grater. As soon as he threw the punch, we both knew the stunt.

So, fine. Barker wanted to play it that way, okay.

It felt good to be winning. I'd dropped my last three, putting me below .500. Not a good record for a kid supposedly on the rise. A rise to the middle. To the punch drunk league with all the stumblebums out there taking licks for nothing more than cab fare home.

My form was on, I wasn't out of breath yet. Hard

work had paid off and no way this joker was going to take this match out from under me with some cheap shots.

I laid three in Barker's gut and had him on the retreat again when the bell rang, signaling the end of the third round. All I wanted to do was keep on punching until he hit face down on the canvas, but that would have to wait another ninety seconds.

In the corner, my manager, Sal, put down the stool and tipped a bottle of water into my mouth. I swished and spat into the bucket.

"Did you see that? He tried to lace me," I said.

"What's that?" Sal turned his good ear to me.

"He tried to lace me," I repeated.

"Aw, he's scared, that's all." Sal had been there and back and seen it all along the way. A salty old-veteran of every fight hall from here to Buffalo, Sal had punched himself silly years ago, then kept it up for another ten years after that. His nose had been broken so many times he'd lost count. Matching cauliflower ears hung like lamps from each side of his head, and he moved with a hitching limp that had finally brought his days in the ring to an end. Why he'd picked up a go-nowhere prospect like me, I'll never know. I was his only middleweight, and I felt the tag was plenty appropriate. My talent was in the middle. The highest I could ever get in the fight game was somewhere between the title fight and the gutter. He knew it and I knew it, like the palooka across the ring and I both knew he threw those laces at me.

Still, Sal treated me like a contender. He may have been punched dumb, but he was no fool. Treat your boys right, and they'll treat you right. Guess he always reminded me of Father Tim in that way. That was enough for me to hitch my wagon to Sal for keeps.

The bell rang for the fourth, and I came out blazing. I backed Barker into a corner straight away, banging body shots into him until he bent at the middle like a little wilting flower. Sucker.

I brought out my uppercut to lift his chin, but that wasn't where the damage came from. The damage came in my follow-up right cross to the now wide-open chin. As many times as I'd practiced the move in sparring, it came as second nature to me.

His chin rose like it was praying to the Virgin Mary, and from there, it came easy. His head snapped to the side, his jaw knocked out of place and staying there. I knew he was headed for the floor, but I couldn't resist one last shot.

Out on his feet, his hands dropped and I laid one straight shot to his face, pulled it a little left, and ran my laces across his eyebrow. The skin split open like a pair of lips gasping for air, and the blood ran into his eyes before he hit the mat.

The ref pushed me back and started to count, but I didn't stick around to listen. I went back to my corner, where Sal waited for me with a big grin. I heard the bell. Fight over. My record came even at ten and ten.

Over Sal's shoulder was Lola, my girl. She comes to every fight, even though I always tell her not to. A lot of guys like to bring their gals to the fights, but I thought it was no place for a lady. Most of them ended up bored, filing their nails and waiting for the bloodshed to be over so they can get home. Still they come, content with their role as arm candy for the big shots as long as it keeps them in mink.

Of course, the crowd at the Excelsior was more a squirrel-masquerading-as-mink than a real fur-and-diamonds crowd.

And Lola was my diamond. She smiled at me, I smiled back. My face wasn't even bruised up that night. No cold steak over a black eye for me. A night out with my winnings, treating Lola the way she deserved. A double in her highball, and dessert after the meal.

Two more fights to go that night and she knew the drill. I'd meet her out front. She couldn't make it to the locker rooms, and there was no reason for her to hang around inside to see a bunch of sluggers she didn't know.

After my three seconds of glory standing center ring with my fist in the air, Sal took me down to the locker rooms.

"Real good, kid. Real good," he said. "You read him like a book."

Easy for Sal to say. He couldn't read any more than I could do Chinese algebra. That part of his head had been punched away a long time ago.

We went through our usual post-bout rubdown, and there was not much to talk about since the fight had gone so well. We didn't talk about what to work on for next time. Mostly because there was no next time scheduled.

"What do we got lined up, Sal? I gotta eat, y'know."

"Yeah, yeah, I know, Jimmy." Sal kept on rubbing,

squeezing a little hard like his mind was somewhere else. "You and me both. None of my boys have been getting much play lately..."

He trailed off, thinking about hard times and empty cupboards. Yeah, things were lean for all of us. Sal past his prime, and me and his other sluggers at the peak of ours. Sheesh, that was a sad state of affairs. His hands dug into my back, taking out their frustration without him realizing it.

"Hey, lay off there, Sal. I won. No need for punishment."

"Sorry, kid." He took his hands off me, rubbed them together to get rid of the liniment oil. "I been meaning to talk to you..." He trailed off again. Not unusual for Sal. He sometimes dropped thoughts like the act of letting them out of his mouth made the whole idea he was trying to communicate slip away.

"Just let me know when we got the next one set, okay, Sal? Maybe after tonight, I can get something a little further up the card, y'know?"

"Yeah, yeah. Maybe, Jimmy."

I hopped off the table and started dressing. "It's just, well, you know how it is, Sal. How I feel about Lola. You know I been wanting to ask her to marry me. I can't do it without two nickels to rub together. Got my eye on a ring, you know. Real diamond and everything."

"Yeah, Jimmy. It's tough times all around."

Just like Sal to make me feel guilty about wanting the best for Lola. Sal had it rough. Not a dime left from his fight days, and when I went on a three-fight losing streak, it made it hard to secure any kind of purse. And him taking a percentage of what I thought wasn't enough to live on? Man, I was a heel for not thinking about him first.

"I'm sorry, Sal. I know I ain't been exactly making it easy for you." Neither had any of his other pugs, but I didn't want to remind him. Rubbing salt in the wound, y'know?

"Well, you see, Jimmy..."

This time he was cut off by a knock at the door. Odd. Not many people made it down the long hall to the locker rooms. Fewer had the politeness to knock.

I looked up, my pants on but unbuttoned and my chest still bare. Through the door came a small man in a fancy suit. Two much bigger men were with him but they stayed outside, bookending the door and looking like they were waiting for something to happen.

"Sal!" the man said. Sal looked down at the concrete floor and sheepishly extended a hand to the well-dressed man.

"Mr. Cardone, good to see you again."

Cardone shook Sal's hand but looked past him to me standing by my locker, half-dressed.

"This is the guy, huh? Jimmy Wyler, right?" He pointed a finger at me, and despite the smile on his face, it felt like an accusation. "A hell of a bout out there. You really showed that joker what for."

He brushed past Sal and held out a hand for me to take. I turned and shook with him. The top of Cardone's head came to my shoulder. It wasn't until he was right up on me that I noticed exactly how short he was. He carried himself like a much taller man.

He aimed that wagging finger at me again. "I came here tonight with an eye on you. Sal here has told me a lot about you."

"That right?" I couldn't figure this guy. He didn't smell like a promoter. Too much aftershave, not enough sweat. The suit, the vest, the tie clip, the pocket-watch chain, and the mirror-shined shoes all said money. But what kind of money?

"Been trying to get Sal to let me near one of his boys for a long time. And you?" He looked me up and down. "You're just the ticket."

I looked at Sal, but he kept his eyes down, away from me.

"Mr. Cardone has a proposition for you, Jimmy," Sal said to the floor. What was with all the "mister" stuff?

"I got a fight for you," Cardone said. "Next week if you want it."

"Sure. I want it." It was what I'd just been on Sal about, so I couldn't turn down an offer just because the guy offering it gave me the creeps. "You a promoter? I never seen you around."

"I'm a promoter of sorts. I put things together. Fights, other things. Entertainments." He lowered his chin and looked up at me from under the brim of his expensive hat. "I arrange things."

He dropped the hints and I caught them.

"How'd you like another one in the win column?"

Cardone asked with a smile. I caught him sliding an eye down across my bare chest.

"Always."

"I think I can," he winked at me, "arrange that for us."

I turned to Sal, who continued staring at the floor. "Is this a fix-up?" I asked. Why not get it out there? I was not much for speaking in codes.

"It's a chance for you to win another one and make a little scratch while you do it."

"So that's a yes?"

For the first time, the smile slipped off Cardone's face. He turned to Sal. "Sal, are we gonna have a problem here?"

Sal didn't react, just stared at his shoes. I figured Sal just didn't hear him.

"Sal?" he said louder.

Sal finally looked up. "No, no, Mr. Cardone. No problem. We'll take the fight. No problem."

The idea of a fix didn't sit well with me, even if I came out on the winning side. Plus, I was upset with Sal not telling me beforehand, but I realized he had been trying to when Cardone came in. Still made me wonder how long he'd been planning it.

Cardone turned back to me. "So, kid, we have a deal?"

Sal spoke with a mixture of pleading and guilt. "It's a good deal for us both, Jimmy. Real good." I pictured Sal's empty gym, his failing health, the string of young fighters under his belt who spent more time face-down on the canvas than they did sleeping in their own beds. Good for him, sure. Then I thought of that ring I had in mind for Lola. The money I'd already put down on layaway. Good for me, too. Maybe.

I looked again at the expensive suit Cardone wore. How much money does a man have to have that makes him carry himself a foot taller than he really is? Must be a lot.

"Did I mention it pays five hundred bucks?" he said.

I felt like I took a glove to the temple. My knees went a little soft. I didn't think he noticed. I learned something about myself right then. I learned I had a price.

ROUND 2

"TOOK YOU LONG ENOUGH." Lola stood on the sidewalk in front of the Excelsior fight hall. A woman like her didn't belong on a dirty sidewalk dodging drunks and salesmen all hopped up on the fights and brimming with fake manhood. Every night she came out to the fights, she must have got a hundred propositions from men offering to take her away from all this.

Lucky for me, she never went with any of them. She waited for me. I couldn't figure why.

I ran out and wrapped her up, twirled her, and set her down before kissing her.

"Jimmy Wyler, you settle down," she said, pulling away from my clinch. "It was a good win, but you didn't take the title or anything." She smiled. Oh, that smile. Something about that grin made me want to punch out the teeth of ten men. I couldn't explain it. It was how a palooka thinks.

"Lola, honey, I'm taking you out."

"Where to? Coffee and a donut? Maybe a hamburger?" She had my number. One sure bet—she wasn't with me for my money.

"Steak and all the trimmings. Ice cream sundae. Whatever you want."

"Sheesh, Jimmy, maybe that *was* the title fight and I just didn't know it."

"Anything for you, baby." I kissed her again.

"I changed my mind. You got knocked loopy. Maybe I wasn't watching that part."

"The only thing I'm loopy for is you, doll."

"Well, then take me out quick, before you come to your senses."

I had thirty-five dollars in my pocket from that night's bout. She didn't need to know the size of my meager roll. What mattered was I had five hundred coming to me. She didn't need to know that either. Let alone how I was planning on earning it.

———

IN THE RESTAURANT, we sat next to each other in a red-leather booth.

"See?" I said. "We're a match." I liked my steak bloody, and so did Lola.

I forked another hunk of good old Kansas beef into my mouth and smiled as I chewed.

"We're a pair all right," Lola said.

"I'm telling you, things are looking up. Won't be long now, and I'll have a big question for you."

Lola said playfully, "I heard that one before."

"No, I'm serious," I called the waiter over and ordered another beer. "And dessert for the lady. Anything she wants."

"We have a nice cheesecake tonight," the waiter said in a fake French accent.

"Jimmy, are you sure you can afford this?" Lola whispered to me.

"Bring it," I commanded the waiter. "With strawberries on top."

"Very good, sir," the waiter said, rushing away. Felt good to have someone call me sir. Still, I felt kind of bad since with dessert and another beer, I'd pretty much spent all of my thirty-five bucks and he wasn't going to get much of a tip.

———

ON THE DOORSTEP of her rooming house, Lola kissed me goodnight. She still tasted like strawberries. I wanted like hell to go up to her room, but the all capital letters of the NO MEN ALLOWED sign above the entrance gave me the brushoff. I could feel the stink eye of Mrs. Lovell peeping through her blinds. For a woman who loathed any kind of lovemaking, she sure was keen on being an eyewitness to any that went on around her front stoop.

"I love you," I said, trying to sound serious and sincere. I probably sounded like a school kid trying to do Shakespeare. You could memorize the words but never get the feeling.

Lola laughed. "Love you too, Jimmy."

I did a skip up the steps and planted one last kiss on her. "I love you more."

"I swear, you've got the gooiest center underneath the hardest shell of anyone I ever met." Like I said, she had my number.

"It's what you love about me, right?"

"Yeah," she sighed. "I guess it is." She'd wrapped her arms around my neck, speaking in that wistful way she liked to do. Thinking about the future. A future with me. I still didn't know how I rated a gal like her, but I wasn't about to let her go.

"Oh, Jimmy. How long until we get our own place, have a couple of kids, settle down?"

"Soon, Lola. Soon." A lot sooner with five hundred bucks in my pocket. 'Course with that ring I had on layaway, that five hundred would be out of my pocket and onto her finger in a jiffy.

"Jimmy, you remind me of my dad. Have I told you that?"

"No."

"He was a dreamer too. He worked with his hands. In a way, I guess you do too."

"Not forever, baby."

"The thing is, my dad made me a dreamer too. Two dreamers like you and me, Jimmy—you think that's a good thing?"

"I can't think of anything better."

Lola. A good Midwestern girl. Going to make a good

Midwestern wife. I knew she wouldn't wait forever, though. The count had started. I needed to make something happen before it got to ten.

She kissed me on the forehead. "Sweet dreams."

"When they're of you, they're always sweet."

"Oh, Jimmy," she scoffed. "Where do you get this stuff? A greeting card?"

She sure didn't love me for my way with words. Best not to question it, best to get on with making her my bride.

I blew her a kiss, did a little Gene Kelly down the street, noticing the lace curtains in Mrs. Lovell's apartment window slip back into place.

———

I WAS SO KEYED up that night I couldn't sleep. Five hundred bucks. Man. Y'know the way some guys can go snow-blind in the Arctic? I'd gone money-blind. It was only after an hour of lying in bed staring at the ceiling that I started to really think about what that money meant.

Dirty money. Crooked dough. The end of my legit career.

So be it. I was never gonna fight for the title. If this let me get out of the racket before I was punch-drunk, better for me. If it let me put a ring on Lola's finger, I'd do just about anything.

And if I became their boy, well, then I could stand to take a few more paydays at five hundred bucks a pop until they used me up. Then I'd be on my way. I could get a straight job and live an honest life. I'd always wanted to work for the railroad. Maybe I could do that. Lola and I could travel all over the country. Maybe even make it back up to Chicago and see Father Tim.

Boy, I'd love to see his face as I walked up the steps of St. Vincent's Asylum for Boys with Lola on my arm and a fat baby on my hip. He'd be proud, so long as he never found out how I got the money to stake my claim.

Once I started thinking about St. Vincent's, it was hard to stop. Those were ten good years. Better than I had a right to expect.

I was eight when my folks sent me away. The youngest of twelve and the farm had died out. I drew the short straw and ended up on the train with a note on my sleeve and no return address. I don't blame them. Hell, I ate better at St. Vincent's than I ever did on the farm.

The things I saw, the people I met there, I never would have had any of those experiences if I'd stayed my whole life plowing dirt.

I still remember VE Day, sitting up in the window looking out as the whole of Chicago all cheered at once. I'd never heard such a racket in all my life. Then the confetti started flying, and people took to the streets. We'd all hung out of those windows watching the world turn into a giant-snow-globe with Father Tim over my shoulder telling me to remember that day, as if I could ever forget.

People kissing strangers, cabbies honking their horns, two guys who climbed a lamp post. I felt like my heart would swell up and break apart and fly away in tiny pieces, just like that confetti.

Then I turned eighteen, bought my ticket for Kansas City and shook hands with Father Tim. That was the last I saw of him or any of the boys.

Something else I remember. The last thing I said to him. He said, "Promise me you'll always be good and do the right thing."

"I promise," I said.

Flat on my bed, wide awake, I saw his face clear as day. When I promised him, it wasn't a lie. Guess when I shook hands with Cardone I'd made it one, though.

Father Tim, he'd understand. Right?

ROUND 3

I CHOSE Kansas City because it wasn't Chicago. It wasn't a small town by any stretch, and had a good history of boxing, but I could still be a big fish in a small pond. Besides, I knew my fists wouldn't get me far in the Windy City. I needed a place where mediocre talent could still make a decent living.

I'd never considered Kansas City would be any more or less corrupt than Chicago. Turned out boxing was about fifty-percent fix. Something about the sport drew an unsavory element. Maybe it was all the blood.

Anyway, there I was back in the locker room of the Excelsior, a place with a little history. Damn good fighters like Jake Hunzinger and Rex Ward had fought there. Solid punchers who never made it to the big time, but if all I ever got was a few up and comers remembering my name before they went out to fight, that was fine by me.

Just the thought of some scared kid about to puke in his spit bucket before his first fight, taking a second to look at the concrete walls, and know that I stood in the same musty locker room and shadowboxed against the same wall imagining my first time, well that just about gave me the shivers.

Sal came limping in. "Showtime, kid."

He smiled wide, knowing his cut of my ironclad victory would be making its way into his pocket soon.

As we walked down the hall to the arena, he went nervously over the plan again.

"So, in the fifth. Not too soon in the fifth, just make it look natural. And for God's sake don't swing using anything you might get lucky with before. Pull your punches, hit him off balance. The fifth, got it?"

"I got it, Sal. I had it the first ten times you told me."

On my way into the ring, I spotted Lola. She liked to sit in the back where it was quieter. I think she just liked to be far enough away so the punches didn't look like they hurt so much. She wasn't like most fight fans, whose biggest hope was to go home with a little blood on their shirt.

She waved to me, and I winked at her. She kept promising to one day stitch my name on the back of my robe. She just had to learn to sew first. I told her there would be plenty of time for embroidery when she was making baby clothes.

I saw my opponent for the first time. A skinny kid with a fat head. He looked like the kind of guy who started boxing because he realized his noggin was so thick he could never be knocked out. Well, he was about to be.

I wondered what it was like from his end. Taking a dive. Was it humiliating? Was he making more than me?

I wondered how long until I found out for myself.

The ref brought us to center ring and ran through the pre-fight mumbo jumbo faster than an auctioneer. The announcer pronounced my name wrong, Myler instead of Wyler, and the bell rang.

One bored sportswriter sat chewing a cigar ringside and refusing to type anything on his Underwood. The radio announcer called the fight with all the enthusiasm of a paint-drying contest. Not that we gave them much to get excited about.

The first was the "feel 'em out" round. We both tried to have an entire conversation with just our eyes. I felt like he wondered if I knew the score.

A couple of body blows, one or two that bounced off his forehead, but neither one of us laid a solid glove on anyone. By the time the bell rang, I figured the scorecards were all as blank and white as a clean bedsheet. The judges had wasted their time sharpening pencils.

Sal admonished me in the corner. "Geez, kid. At least make it look like you're awake out there."

"You said not to get cute and lay anything on him that might get lucky."

"Yeah, but you don't want anyone knowing what's up. Make a show of it, okay? These people still came for entertainment."

"Okay, okay."

I scanned the crowd. Cardone sat in the second row behind the other fighter's corner. A bottle blonde sat beside him, reapplying lipstick from a compact. He wore another three-piece suit. Green, with a silk pocket square. He wore another fine hat too, this one adorned with a peacock feather.

Someday, I thought to myself. Someday. Maybe not the best attire for the railroad, but a guy's got to take his wife out on a Saturday night, doesn't he?

Round two. I think my partner in crime got the same speech from his corner man because he came out swinging.

We had at it like two kids sparring in the basement. He threw more slaps than punches, but every now and then something would land and make me stop thinking about the five hundred bucks.

He got me two good ones across the middle, and I reared back with my combo. Bang went the uppercut, snap went his chin, swish went my right fist, and crack went his jaw.

I heard the sound and my heart nearly stopped. He was falling to the canvas, and I nearly stepped in and caught him.

The ref got in between us and immediately started counting. I wanted to beg him to stop, to shake the kid awake and make him stand up. The ref got to three.

I saw Cardone in the row behind the flat figure on the canvas. He pinched his cigarette tight in his teeth, his hat pushed back slightly on his head.

The ref got to six. I spun my head to the sound of typewriter keys and saw the reporter slapping at his Underwood and chugging smoke signals from his Lucky

Strike. The radio announcer had come alive too, reeling off the referee's counts in harmony.

I turned to Sal in my corner and gave him pleading eyes. He shook his head at me. Sweet Christ, I couldn't even do a fix properly. Then Sal lifted his eyebrows, gripped the top rope, and bounced a little. I turned and saw the skinny kid straightening up.

The ref stopped at eight and then turned, swung his hand down like he was chopping wood, and said, "Fight."

The kid came toward me a little tentative. In a normal fight, I would have charged him, taken advantage of the weakened state. This wasn't a normal fight. I took it easy on him like I was fighting somebody's younger brother, or someone trying to look good in front of his girl, and I was trying to help. I'd done it a few times in the gym, never in the ring. Not with money on the line.

The bell took forever to ring, but finally, it did. I spotted Lola on my way back to the corner, and she held up two thumbs. She never was a student of the finer points of boxing.

"That was a close one," Sal said.

"Tell me about it. I think I aged ten years."

"Try to find something in between, will ya?"

"Don't worry. I'll make it to the fifth. I promise."

Like I promised Father Tim.

I shook the thought from my head, but it plagued me for the next two rounds. I retreated, covered up, swung wide, and tapped on the kid more like knocking on a church door than going for a knockout. I think I even heard someone boo.

The realization of what loomed ahead, what it meant to me, hit me harder than anything the skinny kid threw my way.

He did catch me daydreaming once and a solid shot caught the side of my head. I listed to the right, and might have even gone down if I hadn't hit the ropes. When he didn't follow up and chase me into the corner, anyone in the place who had any doubt whether or not they were watching a fix could be damn sure by then.

I hadn't thrown the punch yet, the bell hadn't rung on the fifth, but the deal was done. I'd sold out for five hundred bucks. The image of that stack of green kept me distracted less and less. The stern face of Father Tim loomed over me. The promise I'd made rang in my ears.

Sal had to call me back to the corner when I stayed in the center, not realizing the bell had rung, ending round four. I made a point of not looking at Cardone.

"Where's your head, kid?" Sal asked me, turning his good ear to hear my excuse.

"I don't know. Just nervous, I guess."

"Well, it's just about over, so you can relax. Now go out there and make it look good."

"I'll do my best." No promises for me anymore.

THE FIFTH ROUND CAME, and we danced for a minute. I started turning up the heat slowly, hitting a little harder, moving in a little closer. The sportswriter stopped typing again. He sat with his arms crossed, watching us with an accusatory sneer on his face. The radio announcer told people about the amazing healing power of Vicks VapoRub.

The skinny kid's eyes invited me in. His gloves dropped a bit, but not so any else might notice. Over his shoulder, I saw Cardone slide up to sit on the edge of his chair, cigarette down to a nub in his mouth.

I stepped up, threw a right at the kid's face. It split the protective cover of his gloves and bounced off his nose. I followed with a left to his gut, which made him double over. I'd gone from sparring power hits to full fight-night swings. Anyone in the place who doubted I could punch was being proven wrong.

A left-right combo to the head was what sent him

down. The kid did a convincing fall and lay still for the ten count, rolling over on his side when the ref got to eight but never showing any signs of getting up.

A small cheer went up from the crowd, but I thought most people were just glad to get us out of the ring so a real fight could break out. I heard a smattering of more boos.

Sal wrapped a towel around my shoulders, the ref raised my hand, and we headed for the locker room like the ring was on fire.

I hadn't worked hard enough to make a girl sweat, and yet I'd never been so out of breath after a fight.

Sal and I didn't talk. He skipped the rubdown. I started to change.

Finally, Sal broke the silence. "Well …"

Like he'd been waiting for his cue, the door opened and Cardone stepped in, followed by two large men in matching suits.

"Not half-bad, kid." He sized me up again, catching me part-dressed like before. "Not half-good either, but not half-bad."

Cardone held out an open palm behind him and one of his shadows slapped an envelope in it. He flipped it around and held it out for me.

I reached for it, licking my lips as I did. Cardone pulled the envelope back.

"You like our little business arrangement?"

An answer got caught in my throat. I didn't like it one bit. It was the money I liked quite a lot. "Sure," I said.

"Want to go another round?"

"Same thing?"

"Close. Now people might expect you to win. So, I want you to lose."

Take a dive. It didn't take long for me to end up on the other side of the fight card. I guess I deserved it after my lousy performance.

"Same price?"

"How does six hundred grab you?"

I guess there was a premium to be paid for buying a fighter's pride. My price had gone up to break the promise I made to Father Tim.

That I still had a price surprised even me.

"Deal," I said.

Cardone handed over the envelope. He smiled the way I always imagined the devil would smile right after he got your signature on a contract for your soul. But there I was, being dramatic. He wasn't paying for my soul, only my back on the canvas.

———

I RUSHED to pack up and get out of there. Sal and I said nothing more than we needed to. Maybe it was the weight of those matching white envelopes in our pockets. Of course, his weighed in a little lighter than mine. After all, wasn't his body out in that ring.

By the time Sal and I got to the sidewalk, we nearly bumped into Cardone and his men on their way out.

"Hey, slow down, slugger," he said to me. "I don't want to be another one of your K.O.s" He laughed, which prompted his boys to do the same, but their hearts weren't in it.

Two men passed us. With the width of the sidewalk open for them, they made a point of passing close, leaving no way they'd be missed. Cardone looked up and made a sour face.

The man in front stopped, smiled a fake smile at Cardone, and snapped a wad of chewing gum in his mouth. "Didn't mean to break up the party." His flunky laughed accordingly. Instantly I knew their roles.

"Ain't it past your curfew, kid?" Cardone said. "Someone leave the door to your crib open and you crawled out or something?"

The guy looked young, I guess. His flashy suit and tie did make Cardone look a little old-fashioned. Mostly I noticed that these two didn't like each other.

"Mr. Cardone, so nice they let you out of the home."

Witty repartee these two had. I turned away from them and scanned the sidewalk for Lola. I saw her walking toward us like the welcome sound of a bell ending the round.

"Guy like you ought to learn his place," Cardone said, the anger growing in his voice.

"I know my place," the flashy dresser said. He leaned in close to Cardone. "Next in line. That's my place." He snapped his gum, baring his teeth as he did. No respect. Whatever beef these two had between them, I wanted no part of it.

Lola reached us, and the tension broke. With a lady present, all parties stood down.

"I'm off for some fresh air," Cardone said. He slapped one of his boys on the chest, and they all moved as a pack down the street. The flashy dresser smiled after him and walked the other way. Sal stood by, mute.

"Hi, Sal," Lola said.

"Hiya, kid. See you, Jimmy." Sal scuttled off quick.

Before she could ask too many questions, I took Lola straight home, begged her off for the night, saying I felt tired even though I had barely moved around in that amateur hour fight.

"You sure you're okay?" she asked.

"Yeah, just beat is all."

"For a guy who just won, you look like someone kicked your cat."

"I didn't eat well today. I oughta know better on a fight day. Just need some iron in my system."

"Yeah, well, remember, whiskey doesn't have any iron in it."

"Don't you worry about me, doll."

I kissed her and said goodnight. The whole walk home, I thanked my lucky stars I had a gal like her. She would understand this mess. At least, I said it to myself enough times I started to believe she would.

Without thinking, I turned and walked six blocks out of my way past a shop window I'd been by a hundred times before.

Still in the window, right above a sign: WE OFFER LAYAWAY. Lola's ring. Well, not yet. I had eighty bucks down. Another six hundred twenty to go. The diamond even shone in the moonlight. It would shine twice as bright on her hand. I stared at it, burning the image into my brain. Every time I thought about the fixes, the dirty money, I'd replace that thought with this picture.

I'd seen cheaper rings. Pawn shop jobs, diamonds no bigger than a snowflake. Lola deserved the best. When I first walked by the jewelry shop, I saw a man come out and get into the back of a limousine, a driver holding the door for him. I knew any place a man like that shopped was the place for me, and that ring was for Lola.

I walked the rest of the way home still seeing that diamond in my head, picturing how it would look on her hand.

I hadn't been kidding about being hungry. However, I was so mixed up my stomach was in knots, so I went to bed without a bite. I sweated off another four pounds in my sleep. I nearly woke up the next morning a flyweight.

ROUND 5

FIRST STOP the next morning was Shinn's Diner. I peeled two twenty-dollar bills off the top of the pile in Cardone's white envelope and bought a paper on my way there. The guy in the newsstand gave me a dirty look when he had to make change from a twenty for a ten cent paper.

I sat in a booth and spread the paper out on the table. I ordered steak and eggs, black coffee, and a donut. I read the paper while I waited. A bunch of junk on the front page, a three-line column in the sports pages about the fight. The only thing that made it from the clutches of that reporter's Underwood about me was, "Also on the card last night..." followed by my name and the skinny kid's.

I was halfway through dipping my steak in ketchup and then the runny yolks of my eggs when I felt eyes on me. I looked up and saw three characters standing over my table. I'd been recognized once or twice in a bar after a fight. Always by some drunk who had been there and always when my face was puffed out and swollen from taking my licks, but never at breakfast the day after when my face was as normal as a bank teller's.

"Can I help you?" I asked through a mouthful of rare steak.

"I believe you can, Wyler," said the guy in front as he smacked gum in wide-open-mouth chews. His two buddies fanned out behind him in a V. The guy took my question as an invitation to sit down, so he slid into the booth across from me. His friends stood blocking my way in case I decided to change seats.

"Name's Whit. I work for an interested party." He didn't extend a hand, and offered up no more details. He dressed like a guy headed out to a dance hall on a Saturday night. His tie loud and wide, his collar undone at the neck. His hat was misshapen, like he'd been sitting on it all night. It added up to someone I felt like I knew, but I couldn't put it together yet.

"What party? Do I know you?"

"You just met me, friend." There was nothing friendly about his tone or the fake smile on his face. His gum continued to snap in his teeth. It started to get on my nerves. I think that was the idea.

It hit me. The guy Cardone had razzed the night before. Some sort of bad blood ran between them. I hoped none of it got on me.

"I think you got the wrong guy, pal."

"Jimmy Wyler, right? Fighter?" Whit put his dukes up and faked a few short jabs, whiffing air out of his nose the way non-fighters think it was done. Now I was curious.

"State your business or leave me alone."

"Next Friday night you're on the card down at the Veterans Hall, yeah?" He didn't wait for me to confirm. "I need you to do me a favor. Well, really a favor for my boss."

"Why do I owe you a favor?"

"Oh, you don't owe me squat. Really, it's me doing you the favor. See, I'm gonna see to it that you win that fight. And I'm gonna pay you three hundred bucks for the trouble." Whit lifted his eyebrows and smacked his gum like I was supposed to be impressed with what he'd just told me. I wasn't.

"Are you offering me a fix?"

Whit spread his arms wide like a preacher asking God for forgiveness. "Did I use that nasty F word? Now did I, Jimmy?" Again he didn't wait for me to answer. "I'm offering you a win. And you did hear the part about the three hundred, right?"

I set my fork down, figuring I wasn't going to be able to finish my breakfast in peace. "First off," I said. "Your prices are a little low. The war's over, you know? We ain't on rations anymore. Second, I can't help you out on that fight. I have a previous commitment."

I was a little leery telling him about it, but I figured on there being some sort of crook's code of conduct. I planned to leave Cardone's name out of it anyway, figuring that wouldn't win me any points after their little sidewalk chitchat. Either way, I was wrong.

Whit stopped chewing his gum. He brought his arms in and leaned on the table. "I don't recall asking you for permission."

I didn't know what to say. He didn't seem to want to hear no, but that's all I had on my tongue.

"Next Friday," he said, low and mean. "You get the win. Now, what's the confusion here?"

"I told you, I'd like to help." I sounded weak, but he had me backed into a corner before I even knew the bell had rung. "But I got other arrangements for that fight. Honest. Maybe we can work out another night. I play ball, it's just not on that night."

Amazing how weak my knees got when I didn't have my gloves on. All of a sudden, I was acting like a professional diver offering my services to the lowest bidder.

"I appreciate the offer, Jimmy. Really, I do. But it has to be Friday night. My boss insists." Whit took the gum out of his mouth, perched it on the top of his index finger like it was gonna do a trick or something. He reached over to my plate with his other hand and picked up a cut section of steak with his fingers, dragged it through the broken egg yolk, and slid it into his mouth. "I insist too."

"Look, Whit, I just can't. I—"

Whit nodded to his pals, and each one grabbed one of my arms. My hand hit the table loud like a gunshot, and the three old timers at the counter turned to watch. The waitress froze with a pot of coffee in the aisle between tables.

Whit slowly put the gum back in his mouth, chewed twice and picked up the ketchup bottle. He flipped it over in his hand, gripping the stubby neck of the bottle, and smashed it on the table. It bled ketchup onto the floor and across my newspaper. I started breathing too hard and too shallow and had to remind myself to slow down, not hyperventilate.

Whit leaned across the table, his tie dipping into the pool of red. He pushed the jagged edge of the broken bottle against my hand. I felt the sharp edges dig in, but he stopped short of breaking the skin.

He squared a stare at me that drained the blood from my face.

"Don't make me repeat myself, Jimmy. I came in here to tell you what's what. Now, do we understand each other?"

I nodded my head, my throat too tight to speak.

He pushed a little harder on my hand and then pulled the bottle away. The two men let my arms go. I looked down at my hand, but couldn't tell if I was bleeding or if it was just ketchup.

The cook had come out of the kitchen to check on the ruckus. No one moved to help me, though.

Whit brushed his tie off and stood. "You owe me for a new tie. You'll have plenty of cash soon enough though, right?"

He slapped his pals on the shoulder, and they followed him out like rats trailing after the Pied Piper of chewing gum.

ROUND 6

I PAID for my breakfast with the change from my newspaper. Twenty bucks minus ten cents ought to cover my meal, the broken bottle, and then some.

My first thought was to go see Sal. Cardone had been so nice about everything, and Whit had been the opposite. Cardone had to let me bow out if I promised him another fight for less money, right? Even knowing Cardone paid so much more than Whit's mystery boss made me feel like he had to be an okay guy. A businessman.

I found Sal at the gym. His overstuffed office in the corner of an open gymnasium, which permanently smelled of sweat, sat like a fishbowl where he could watch everything. Two young kids with thick eyebrows I pegged as brothers sparred in the ring while Nick, the sweep up man, ran a dirty mop around the floor.

Sal was a happy man that morning.

"G'morning, Jimmy."

"Hiya, Sal."

"Why do you look so glum? You ought to be on cloud nine, all the dough you're into these days."

"You know what they say, money doesn't buy happiness."

"Like hell, it don't." He laughed like a child. Sal had to be over fifty, but with all those blows to the head, he more often than not seemed awfully childlike. The way he sat there all excited about our illicit deal made me think he was as gullible as a child too.

Me, I had no excuse. Money blind. That was all I had to lean on.

"Sal, I want to talk to you about next Friday."

Sal whispered, a big grin on his face like we were a pair of boys out in the woods telling secrets. "You want to know what my cut is for that fight? Two hundred." He giggled again. "You know what that means? I'm gonna get my operation."

Punch-drunk no one can fix, but Sal had seen a doctor who said he could take care of his ears. Sal had gone almost all the way deaf in one ear, and for all the ringing in the other, he might as well be deaf in that one too. The doc was going to cut away a lot of the puffed-up cauliflower ear tissue, some you could see and some he said was deep down inside. Back in Sal's day, boxing a guy in his ears was commonplace. So were kidney punches. I didn't know how any of those guys made it out alive, especially after as many fights as Sal had.

"That's great news, Sal."

"Yep. I got six coffee cans full of dough just waitin' on

this last little bit. Then I go up to Kansas City General and let the doc have at it. Hey, do you think I'll get one of them real pretty nurses?"

"I'm sure you will, Sal. Ain't they all pretty up there?"

"I guess you're right." He got a little sad, I thought. Regretful, maybe. "You know, Jimmy, I hate to say it…but I shoulda done this years ago." He looked at me and laughed a bit. I knew he didn't mean the operation, he meant the fix. His eyes were watery, like he remembered an old dog he'd lost or something. "I've had offers before for my boys. Had offers when I's fighting. Never took a dime, though. Maybe if I had…" He looked around his sad gym. "Maybe I'd have been better off, is all."

Sal already forgot I'd asked to speak to him about the fight. I let it drop. Who the hell was I to tell him he couldn't have his operation? And who was I to get him in Dutch with Cardone over my problem? No, whatever I did, Sal had to stay out of it.

That much I could promise. And it was time my promises started to mean something again.

———

THE NEXT TWO DAYS, I kept to myself. I didn't call Lola, took all my meals out from the lunch counter a block away from my apartment.

Wednesday I went into the gym. One way or another I was going to fight on Friday night, so I might as well show up in shape.

The heavy bag never knew what hit it. I punched until my knuckles were swollen and sore. I swung until my elbows hurt from all the sudden stops. The poor Negro kid holding the bag for me was scared. I could see it in his eyes. He was more scared to let go and take off, fearing what I'd do to him. He cowered behind the bag and tried to wait me out. I had twenty rounds of slugging inside me, though.

I punched at Whit's face, and at my own.

Once I'd let the kid off the hook, I stepped over to the speed bag and started tapping out a rhythm. The mesmerizing sound and the sweet, sweaty funk of the place put me in a trance. I thought of a million ways the night could end, none of them good. I tried to weigh who it would be worse to make angry. Who would understand more?

I hadn't taken any money from them yet, either one, so maybe that bought me a little leeway. My fee was chicken feed, though. I knew that. The real dough in a fix was the bets, and those were already coming in. In tiny bookie joints, back rooms in bars, street corners under yellow lamps, bills and markers were changing hands. Not even half the bets that would be placed on a title fight, but so far they hadn't got any of those guys in on a fix. As far as I knew, anyway.

The speed bag at Sal's gym hung in front of a mirror. You were supposed to study your form and make corrections as you go. I looked dead into my own eyes. I didn't like what I saw there.

I'd taken money to throw a fight. Didn't matter what

end I came out on. My ego might hurt less if I stayed standing, but a fix was a fix. And I was part of the fraternity now.

I stopped punching and let the speed bag swing to rest. I swear it let out a sigh of relief. The room stayed noisy with other fighters slugging each other, the slap of leather on the heavy bag, on flesh. The shouts of a corner man coaching his sparring up-and-comer floated on the air like the smell of spit and wet canvas.

Put me out in the country with nothing but the crickets at night and I'd go nuts in no time flat. But there, in the gym, with the noise swirling around me, I could tune everything out and focus completely on my own face. The bastard who'd let me down.

I stepped up closer to him. I tightened my fist inside the thin practice gloves, lighter than the full boxing mitts I used in the ring, but also less padding to protect my knuckles. I glared at the face. Tried to stare so hard time would go backward and I could make the choice all over again. Make it the right way this time.

I punched him square in the jaw.

The tangled knots of sound inside the gym came to a stop when the mirror shattered down the wall. Shards of glass landed in a pile at my feet, long swords of mirror view of the ring behind me stabbed down into the worn-wood floorboards.

All eyes were on me. All but my own. I stood alone without my reflection. Just me. No one else to blame. The way it should be.

I turned and left without a word.

ROUND 7

THE BELL DINGED above the door to the jewelry store. I stepped in feeling the way I always did there—out of place. The man behind the counter wore a starched suit and a gold pocket watch chain, silk kerchief in his pocket matching his tie. All class.

"Hi there," I said. He recognized me. Must not get many of my types down there.

"I thought we'd seen the last of you, Mr. Wyler."

"Sorry. Guess it has been a while."

"Six weeks." He stood a few inches shorter than I did but somehow managed to look down his nose at me. "Six weeks without payment."

"I know. That's why I'm here." I took a twenty out of my pocket. I'd added one to replace what I spent the day before. Something nagging told me not to drop the whole load on him yet. I might need it.

I handed the bill over. "This makes a hundred even."

"Mr. Wyler, perhaps we'd better cancel your

contract. A full refund of course. If you cannot meet the specific payment plan–"

"No. I'll have it. Next week. All of it." I tried to step back, not sound so desperate. "I have a big deal coming in. I'll have all of it. Next week, I swear."

He sighed like a man who'd heard it all before. "I'll give you until next Friday. How does that sound? By then, if nothing happens…" He said it like he knew nothing would. "Come back and I will refund your money in full. Minus the five dollar deposit."

"I'll be in. I swear. You can count on it."

He sighed again.

———

I WENT from the jewelry store to a department store. A regular shopping spree. I went to the men's department and picked out a tie matching what I remembered Whit wearing. The brightest one on the table. The salesclerk asked if she could gift-wrap it for me, and I nodded yes.

In one quick morning, I'd drained the money I'd lifted from the envelope already. Worth it if it bought me my life back.

I'd done some asking around and found out where to find Whit. No matter how many people I asked, though, no one knew or no one would tell me the guy he worked for. It made me even more worried.

Whit kept time on Wednesday afternoons at a gym over on Highmore. The one bit of information I did get about him was he recently started running the fight game for the mystery man. Trying to make a name for himself. The beef between him and Cardone had been sizzling for a few months now. Cardone accused him of stepping in on his game, and Whit didn't deny it. He aimed to take over, and didn't care who knew about it. Talk like that though, you'd have to back it up eventually.

No ring experience in his past, but Whit sure seemed to like pulling the strings behind the scenes. He had a pretty tight grip on my strings, for sure.

I walked inside with my thin tie box under my arm like I'd come calling for a date.

Whit stood ringside, his shirtsleeves rolled up to his elbows, hat pushed back off his forehead, and his jaw working another gob of chewing gum.

"You don't keep those gloves up, boy, he's gonna knock your block off, and you're gonna deserve it."

His accent caught up with me. Pure Chicago. I felt no nostalgia.

"Get 'em up, you crumb bum!"

The two boys in the ring were no more than teenagers. They wobbled around on newborn pony legs and swung their arms like they were reaching for a pillow to lie down.

A short man next to Whit saw me and tapped his boss on the shoulder. Whit looked at the man, who nodded his head in my direction. Whit turned and broke into a smile, chewing all the while.

"Take a break, you bums."

The two boys in the ring nearly collapsed. Reminded me of a couple in the third day of a dance marathon.

A small section of bleachers was set up for people to watch the fights. They were empty except for a Hispanic kid tying his shoes on the bottom step. Whit motioned me over.

"Beat it, Spic," he said. The kid scrambled away, one shoe on.

I sat down. Whit took a seat one row higher than me. Mind games. He might not have had any time in the ring, but he knew the way behind an opponent's defense.

"What's that you got there?" He lifted his chin at the box under my arm.

I looked down like I'd forgotten about the tie, and I guess I had. Other things on my mind, y'know. Things like counting up all the bodies in the room in case things got ugly. The two tired kids had retreated to the sidelines and were sucking down water, four other young men jumped rope or worked out here and there. Then there were three men who stood by watching Whit and me, apparently with no other plans for the afternoon. There was a dark door to a locker room. Not knowing what lay beyond it frightened me in a way I hadn't been since my boyhood at St. Vincent's, convinced there were monsters in the closet.

"For you," I said, handing over the box.

"Mr. Wyler, you shouldn't have," he said sarcastically as he untied the ribbon. Whit lifted out the tie and gave a wolf whistle. "Slick. Just my style. Thanks, Jimmy."

"A peace offering. Y'know, after our first meeting didn't go so well."

"I thought it went just fine." He smacked his gum and

held up the tie over the one he had on. Ugly on top of ugly.

"I appreciate you making the gesture toward our new partnership. You got class, Jim."

"About that..."

Whit put the tie back in the box, started chewing more slowly. "You see, the thing is, I'm kind of stuck between a rock and a hard place." I did my best to look him in the eye. "And you're the rock."

"Spit it out, Jim."

"I was hoping we could come to an agreement. Like I said, this weekend's fight is just not a good one for me. But if we could do it another time–"

"Jimmy."

"No, just listen. I'd gladly do you a freebie. No charge. Just if it isn't this weekend–"

"Jimmy." He held up a hand, and I obeyed like a dog. I chewed a hard lump of anger and wondered how much more I could swallow before I got full. After all, talking wasn't usually how I solved a dispute. "Is it Cardone?" Whit asked.

How the hell did he know that?

"I can see by your face that it is." He shook his head like he was exhausted already at the lesson he was about to give me. "Jimmy, Cardone is small-time. A hood. I represent a large interstate organization that can—and will, mind you—eat Cardone for lunch. Trust me, Jim. You do not want to hitch your wagon to him."

"It's just that I already promised–"

"So un-promise." I noticed the men watching us drifting closer.

"It's not that simple."

"Jim, let me explain. I don't like Mr. Cardone. He stands between me and what I want. And anyone who stands between me and what I want, well, that ain't a good place to stand." Whit spat out his wad of gum onto the bleachers and reached into his pocket for another. He grew more agitated. "Treats me like a child, that meatball. Thinks he can push me around and no one will notice. Joke's on him because I got a lot of guys noticing me. Big time guys. Bigger fish than Cardone. He's a freakin' sardine next to the guys got my back."

Whit chomped on his gum as if he was angry at it.

"I don't know anything about that—"

"Well, now you do. If that greasy eye-tie wants to disrespect me and stand in the way of my upward mobility, he's got another thing coming." The peanut gallery chuckled, and one of the bigger guys put a finger gun to his head and mimed pulling the trigger. The moment of dark levity seemed to calm Whit.

Whit leaned back, putting his elbows on the bleacher seat behind him. "What do you want me to do, Jimmy? I already have an investment in this fight. I have money coming in based on a certain outcome. An outcome that those big fish I was telling you about are curious to see if I can deliver. This is a test, Jimmy. And I need to get an A. And now you tell me you can't provide the outcome I promised them? What am I supposed to do?"

"I...I don't know." I really didn't. No sense lying. I'd

been thinking three days about it, and I didn't have a solution other than him letting me off the hook.

"Tell you what." Whit stood, leaving the tie box behind. "You're obviously lousy at negotiating." That got another chuckle from the peanut gallery. "So I'm gonna let you do what it is that you do."

Whit stepped down off the bleachers.

"I got a guy," he said. "You go, oh, let's say...four rounds with him. You put him on the floor, I let you walk. What do you say?"

What could I say? "You mean it?"

"I'll still take you up on that freebie." He winked and open-mouth-chomped his gum.

"Yeah, okay." I regretted nearly punching my arms to rubber at the gym the day before. I really regretted it when I saw my opponent.

Whit nodded, and a guy whistled. That dark locker room door opened, and it held just the sort of monster I thought it would.

———

HE WAS APPROXIMATELY the size and shape of a boxcar on the Santa Fe line. Tall, head shaved, and broad shoulders. His chest stuck out square and firm like a bank safe. At the end of his steel beam arms were a pair of anvils for hands.

He must have noticed the look on my face because he smiled. His two front teeth were missing. Guess I knew what he wanted for Christmas.

"Jimmy, meet Vic," Whit said. He spat his gum out on the floor and unwrapped a new stick, folded it into his mouth while one of the lackeys he kept around picked up the spent wad and put it in a trash can.

"I don't have gloves," I said.

"Sure you do." Whit snapped his fingers and a pair of bag gloves, thinner than regulation, sailed into the ring. They landed hard on the deck the way I figured I would in short order.

"What did we say?" Whit asked. "Four rounds?" The guy to his left silently nodded. "Well then, ding ding."

"I don't have shorts," I said.

"Look, you wanna do this or not?"

I couldn't walk away from the opportunity to get out of the deal, no matter how slim my chances were. I might land a lucky punch. Yeah, and Ava Gardener might waltz in here and ask me to make love to her.

I climbed between the ropes and stripped off my shirt. My trousers and shoes couldn't have been worse to fight in, but they would have to do.

Vic pounded his meaty fists together, slapping the leather of his gloves with fierce whaps that made me jump. He looked up at me and smiled his toothless grin again, then beckoned me forward with a "come on" wave of his hand.

I once saw a guy box a grizzly bear at the Kansas State Fair, and as I took the long walk across the ring to where Vic waited for me, I felt downright jealous of that bear-fighting man. He'd had it easy.

No sense waiting for the fight to come to me, so I

barreled in the last two steps and came at his head hard. Body shots were not going to get the job done, not with that solid iron gut of his.

He covered up and let my punches ricochet off him like bullets in a Superman comic book. I didn't want to punch myself out, so I eased off and braced myself for what he had in store for me.

Vic opened up like a deadly flower and came at me. I saw a newsreel once about the men who operated the howitzers on Omaha beach. This guy carried one of those guns on each shoulder. Twin barrels of destruction aimed my way.

My hands went up and immediately came crashing back into my own face. Once, twice, left, right, until he had me backed all the way across the ring and pinned against the ropes. You'd think I'd never been in a fight before in my life.

I bent side to side, doing a decent job of avoiding his tree trunk arms. I had speed on him. It took him a lot longer to move the steel heft of his body or to reset his punches. It was my only hope. I struck out with a wasp-like stinger at his chin, caught him off center, but enough to make him notice me again.

I got low, a move I hadn't used in years. When a guy towered over you, dip as low as you can. His punches had no steam when they go straight down to the floor.

The trouble with this bout—no referee. Vic smashed a hand down on top of my head like he was cracking walnuts. I started looking around for the bowling ball I thought must have been dropped on me. I sunk one in his gut, right on his belt line. I'd punched parked cars with more give.

I snuck out under his arms and got myself away from the ropes. My foot speed might be able to save me, for a little while, anyhow.

Vic came thundering across the canvas, chasing me. The crowd around us hung on the ropes jeering and catcalling like a Roman coliseum. As I ran away, I heard a few unsavory assessments of my skills in the ring.

I set my feet again a safe distance away from the ropes. Vic continued his charge. I dodged first, then came up fast and planted a glove in his ear. The thin bag gloves bruised my knuckles on the thick bone of his skull, but I knew how much a good shot to the ear hole hurt. I could tell he'd been stung. He spun to chase me again as I shuffled my feet around to his left.

He swung a wild arcing right that I outran. This was no textbook lecture on boxing. Maybe on pure survival. That I was still standing should have won me the decision by itself.

I put two more in his ear, trying like hell to make it ring as loud as Sal's. I realized then I had two things on my side, my speed and my anger. Now that I didn't have to worry about making nice with Whit, I could let that tiger out of its cage.

I swung hard for the bad decisions I'd made. I swung again for letting down Father Tim. I swung again for not being the man Lola expected me to be. I jabbed to his gut for each dollar with which I let myself get suckered. My loafers slipped across the floor, my knuckles aching from the too thin gloves, but I kept punching. The shouts from the sidelines grew louder. The old familiar sound of a sold out fight night. I let it take me away to that different mindset.

Anger drove my fists. Anger at Whit. Anger at myself.

The anger wasn't enough.

At some point shortly into my barrage of angry punches, Vic decided he'd had enough. He dropped his defenses, let two blows bounce off him like nothing more than mosquitoes, then threw a left jab at my nose, stopping me dead in my tracks. The right hook I never saw coming.

I started falling to my right, my knees not responding to my commands to stay locked. Vic wasn't through. He threw a left hook, catching me on the way down and lifting my body up again, and sent me falling to the left. I hit the ropes but still didn't fall.

I was being held up.

Two guys who had been shadow boxing in the corner before and one of Whit's right-hand men held me upright. A punching bag for Vic. Where was the damn bell? Oh, right. This was Whit's fight in Whit's place with Whit's rules. No bell was going to save me.

Vic came charging in and went to work on my gut. I thought back to the grizzly bear. The guy punched the sad looking bear for a round and a half, making a show of it for the crowd, the bear on a thick chain. Three shows a night at state fairs all across the Midwest. The night I watched, the bear had had enough. The guy got cocky, stepped too close. The bear grabbed him.

It would have been over in seconds, but then we all realized the bear had all its teeth and claws removed. Still a bear, though. Just using powerful slaps of its huge paws the bear pounded that guy silly. Took four guys with baseball bats to pull the bear off.

The vivid image of the bear blurred in my brain as Vic's hairy chest came at me again and again. If not for the bald head, I would swear the bear had retired to this gym and had been brought out of that dark locker room just to knock me into next week.

"That's enough!" Whit shouted.

Vic stood down obediently.

"Kid's still gotta fight for me Friday night."

I figured it was why Vic had been working over my midsection instead of my face. Not sure what difference it would make, I'd gone to pudding inside.

The hands let me go, and I sank to the canvas. There were back-slapping congratulations to Vic. Yeah, well done. You beat a guy half your size. What a hero.

Whit threw me my shirt. It landed a few feet away but I stayed where I was, trying to keep my insides where they were—inside.

He said, "See you Friday night." Then everyone ignored me, going back to their business like I didn't exist.

ROUND 8

I WAITED over four hours for Lola to get home. I huddled half a block down from her rooming house in a doorway, like a bum. My ribs ached, my hands hurt. My pride hurt worst of all.

Lola got off work like a normal person at five p.m.. She did secretarial work for an office downtown. They built bridges or something, I'd never known exactly. I knew the risk of coming to see her, but I had nowhere else to go.

A cable car rang its bell as it pulled away and Lola walked up the street with two other women who had gotten off. I pushed my back into the hard stone of the building, trying to make myself invisible. The two other women peeled off and went their own ways. Lola walked up the steps to her place. When she reached the third step, I came out of the shadows.

"Lola."

She jumped, then smiled when she saw it was me.

"Jimmy! My God, you scared me." She noticed I wasn't right. "What's the matter?"

Lola was used to seeing me banged up. It was my job, after all. In our time together, she'd practically become a part-time nurse looking after me.

"Just a little knocked around is all. Can I come inside?"

She swung her head to see if Mrs. Lovell was watching from her window. The curtain remained in place, but that didn't mean the old bat's all-seeing eyes weren't on us from some other place.

"You know I can't, Jimmy."

"And you know I wouldn't ask if I didn't need you."

"We can go to your place."

"I've been out here for four hours. I don't think I can make it to my place. You might as well dump me at County General. Or go ahead and dump me in the Missouri River."

"Jimmy..." She huffed, exasperated.

I gave her my best puppy-dog eyes, strained through a gut full of pain.

She threw another look at Mrs. Lovell's curtains and whispered, "Come on, be quick."

———

LOLA PUT antiseptic on my wounds, though they weren't much to see. The kind of scrapes you get picking apples, not much more than that. I knew the worst of the damage was on the inside. I wanted to ask what a broken rib felt like, but figured Lola wouldn't know any better than I would.

I sat on her couch in the single room, her bed all of two feet away, a washroom, and that was about it. The kitchen was down the hall, and all the girls in the rooming house took turns cooking. Lola had the curtains drawn. I felt like a real fugitive hiding out from Johnny Law. I also felt like a fool for getting in Dutch.

"So, what was it? Some hotshot kid? Or were you the hotshot trying to prove a point?"

"I guess I was trying to prove something." Sweet Lola. Assuming my ego had got me in trouble, not my greed. I weighed my options to tell her or not. She would be understanding, sympathetic. She'd hold me and tell me it would all be okay. Maybe.

She might be angry, disappointed in me. Disgusted by my actions, getting involved with mobsters and fight-fixers. Would she care that I had done it for her?

No, I couldn't say that. None of the blame for this could fall on her. It certainly wasn't her fault I couldn't afford an engagement ring on my regular purse money.

I had to lie. I could see now how easy it was to go from one bad decision to another like a chain reaction. This one led to the next one, which led to something worse coming down the road. I stopped myself from speculating what something worse might be.

"Don't you have a fight in two days?"

"Yeah," I said, and left it at that.

She watched me gingerly try to sit up. She furrowed her brow at me. "You sure you're okay?"

"Yeah. I've had much worse." Lies on lies on lies. Father Tim would tan my hide if he could hear me now.

"It's my night to make dinner, so we've got to think about how to get you out of here."

"Can't I stay?"

"For the whole night? Do you want me to get kicked out?"

"I can be quiet."

"Can you be a girl? Because if not, you can't stay here. You know Mrs. Lovell's rules. She kicked out Cindy last year for having her brother in her room after hours. Her *brother*."

Her emphasis pointed out I was, in fact, a much worse offense. Just as well. If I stayed the night, it would mean a whole night of lying to Lola, of not telling her the truth eating me inside worse than Vic's gut punches.

———

THURSDAY CAME, and I still didn't know what to do.

My workout was lackluster, to say the least. I tiptoed around the ring, trying hard not to rotate my midsection since every time I did, my ribs exploded with pain. I covered it okay, I think. But there was no fire behind my punches, no speed in my steps. Yesterday's single round with Vic had me boxing like I still had training wheels on.

I wasn't supposed to be swinging for the fences or anything, nothing to tire me out the day before a fight. Just a refresher to make sure my footwork and hand placement were forefront in my brain come fight time. I'd always told Sal from the get-go that I knew that stuff in my sleep. What I needed was to lift more weights, build some bulk in my arms. I could dance around doing Swan Lake all day, but if some big lug hit me with cannon balls for fists, I was sunk.

In private, before I even laced on my gloves, I asked him what the point was, given that Cardone was paying me to take the fall. I conveniently left out the other half of the equation.

Sal was insistent.

The young gun he put in to spar with me must have thought he was hot stuff. He landed more punches than he had a right to. He popped me a good one in the nose, and he saw my stunned expression. He left that ring like he'd just beaten Rocky Marciano.

Sal stared me down, as disappointed as the nuns at St. Vincent's. I knew that look well. I'd been seeing it in the mirror for the last week.

"What's with you, Jimmy? You have a fight with Lola or something?" I always thought Sal wanted Lola for his daughter. He never did have any kids. I'd have to do in a pinch. Great. Another father figure I'd let down. Of course, this one was in on the take. Well, like father like son.

"No, Sal. Nothing like that. I'm just...preoccupied, that's all."

"Well, you'd better focus, or you'll have another scare like last time."

"There won't be any scare."

"If you get into the ring like you just did, a guy could knock you out with a broken arm and a stiff wind."

"Aw, leave it alone, will ya, Sal?"

He tossed me the towel from around his shoulders. "Hit the showers."

I stood under the water, letting it run hot as I could stand, and thought of ways out of the mess I was in. Running away came up over and over. Maybe Cardone would let Sal keep the money if he knew Sal had nothing to do with it. Sal could claim I was an impetuous, hotheaded kid, and who knew why I'd taken off?

Then again, Sal would be left behind to pay for my mistakes. If I did hit the rails west for Los Angeles, or maybe back up to Chicago, Sal would be the only one behind to make up for Cardone's losses. And who knows what Whit would do when he came calling. Just because he'd bypassed Sal to get to me, didn't mean he wouldn't look him up when I split town.

And then there was Lola. It wasn't like we were a secret. It would be easy to find out about her and where she lived. And it wasn't like Whit and guys like him kept family or girlfriends off limits. Cardone, too, had been swell so far. But what would happen if I bailed on him? A kind and benevolent mobster was still a mobster.

And when there was money on the line, all bets were off.

When I got out of the shower, Cardone was there. Sal was talking to him with his hands nervously lacing and unlacing his fingers, his head bowed slightly the way you would talk to a bishop or something.

"Ayy, there's the boy," Cardone said, throwing a few air-punches in my direction. He looked over my towel-wrapped body approvingly.

"Hiya, Mr. Cardone," I said.

"Sal here was just telling me about his operation. Good news, I say. Good news."

"Yeah," I said. "Been a long time coming."

"Well, I can't promise nothing, but if things keep going well, I will have more paydays for you boys. It ain't exactly a long-term job like working at the post office or nothing." He stepped closer and slapped my bare chest. "But it pays a hell of a lot better, am I right?"

Sal laughed and I tried to muster up a smile, but it died on my face.

"So, what do you say, kid?" Cardone asked. "Fourth round is a charm? Worked for us the first time, right?"

"Fourth round. Got it." Whit said his guy would go down in the third. I thought maybe I should tell Cardone about Whit, about the things he'd said. Cardone being a losing prospect, and all that stuff he'd talked about. Then what? All Cardone was going to say is I should stick with him. And did one lousy fighter on a random Friday night warrant sparking a mob war? I doubted it. Either man would let me twist in the wind rather than start a street fight over who called the shots in the low-rent boxing halls of Kansas City. I'm sure neither man saw this as the pinnacle of his career. I was nothing but a steppingstone, and I was starting to get shoe prints on my neck.

"Mr. Cardone, can I ask you something?" I felt like

I'd just dropped my gloves in the middle of a bout. I was wide open and primed to take a big hit.

"Sure, kid." He kept his genial expression on his face, but I saw something more sinister pass behind his eyes.

"Does the other guy know?"

"About round four? Hell, no. Why would I bother paying two guys? Your first time, I paid you to make sure you'd play ball. A test, if you will." He slapped my bare chest with the back of his hand, friendly-like. "Now I know I can trust you. Saves me some dough."

He smiled, and I tried to force one out. So, I knew the score. Only one of us was losing sleep over the fight. Maybe paying two guys was why Whit paid so low.

"I met your friend Whit," I said. I let that fly out of my mouth before I had the good sense to think twice. Just the way I wanted it. If I'd stopped for a second, I would have kept it in, but I had to know Cardone's side of things. I got it quick.

The genial smile slid off his face. The friendly neighborhood mobster I'd known had left the building, replaced by Al Capone's ghost. A seething, remorseless man.

"That scumbag ain't no friend of mine. He talked to you?"

Scared into submission, I retreated back to my corner. "I only seen him in passing," I said. "I saw you two talk once. I thought maybe–"

"You thought wrong. That little punk has been up my *stronzo* for a year now, trying to prove what a big shot he is. Every time I squash him, he pops up again like the cockroach he is." Cardone took a moment to compose himself, straighten his tie, and shoot his cuffs. "Little children oughta know their place, is all I'm saying."

Sal, sensing the tension, tried to change the subject. "Mr. Cardone, any time you wanna do business, I'm your man. I got a lot of up and comers. Some real tough kids. I could talk to them for you. I'm sure they would be on board."

Cardone softened back to the well-mannered gentleman I'd come to know. "As long as you get your cut, huh?" He smiled widely at Sal, who ducked his head as he smiled back. "We'll see, Sal. We'll see. Got to be judicious. If we go out and fix every fight...aw, I don't want to bore you with business talk." He turned back to me. "You just keep those mitts up, *capiche*?" He leaned in and slapped my chest again with the back of his hand. "At least until the fourth round, eh?" He winked at me and turned to leave, slipping a cigarette into his mouth. When he opened the door to leave, I saw his two bodyguards out in the hall, waiting on either side of the door.

"Sal, can I ask your advice?"

"Sure, kid, sure. Anything."

I didn't know what I was doing, but I needed someone in my corner more than ever. "It starts with, I gotta tell you something."

"Whatever it is, kid. I knew something was wrong."

"It ain't Lola or anything. I wish it was." The locker room at Sal's gym was small. Two rows of steel lockers painted a red that reminded everyone who used the gym of blood. Nosebleed blood specifically. A single bench ran down the middle between the two rows of lockers. I sat on the worn wood while Sal stood over me, reminding me of Father Tim at confession.

"I got a problem, Sal, and I don't know how to get out of it."

"You gotta speak up, kid."

I hated to do it, hated saying the words out loud at all, let alone for anyone to hear. "I said I've got a problem, Sal. A problem I don't know how to solve."

"You can tell me."

"I never should have got into the mess with Cardone." I could feel Sal tense up, the two hundred bucks slipping through his fingers. "I'm really behind the eight ball on this one. I'll take the dive tomorrow night. That's no problem. I never want to do it again."

"That's all right, Jimmy. I understand."

"No, you don't." My volume increased all on its own. The stress and anger I felt toward myself caused my blood to boil. "I have another fix. For the same fight. Only it's with someone else, and it's the opposite result."

Sal's face screwed into confusion. I explained, "Another guy came to me about Friday's fight. Said he wanted me to win it in the third. You hear me, Sal? I'm in deep with two different guys who want me to do two different things." Sal was starting to get it. "What do I do, Sal?"

"You told the other guy about Cardone?"

"Yeah. That didn't go over. There's some kind of beef between them. I get the feeling Whit wants what Cardone has, and I'm caught in the middle."

"Hmmmm." Sal thought for a while. I could tell it was hard on his brain. Finally, "I don't know what to tell you, kid."

I'm not sure what I expected. Sal was no mastermind. If you couldn't slug it out in the ring, Sal didn't know how to solve most problems. At least I felt a little bit better about him knowing the score. One less person I had to lie to. I could see the worry on his face, though, and I felt bad about handing him my burden.

"I'll figure it out, Sal. Don't you worry about it. Your money's good as gold."

He forced a grin and nodded. I watched his cauliflower ears, puffed and misshapen. In a way, I envied Sal. His life was one of simplicity. All life's mysteries were solved within the ring. Philosophy, religion, manhood—all started and ended inside the square.

My troubles were just beginning.

ROUND 9

I CALLED LOLA, had her meet me out at the soda shop around the corner from her place. Fontana's Fountain had become our spot. During the long wait while she pondered if I was worthy of being her boyfriend, I'd spent a Cadillac's worth on ice cream sundaes, vanilla Cokes, and banana splits.

The familiar candy-colored decor of the booths gave me no comfort as I waited for the right moment to ruin her world. Felt eerily similar to waiting for the perfect instant to level a right hook across someone's chin. I feared it would hurt her just as bad.

I left my chocolate milkshake alone even as Lola reached the bottom of her strawberry shake. She slurped the last of it and looked at me, frowning.

"Jimmy, you're still blue. Just like the other day. Did that kid you sparred with really get into your head that bad?"

I pushed away my melting shake.

"Lola, tomorrow night. I need you to do something for me."

She sensed the seriousness in my voice. "What, Jimmy?"

"I want you to pack a bag. Be ready to leave town."

"Leave town? Where?"

"Chicago. I'm going to take you there. Well, maybe. I just want you to be ready, is all."

"You want me to be ready to leave for Chicago, but you're not even sure you're going to take me? Jimmy, I'd love to get away for a weekend, but why so secretive about it?"

"Not for the weekend, Lola. For good."

She stared at me for a long time, trying to match the look on my face with my words. She put two and two together and came up with trouble. "Jimmy, you're scaring me."

"There's nothing to be scared of," I lied. I didn't come close to believing it, and I doubted she did either. "It's just, I need to know how tomorrow's fight goes before I can promise anything."

She scrunched her eyebrows together in that way I usually love. "Is this you trying to be romantic? Because it's not working at all, Jimmy."

"No. I really need you to be ready." I hated frightening her. I hated lying to her too. The less she knew, the better. And if I made it out of this and she never had to know? Even better still. "Will you promise me?"

"Yes, Jimmy. Okay. If you insist."

"I do." It was no kind of proposal. Maybe no way to start a life at all, but I had to get her out of town, or I'd wonder forever if she'd end up paying the price for my mistakes.

I walked her home, gave her a dispassionate peck on the cheek, and said goodnight. Then I went back to my room and packed a bag of my own. I didn't take much, but then I didn't have much. I packed my gym bag. Smaller than a regular suitcase, but one I could bring to the fight tomorrow without rousing any suspicion. I put in three shirts, two pair of pants, and two ties. Socks, underwear, and a belt. The rest of the space I'd need for my gloves, shoes, and trunks.

I took the one photo I owned, of me and Lola arm in arm, out of the frame of the mirror where it was wedged and slid it into the bottom of the bag. Next, I took the envelope of cash from Cardone and split it in two. I put two hundred of it in another envelope, and the two hundred and forty bucks I had left over I kept in the original. I put both envelopes at the bottom of the bag.

Finally, I got into bed and stared at the ceiling. It felt like looking up from the bottom of a grave.

———

FIGHT NIGHT, and Veterans Hall was about half-filled. We were up third on a four-fight card. Me versus some guy named Kelly. The Fightin' Irishman, it said in quotes under his name on the poster.

I knew whose side Kelly was on. I wondered how his negotiation with Whit had gone. Better than mine, or was that just the way Whit did business? Either way, Kelly expected me to put him down in the third. I still wasn't sure what I was going to do.

I found Sal in the locker room. The Vets Hall was a big place, wood floors in the lockers that creaked. The walls were always sweating from the steam in the showers.

We grunted hellos to each other. Sal waited for me to tell him that I'd come up with a brilliant plan or that I'd worked it all out with Cardone.

I hadn't.

"So, what goes on tonight?" he asked. His voice shook like I was Marilyn Monroe and he was asking me to dance.

"Sal," I said, "I have no idea."

"Jesus, Jimmy." He crossed himself. I'd never seen him do that before. I almost asked him to do one for me, but I didn't feel I deserved it.

We stayed underground in the locker room through the first two fights. I taped my hands in silence. Sal checked my work, rewrapped a section. We avoided each other's eyes while Sal laced my gloves. The pre-fight rituals calmed both of us down. The slow and steady rhythm of getting ready to fight was something familiar to us. The silence wasn't unusual. We didn't need to speak.

A stubby guy in a vest and a rope for a belt pounded once on the door, then charged in.

"Two minutes," he barked, and was gone.

I slapped my gloves together twice, nodded my satisfaction with the fit.

"So, when do you..."

"I dive in the fourth," I said, telling him what he already knew about my agreement with Cardone. "I win in the third."

Sal shook his head. Without a word, he slung a towel over his shoulder, lifted the spit bucket and stool, and held the door open for me. I picked up my bag and took it with me.

"Don't you want to leave that here?" Sal asked.

"Not tonight. Might need it."

Sal had given up questioning me.

————

THE CROWD HAD FILLED in during those first two fights. The place was noisy and smelled like popcorn and beer. A ring announcer with a nasally voice and wearing the usual black bow tie took the microphone hanging down from the rafters. He droned over the PA for a minute, but I heard none of it.

Sal nudged me at one point and I raised my hand over my head, assuming the man had said my name.

I watched Kelly on the other side of the ring. Bright green silk robe with a shamrock on it. I wonder how he felt being propped up as nothing more than a Mick in two gloves. And some people in the crowd either loved him or hated him already because of it. Fickle fight fans.

Choose your man based on whatever caught your eye. I'd known guys who could watch Joe Louis punch out their own mother and still would say a Negro can't slug his way out of a wet paper sack.

Judge a guy for the color of his skin or what island his parents came from. Go figure.

I wished my decision was that easy to make.

The referee beckoned us to the center of the ring. Sal put a hand on my shoulder.

"Good luck out there."

"I thought the Irish had all the luck." He didn't laugh at my joke.

"I'm here in your corner. You know that."

"Sal, if it goes like I think it's gonna go, do me a favor and deny you knew anything. Keep your trap shut. Do whatever you can to keep that two hundred bucks."

The ref hollered for me to join them. I patted Sal with my glove and went to center-ring.

Kelly shuffled his feet, a tall, pale kid with sandy-blond hair and a still-healing cut over his right eye. He wasn't the only one who should have sat out another week or two. He also wasn't the only one getting an extra payday for this bout.

I could feel him sizing me up, taking in the fact this was the other guy who took dirty money to throw this fight. I felt judged, but I didn't know why.

I ignored the ref's usual patter, knowing when to touch gloves only by the cadence in his voice.

On my way back to the corner, I saw Cardone in the

stands, dressed to the nines with a girl on his arm. He sat about halfway up the sloping rows and munched on a box of popcorn. He looked like a guy without a care in the world. For the first time, I got incredibly angry at him. I wished like hell he was the guy in the green trunks across from me so I could beat him silly for getting me into this mess.

I scanned the crowd for Whit and almost missed him. I spotted Vic first. The giant who'd beaten me two days before sat next to Whit. Three other men I recognized as Whit's shadows, and at least two of them were the ones who held me up against the ropes while Vic beat me.

It certainly wasn't the first time I'd been angry at them.

Suddenly I became the spectator. I saw one of Cardone's men tap him on the shoulder, point to where Whit sat with his crew. Cardone said something angrily, flecks of popcorn flying out of his mouth. The angry ghost of Capone was back. He placed a row of fingers under his chin and flicked it out quickly and aggressively toward Whit. Some sort of insult.

Whit and his boys laughed. The gap in Vic's teeth stood out even from that far away. They sat like the jester and his court, come to dethrone the king. I felt more for Cardone. If the fight was between them, I knew where my money would be. But being on one side or the other didn't help me in the ring. Either way, the outcome would be the same for me.

The bell rang, and I felt like I was being swept away in the tide.

The crowd urged us on, angling for blood. I took it the first two fights didn't deliver much in the action department and the place had gotten antsy. Kelly kept a respectable distance, taking his time. Waiting for the third.

We slapped leather like a couple of school girls and the crowd was quick to boo. I recognized the radio announcer as the same guy from my fight at the Excelsior. He already thought I was a slug, and I wasn't helping his argument any.

I threw a combo just to prove to myself I still could, and Kelly covered up. I didn't follow it up, letting him escape and dance away. As I turned to follow him, I could see Sal across the ring hanging his head like the day Roosevelt died.

I chased Kelly, and when I caught him, he stood still on lead feet, inviting me in. I jabbed him three times fast, then whiffed a wide hook past his face. He stepped forward and grabbed me in a cinch.

"What's with the light touch, pal?" Kelly whispered in my ear. "Whit pays us to make it look good, not just for the decision. Make with the punches already. Just no chin shots, and I'll be fine until the third. Don't you worry about me. I've taken dives more times than the U.S. Navy."

The ref stepped in and broke us up. It was all out on the table. We knew the other was in on the fix, and The Fightin' Irishman had imparted some of his expertise. If he went down on a feather punch, maybe I could claim to Cardone that I knew nothing about it. That Whit had set up the dive on his end and not consulted with me at all.

It was a big risk and a big assumption that Cardone would never check up on my story. By then, I could be in Chicago with Lola.

To emphasize his point, Kelly tagged me on the nose twice. We had a short dust-up right before the bell rang that seemed to ignite a little fire in the crowd. I wondered how many of them had money on the fight. How much of that sucker dough was going to make it into my pocket?

I searched the crowd for Cardone and Whit as I made my way back to Sal. Neither man seemed terribly interested in the fight yet. Whit and his boys laughed at something, not a single one of them looking toward the ring. Cardone whispered sweet nothings into the ear of his lady friend, ignoring his enemy across the room. She smiled and blushed at whatever the old charmer had said.

"Have a nice nap out there?" Sal asked.

"We were feeling each other out."

"You were picking out china together is more like it. I don't care what you do in the end, but when you're out there on that canvas, you represent me. And if you can't fight like a man, I might as well throw this towel in right now."

I'd never seen Sal so angry in the corner. I needed to remember this was getting to him almost as much as it was me.

"I'm sure Cardone will still give you your money, Sal."

"We won't even make it to the fourth?"

"What am I supposed to do? Go a whole round without hitting him?"

Sal had that pained losing-my-money look.

I slapped my gloves together. "I'll see what I can do."

"What, Jimmy? What can you do?"

I had no answer. For the first time, the bell saved me from the corner.

ROUND 10

ROUND TWO BEGAN as a slow dance between partners who didn't like each other. We shuffled around,
never getting too close, acting like we didn't want to
touch. Kelly threw some punches and I threw a few, but
each landed on gloves or whiffed in the air.

I heard the radio announcer say something about a
"lackluster fight so far," and the two of us in the ring
moving "like sleepwalkers." I found it hard to argue, but I
still wanted to punch him in the face, or better yet, in his
honey-toned throat.

Lines of patrons were up in the aisles on their way for
more popcorn and more beer. The main event was two
heavyweights, and most people had given up hoping for a
drop of blood until the big guys hit the ring.

I spotted Lola because she moved against the crowd.
In her hand was a suitcase. I wished she hadn't come at
all. I hadn't told her emphatically to wait for me outside
or at her place. Since she'd been in the habit of coming to

all my fights, I guessed she figured whatever trouble I had didn't have anything to do with the bout that night. Boy, was she wrong.

With my head turned, Kelly landed a punch to my temple that blurred my vision. I stumbled and took a knee, shaking my head to bring my world back into focus. The people still paying attention perked up and cheered. I heard more than a few calls to "Finish him!" I wasn't sure if they had it out for me or if they just wanted this dud of a fight to be over with.

I looked up at Kelly, and the expression on his face was confusion. Everything in the book said to charge me, put me down with another sock to the head. But Whit's eyes bore into his back and held him frozen in place.

Luckily, the ref stepped in and backed Kelly off. He gave me a standing eight and looked me in the eye, asked, "You okay?"

"Yeah," I said.

"Fight!" he said, and chopped down with his hand.

"A little bit of excitement snuck into the second round, folks," the announcer said. "Like a jolt of strong coffee into this dreary quicksand match. And speaking of coffee, Chock Full 'O Nuts is your choice for that first morning cup."

He rambled on with his ad copy and I tried to tune him out. I wished they would sit in a booth in the back like a baseball announcer. They all liked to claim they needed to be up close to give the listeners the full experience. The sights, sounds, and smells. I could have saved him the trouble. Every fight hall in America smelled like stale sweat, stale popcorn, and stale beer. They all sounded like desperation. The desperation in every punch the poor kid from the streets slugged out to maybe make it to someplace better. Every desperate shout from the guy in row three who was on the tail end of a losing streak and couldn't buy his way out of trouble. The desperate pleas of a woman who wanted to go someplace decent and nice for a change. And above all, the desperate cries of blood-hungry fight fans growling like spectators at an execution.

I knew I shouldn't, but I caught Lola's eye again in the stands. She hadn't sat down, that crinkled brow look of concern on her face from seeing me get hit. She wore white gloves, her best skirt and jacket, a pillbox hat. Her traveling clothes. She didn't belong in a place like Vet's Hall on fight night. She didn't belong with a palooka like me. I vowed right then to dedicate the rest of my life to making her decision to stay with me worth it for her.

I swung at Kelly's midsection, working him over like a ball of dough. He tightened his iron abs and took what I gave him. He could have taken ten more rounds.

Kelly wrapped me up again, taking the time to make another meeting out of it.

"Is this your first time at the dance or something? Make it look good." He broke off with me and swung at my head.

I swung back and connected. It felt good.

We had about thirty seconds left in the round, and we lit up the place. We traded frustrated punches, angry uppercuts, and jab after jab where I saw only Vic's face instead of Kelly's.

By the time the bell rang, I was winded, and the crowd had gotten interested again. I even heard the announcer chime in as I headed back toward Sal, "Looks like we have some life yet in these two pugilists. A flurry of punches like midwinter snow fell on the ring late in round two. Can they keep it up? We shall see right after this word from our sponsor, Sterzing's Potato Chips."

Sal put out my stool, wiped sweat off my forehead with his towel. At least I had worked up a sweat this round.

"Round three, Jimmy. What are you gonna do?"

"He wants a fight, I'll give him a fight."

"You gonna put him down like that other guy wants?"

"Maybe Cardone will think it's an accident."

"What if he don't?"

Easy for Sal to say. He'd only dealt with one half of the equation.

"Look, Sal," I said. "Whatever happens, I got you covered. Hand me my bag."

"What?"

"Hand me my bag," I said louder.

Confused but beyond arguing, Sal handed me my gym bag. I unzipped it and reached to the bottom, awkwardly shoving aside my clothes with my gloved hands until I saw the white of the envelope.

"Grab that," I said. "It's for you."

Sal reached in and took the envelope just as the bell rang for round three. I stood. The referee had to scold Sal to take the stool out of the ring. Sal couldn't take his eyes off the envelope.

I kicked the stool aside, and it slid out onto the floor. Sal had peeled the corner up on the envelope and now ran a thumb across the two hundred bucks inside. I turned and headed into the ring, as curious as anyone in the place about what might happen next.

ROUND 11

THE BELL RANG AGAIN after I'd taken two steps into the ring. Both Kelly and I looked around, confused. The ref was at the ropes shouting into the crowd.

A fight had broken out in the front row. Two drunks and another two of their drunk friends had started their own match when ours wasn't up to snuff.

The ref could have shouted all night long, and it wouldn't have done any good. The crowd around the men was finally getting the blood it wanted.

Drunk fights were always ugly affairs. No gloves, no technique. The first thing to go were the knuckles. A couple of would-be tough guys spent the night drinking beer and watching the pros do it, and all of a sudden they thought they knew all there was to know about the sport. Bare fists pummeled into faces. Joints popped on cheekbones and skin split over knuckles and on lips.

After that first exchange, things usually slowed down into more of a grappling match than boxing. These guys were determined, though. One wore a green suit that was already stained with blood from his own nose. The other wore gray pinstripes and was leaking bloody saliva from his mouth. I didn't know him before, but I'd have bet you dollars to donuts he came in with more teeth than I saw in his mouth.

The two friends came around and took up the main action, working like tag-team wrestlers. They were slightly smarter and started with gut punches. Both guys were a little heavy, so there was plenty of target. One fat guy sent another backward, but the crowd of blood-thirsty savages behind him threw fatty back into the mix.

Kelly and I stood and watched in stunned silence. I couldn't hear any of what was being drunkenly slurred between them, so I had no idea what the beef was about. I knew it bought me a bit of time, so I wasn't complaining.

Two thick guys came down from the lobby. Ex-punchers from the looks of it. Hired security now. Both of the men who came to stop the fight could give lessons in broken noses.

The radio announcer was up on his feet and calling the fight in the stands like the heavyweight championship.

"You wouldn't believe it, folks. The action in the stands tonight is more exciting than anything going on inside the ropes. Our amateur sluggers could teach the pros a thing or two on this night."

The fat men had started aiming for the face.

"OH! A solid right to the nose, and one man is down.

Better call the doctor, folks, or better yet a chef, because that side of beef is done."

The two bouncers arrived but quickly found they had their hands full with the foursome. All four men lurched and stumbled, slipping on pools of their own blood. The screaming men surrounding the fight tried to make a human blockade to keep the bouncers from breaking it up. A crowd like that was the type of guys who could never get enough, and the ones who usually paid were their wives when the jerks wanted just one more bloody nose.

The fat man still standing turned to the crowd and held his hands over his head in victory, ignoring the blood that coursed down his face.

"Looks like we have a winner, folks," the announcer said. "Get that man a pair of gloves and send him in the ring. Heck, send my Aunt Sally. Anything is better than what we've seen so far."

The bouncers got to the melee, and in no time, had the two original fighters apart. The man in the green suit took a beer-soaked swing at one of the old pros. That did not go over well. The pro let go of the man's lapels, set his feet, and plowed a right fist across his jaw so hard I thought it would come off and land in the last row.

The green-suited man was unconscious before he hit the floor. He'd wake up in a drunk tank tomorrow with the worst headache he'd ever had.

It took another two minutes for the excitement to die down. I found Whit in the stands laughing with his boys, enjoying the chaos. Cardone was shielding his date's eyes from the blood as the men were taken up the aisle right past his seat.

Lola sat stiffly in her seat. If it wasn't for me, she would have never set foot inside a fight hall. I kept telling her not to come, but she said if anything happened to me, she wanted to be there to see it, or otherwise, I'd make up some fool story about it the next day.

The bell rang again and the ref called, "Fight!"

Kelly and I stood for a few long seconds, not knowing what to do. The crowd was still on its feet, milling around, turning fallen chairs back over. No one paid much attention to us inside the ring. We weren't the ones putting on the best show.

But show time started now.

Kelly stepped in close to me, giving me the opening. I didn't take it. We slapped gloves a few times with about as much punch behind them as if we were playing pat-a-cake.

The buzzing mosquito of an announcer started in again.

"And back to the ring, where apparently it's still nap time for the toddlers. Perhaps one of our new sponsors is Elmer's Glue. At least that would explain what's on the bottom of the feet of Kelly and Wyler as they shuffle lifelessly around the ring."

Kelly looked me right in the eye, lowering his gloves slightly to make it easier for me to get a shot through. The seconds ticked off.

I saw Whit in the stands over Kelly's shoulder. He had taken a sudden interest in the bout. He and Vic and the rest of his boys all watched the ring like a strip show might break out.

Kelly came at me with a few jabs, which I batted away. I sent a few meaningless shots into his gut.

My body was torn. I wanted to send him down to the canvas, have it all be over with. Take my licks from Cardone and put it all behind me. But then I saw Sal in my corner, the white sprout of the envelope poking up from his belt.

He had his money. Even if Cardone took his share back from this fight, he'd still get his operation.

Kelly swung at me again, begging me to come and get him.

I stayed neutral, unable to decide. The rage of indecision burned red in my brain and I forgot where I was for a second. I saw Vic lean over to Whit and complain. Whit shut him down with what I expect was reassurance I would come through.

Regret weighed down my gloves, dragged my feet through the mud. The long list of things I never should have done hung like a noose around my neck, all the way back to never should have left Chicago.

I swung at Kelly just to have something to do. He took the chance and stepped into the punch—a punch that couldn't have knocked over a house of cards—and Kelly went down.

The crowd booed, and the sound bored a hole in my skull. Kelly was no actor. He fell like a kid play-acting and hoping for a gumball after a scraped knee. I didn't want it to go this way.

The referee stepped over Kelly and started counting. He'd seen enough fights to know a fix, but he did his job just the same. Kelly rolled around like he'd been knocked loopy, but I knew as well as anyone in the place that he could have stood up and recited the Gettysburg address if he wanted to. His brain wasn't scrambled in the least.

"Kelly's down, and for no earthly reason," the announcer raged. "A hit as soft as a pillow put him on the canvas, and it makes this reporter think of the days of Al Capone and the rackets. A disgraceful showing tonight at Veterans Hall, one I would think the boxing commission will soon look into, along with both these fighters. Men who are a discredit to the sport of kings."

Something in me popped. I had been holding back hitting for so long that I had to hit something, someone, right then.

I turned and lunged through the ropes, reaching for the announcer and his big silver microphone. He leaned away from me and snatched up his mic in one hand, started calling the play by play of the attack.

"My goodness, ladies and gentlemen, the fight has come to me now."

I didn't let him finish. I slapped the microphone out of his hand and punched him square in the chest. I heard him wheeze for air over the roar of the crowd. It had gone from a real dud to the best fight night of the year.

The ref had stopped counting over Kelly and ran to the ropes, where he grabbed me around the waist and tried to haul me back inside the ring.

There wasn't the power I wanted behind my

punches, but I got in three more good shots on the bastard announcer before I let myself get pulled back.

The scoring table roiled in chaos. The front three rows were on their feet, cheering me. They would have voted me for president right then.

I turned and Kelly was up, looking over at the side of the ring with a lost look on his face. Was this part of the set-up? he seemed to be asking.

"What the hell was that all about, kid?" the ref asked me angrily.

I didn't have time to answer. The bell rang. End of round three.

ROUND 12

KELLY WANDERED BACK to his corner in a daze. He kept looking over his shoulder at the spot where he'd hit the canvas as if he were expecting to still see himself there.

I stopped before I got to Sal and turned to the stands. Whit and his boys were up and stomping out. I saw Vic point in the direction of Cardone, but Whit slapped his hand away and tugged his hat down tighter on his head. He was angry, that much was clear. What he might do about it was clear as mud.

I sat down on my stool and Sal began rubbing my shoulders.

"Well, your bed's made now, I guess," he said.

I watched for Cardone and found him in his seat sipping a beer. Nothing too out of the ordinary. I wondered if he thought my outburst with the reporter was merely a ploy to get the fight to go into the fourth, and would he be proud of me? I'd hate to have to tell him the microphone jerk simply made me mad.

"Well, are you?" Sal asked.

"What?" I said. I'd missed the question.

"Are you going down in the fourth?"

"One way or another, I'm going down for sure real soon."

I still had a chance to play dumb with Whit. Kelly had got up off the mat, all I did was act on a personal grudge. Could be he'd understand.

My deal with Cardone could still stand. The trick was that Whit knew I'd had my deal with Cardone and now I'd be choosing sides. Something told me Vic would be paying me a visit to finish what he'd started.

I looked for Lola in the crowd. She sat on the edge of her seat, looking more nervous than usual. The air had that feeling in it. If you cut through the sour sweat and the cigarette smoke, you felt it—something about to happen. It was what you wanted in a fight hall. The impending knockout, the haymaker punch that sent a guy to sleep. This hummed in the air a little different, though, and I could see Lola felt it too.

A hand clamped down on my shoulder. I turned, expecting to see Whit with a razor in his hand. It was the manager, Mr. Foy, a pudgy man with a loose tie and a drooping mustache.

"Listen up, Jimmy, I don't like that stunt you pulled." Meaning attacking his ringside reporter. "Normally, I'd toss you out on your ear, but I haven't seen a crowd this into a fight in a dog's age, so I'm gonna let you keep going.

You work 'em up, get 'em good and thirsty. But no more monkey business, you understand?"

"Yes, sir."

"Okay, then." He patted me twice on the shoulder. He aimed a thumb at me over his shoulder as he talked to Sal on his way down off the ropes. "Keep your boy in check, Sal. The fight stays in the ring."

"Got it," Sal said. He turned back to me. "Rules get thrown out the window when they're screaming for blood."

"More like when they're screaming for beer."

The bell rang. I had no idea what to expect from Kelly this round. I got my answer quick. He came at me like an angry hornet. I took it his payday was ruined, so his only satisfaction of the night would be to beat me inside out.

For the first time, I saw what he was made of. He threw quick punches in combos of three and four. It was like fighting a hummingbird. A hummingbird with a decent right.

We slugged it out for a few seconds, an honest-to-goodness boxing match. And a good one too. My brain slipped back into fight mode, and I tuned out the crowd, the noise, the jerk with the microphone, who had retreated to a chair in the front row, out of arm's reach.

Kelly ran through a flurry of punches twice more and then wrapped me up in a hug usually reserved for returning war heroes. He spat in my ear as he talked this time.

"What the hell do you think you're doing? You have

any idea what Whit is gonna do to us? It's all your fault, and I'm gonna damn well tell him so."

The ref stepped between us and pushed us apart, reciting the usual warning with no emotion behind it.

Freed from the clinch, I had a clear view of Cardone in the stands. He sat up, watching the round eagerly, waving away the girl who tried to interest him in her new ring. Behind him, I spotted movement. Not unusual in the stands, but it struck me the way several bodies moved at once.

Whit and his boys. They marched a military line, coming up on Cardone from the back. I'd been too young to enter the war, but I knew an ambush when I saw one.

I stepped up to the ropes and shouted, "Hey!"

The crowd in the front row pelted me with old popcorn, telling me to get back to fighting.

"Say hi to your mother for me after the fight," some guy yelled.

The ref behind me yelled at me to come back in. Cardone stared at me, and I read his lips saying, "What the hell?"

I couldn't think of how it mattered whether Whit got to Cardone or not, only that I didn't want anyone to get hurt over my stupid choices. Kelly sidled up beside me and planted a right hook in my ear. I shook off the blow and came back at him with a left cross that caught his chin and sent him spinning.

I left him there to hit the mat on his own. Tossing glances out to Whit's team advancing on Cardone, I made for my corner. Sal climbed the ropes to meet me.

"What is it, Jimmy?"

I grabbed the towel off his shoulder and turned, flinging it into the ring. The ref had his back to me as he stood over Kelly counting to ten. The crowd focused on the prone body lying on the canvas. My eyes focused on Cardone.

The towel hit the mat. No one noticed. Too late anyhow.

Two of Whit's men straddled either side of Cardone as Vic clamped a mitt over the girl's mouth. Whit reached from behind and dragged a knife across Cardone's throat. Cardone's two men sat one row in front of him, eyes on the action in the ring, and maybe a little blurry from all the beer. Whit's men made a good shield from the crowd, who weren't watching anyway, but I could see it all. No one else noticed the murder among them. If only they could see the blood, they'd all be on their feet shouting for more.

Cardone's head flung back, his mouth open, but I could tell no sound came out. No one near him turned. Whit's hand spread across Cardone's forehead, pulling it back. A fine spray of blood jetted out, and the popcorn box in his lap turned red. The girl's eyes went wide, and Vic's knuckles went white keeping her in place.

The referee reached ten, the bell rang. The ref turned and saw the towel, he looked up at me, confused.

I turned to Sal. "We gotta go."

I checked quickly to see that Lola was still in her seat. She stood in the aisle, knowing this was no ordinary fight, her suitcase already in her hand. Good girl. Damn good girl. If she had let me talk her into waiting at her place, I'd never make it there. This way, we could both run together and have a chance. How much of a chance, I wouldn't bet on.

I hopped between the ropes, pulling at the laces of my gloves with my teeth. The crowd cheered the best bout of the night. Knockout. Just what everyone wants to see.

The first gunshot was nearly buried under the sound. I turned, pulling one glove off, and saw Cardone's two men had finally caught on. The first shot came from Cardone's men. All at once, four other men within spitting distance of each other all drew their guns and started blasting.

The place nearly came apart at the seams. People ran three directions at once and all into each other. I tried to make it up the aisle toward Lola, tugging at my second glove, stubbornly still attached to my fist.

The aisles filled in like flood water rising, only with bodies churning in whitewater swells. For a second, I felt grateful the glove remained on my left hand. I punched a few guys out of my way, sending them sprawling onto the folding chairs in the aisles. More gunshots. Someone screamed like he'd been hit. The guys I punched had no idea I'd probably saved their lives. Flat on the deck was the safest place to be. I stood straight and tall as I tried to reach Lola.

I bet that announcer was having a field day with this.

I spotted Lola ahead, and she saw me. She fought to stay upright in the rushing tide of bodies fighting toward the exit. I cold-cocked a fat guy in a hat and shoved another guy with his jacket on inside out.

A man ran past me in the aisle with track-star speed until another shot rang out and he fell, a bright red hole in his back. Whit's men and Cardone's men had spread out and were shooting blindly over their shoulders like in a Jesse James movie.

I saw one of Whit's men take a bullet to the head. He fell and a man in the crowd caught him, realized what he had, then dropped him quick.

I reached Lola, grabbed her hand in my ungloved hand, still with tape on it, and pulled. "Come on!"

She followed me, bouncing her suitcase off the shins and hips of men running for the door as we made our way against the tide down toward the ring. The shooting slowed now that some of the men were dead and some had made it to safe hiding spots.

I saw Sal standing dumbfounded by our corner, huddled with my stool against his chest as if that would stop a bullet. We reached him and I stooped down to pick up my bag, chewing open the knot in my glove as I did.

"Sal, get moving," I said.

"What the hell is all this?" he asked.

"Nothing but trouble." I checked his waistband; the envelope was still there. "Go. Get out of here."

Lola clutched my arm. I could feel her terror in the sharp fingers digging into it right through her gloves and in the tremble in her body.

"Sal," I said, "we have to go. I'll call you." I lifted my gym bag and took Lola's hand. A bullet pushed past my face, blowing on me with hot breath as it passed. It landed in Sal's neck. In one side and out the other. His hands opened, and the stool fell to the floor.

I watched his confused face go slack. Lola screamed and buried her head in my shoulder blades. I turned to see Whit halfway up the aisle with a gun pointed my way. Guess he blamed me for all this, and I couldn't disagree.

When I turned around, Sal had already slumped to his knees, the envelope tumbling out onto the fight hall floor, spilling money on top of a growing pool of blood.

I pulled hard on Lola's hand and made a weaving course for the exit.

ROUND 13

WE BURST out the side exit and into an alleyway. I cursed Lola's good shoes, the ones I knew she would never leave behind. The heels were too tall and made it hard for her to run. Still, I pulled her along as fast as she could take as we made for the street.

The sidewalks reminded me of the hysterical citizens in *War of the Worlds*, mine and Lola's last date night. Men ran from Veterans Hall like their lives depended on it. For me, it really did.

We made it out of the alley and to the sidewalk. I spotted two cabs waiting by the curb, the drivers out of their cars and looking at the doors of Veteran's Hall hemorrhaging people. They had that look of confusion that set in right before you decided if these people were running, then I'd better be running too.

I pushed through the stream of runners, dragging Lola behind me, and made it to a bright yellow cab.

"Hey, buddy, let's go."

He turned to me, stubby cigarette burned down to ash in his fingers. "What the hell's going on in there? A fire?"

"Just get in and drive." I opened the door and reached back for Lola. Seeing an open door, a guy in a dark blue suit and wild hair that used to be combed over a bald spot ducked in between Lola and me, slipping into the seat.

"Hey!" I shouted and reached into the cab. The driver was so mesmerized by the street he never noticed us.

I hauled the guy out by his lapels. The man's hair stood even higher as I brought him back to the sidewalk. "This ain't your cab, mister."

He didn't know which way was up. Probably the first time in his life, he heard gunshots. He saw my solid expression, my unwillingness to debate the situation. I didn't think he even noticed my bare chest or my boxing trunks.

He swung at me with arms loose as wet noodles. I pushed him back from me and rammed a fist into his nose. His hair stood straight up as he fell to the sidewalk, arms flailing to grab something that wasn't there.

Behind me, Lola got clipped by a guy running past. She teetered on those high heels and fell down. I was there in a flash to lift her back up. I knew the street was too dangerous for us.

"It's all right. I won't let you go," I said. I doubted it was any comfort to her.

I turned back to the cab and pushed Lola in, tossing her suitcase in after her. I pounded my fist on the roof to get the attention of the driver, who still gawked by the mayhem on the street.

"Let's go!"

The cabbie snapped out of his daze and slid into the driver's seat, tossing his nubby smoke as he did.

"Train station," I said. "Step on it."

That damn jerk who tried to take our cab. That drunken panicked fool. If it wasn't for him …

Whit and Vic hit the sidewalk. Vic saw us immediately. Must have been looking for the cabs. He shot out an arm with a finger like a dagger on the end of it, aiming right at my heart. Whit followed his point and spotted me, gym bag in my hand, door open.

I flung the bag in ahead of me and sat down quickly, slamming the door.

A car skidded to the curb, Whit's driver Johnny-on-the-spot to pick up the boss man. I bet he was wondering more than anyone what the hell had made everyone flood out of Vets Hall.

A second car joined them at the curb. Whit's buddies, minus one who was still face-down on a row of broken chairs inside the hall, busy painting the floors red from the bullet hole in his skull.

I pounded on the back of the seat. "Get moving!" I yelled.

Lola's eyes were terrified, her body rigid, her mouth a grim line. The red of her lips reminded me of the blood on Sal's neck.

The cab driver finally jerked away from the curb. Whit yelled something at his boys and then took a potshot at the cab with his revolver. Our cabbie ducked in his seat.

"Jesus, Mary, and Joseph!"

"Just keep going," I said.

"Is it a raid?"

"Yeah. Just drive." As long as he had an answer, it didn't matter to me what he believed.

I turned in my seat to see the second car take off after us, right on our heels. Whit still stood on the running board of his car and fired another shot. Not even close.

"I hate to tell you pal, but you got company," I said.

"Hey, hey, wait. This ain't my problem."

"It is now," I said. "You'd better get moving."

"You ain't got a gun, do you?"

"No, but they do, and that's enough."

The driver knew the city streets, so we had that advantage. I clutched Lola's hand in my taped one and squeezed. She squeezed back—hard.

"It's gonna be okay," I whispered to her, subtly pushing her down in the seat so her head was below window-level.

"Jimmy ..." was all she could manage. She was a tough kid. I had never expected to find out how tough.

I dug in my bag and pulled out my wristwatch. 9:40. The train for Chicago left at 10:00 on the dot. Plenty of time to get there if nothing went wrong.

The cab driver should have won a medal for valor. He wove between cars and squeezed through yellow lights to make sure we kept moving. The Friday night traffic wasn't bad, but it kept us switching lanes and dodging buses.

The car behind us kept pace, squealing tires a lot more but sticking to our bumper. I started to recognize streets that I knew ran close to the train station. Still a good half-mile off, but closing in. If they followed us right to the door of the station, though, that was no good.

"Can you lose them?" I asked.

"What in the hell do you think I'm tryin' to do?" the cabbie said as he hunched forward in his seat, licking sweat off his upper lip.

"If you get to the station and they're still on us, keep driving."

I felt the tap of a fender on our back end. The rear of the cab started veering away, and the whole car angled to the left. I wrapped my arms around Lola and braced for the crash.

The cabbie kept us from flipping over. That much was a miracle. The cab swung into the oncoming lane. The cabbie pressed the brakes. The car behind us backed off and let us swing out of control. We went up on the curb, the front wheel bouncing up and both tires popping loud as gunshots.

The front end of the cab went through the window of a drug store. Thankfully, it was all closed up. The storefront shattered and threw bits of glass over the car like spring rain. Like that confetti on the streets on V-E day.

The cab driver pitched forward, and his head hit the steering wheel. He slumped back into his seat, out cold. Lola and I slammed against the back of the seat, my arms taking the brunt of it for Lola, though when I looked at her, she already had the workings of a great headache.

We both took a second to get our breath and our bearings back, the music of falling shards of glass to accompany us.

"You okay?" I managed.

"Yeah. I think so," she said weakly.

"Stay here."

I hated leaving her, but I wasn't going to sit like two ducks in a pond and wait to be shot.

I opened the door and started a whole new cascade of falling glass. I waited for it to pass, then slid out on the side of the drug store. I was blocked by the bulk of the steaming car.

Someone screamed, and I heard someone else yell for somebody to call the police. Then I heard, "He's got a gun!"

Since my hands were still taped, I took the risk of putting my hand down and scooping up a fistful of glass. Nothing sliced my hand, so I spun out from behind the car and took two steps forward, seeing the two approaching gunmen as they stalked the wounded car and the people they thought were inside.

I flung my arm out and tried my best to aim at their eyes. A cloud of tiny shrapnel sailed across the space between us, and by the time they turned to look at me, they each got a spray of broken glass to the face. Both men screamed but I didn't wait to see how badly they were hurt. I stepped forward and knocked the gun out of the hand of the man closest to me, then put a firm right cross over the bridge of his nose.

He went down and I stepped over him to the other man, clutching at his eyes, gun still in hand. I saw the small crowd of onlookers. Some had gotten close, wanting to help, but then backed off when they saw the guns. Now they watched as I raised my fist again and pounded a right into the other man's cheek. I grabbed his shirt with my left and ran three more rights to his already bloody face.

Finally, he dropped the gun and slid out of my hands. My knuckles ached and were already starting to swell.

I crunched over the glass to the cab, opened the door, and reached for Lola. I pulled her onto the sidewalk, trying to steer her away from seeing the two downed men. I bent back inside and grabbed our bags.

I turned to the closest onlooker and said, "Call an ambulance. The cab driver needs help." I left the other two out of it.

I took Lola's hand and started running for the train station.

ROUND 14

MY HANDS THROBBED. It had been quite a while since I'd punched someone without gloves on. The tape had done little to protect me, and I hadn't been pulling any punches.

With Lola's wrist in one hand and our two bags in the other, I needed to take a rest six blocks away from the scene of the taxi crash.

We were only another five blocks from the train station, and I could see a bank clock across the street that read 9:48.

Safe now that nobody was following us, I sat down on the stoop of a three-story walkup. Whit had gotten greedy with those gunshots and missed the chase. That cabbie was such a pro that by the time Whit had gotten in his car, there would have been no way for them to catch us.

I sucked for air and massaged my aching knuckles.

"Johnny, please tell me what's going on," Lola said in a weak voice. "I've never seen you like this. I'm...I'm scared."

I pulled her down to sit next to me. Her body stiffened. I wondered exactly what she was scared of.

"Those men," she said. "You hurt them."

"Or they would have hurt us."

"I've just never..."

"Lola, I'm so sorry."

"Don't be sorry, just explain."

I did my best. I studied her face for disappointment, for the moment she would stand and walk away from me forever. But she stayed.

"And you knew it was going to end like this, and you didn't tell me?"

"Honestly, Lola, I had no idea what would happen tonight. I couldn't have predicted this. I never would have let you get within ten miles of this if I had known."

I searched her face for some indication she believed me. She stared at me, her eyes blank.

"Jimmy, you're not a bad person."

Was she telling me that, or herself?

"What you did was stupid. What happened tonight made it worse."

"I know, I know."

"Tell me we can start over." Her voice pleaded, worry dripping off every letter. Still, I'd never heard sweeter words. All this time I'd been thinking I was saving Lola, when here she was saving me.

"We can. We can, Lola." I grabbed her and held her, wanting to take so much back. I did it for you, all for you, I wanted to say. But that would make her to blame. And it was me. Only me.

Sal was dead because of me.

I started crying, something I hadn't done since St. Vincent's. Around there, if you didn't toughen up and learn not to cry pretty quick, life became that much harder. Secretly, each of us boys went to Father Tim on our own and cried our eyes out over our lost parents, our sad little lives. And Father Tim never told our secret to the other boys. A secret we all held.

Lola stroked my hair. She'd been more to me than I ever could have expected. I'd do anything for that girl. Anything legal. My days of handshaking with the rackets were over. So was my time in the ring. A new start. A legit job. Chicago.

I looked up at the clock again. We had just enough time, but we had to move.

Lola took off her shoes and held them in her hand as we ran the last five blocks.

————

I PULLED Lola to a stop across the street from the station. We sank back into a shadowed alcove and I watched the doors, looking for any sign of trouble.

I reached into my bag and pulled out a shirt and pants. I changed in the darkness and tossed my boxing trunks into a bush, happy to be rid of them forever. Lola put her shoes back on.

There was a big clock out in front of the station, mocking people running late for the trains. It let me keep an eye on the time so we wouldn't have to come out of our cover until we absolutely had to.

"We'll get tickets on the train," I explained to Lola. She started to shiver in the night air. "Are you sure you still want to come with me?"

The pause waiting for her to answer felt longer than any ten-count I'd been on the losing end of. Finally, she nodded. "I'm not sure of very much right now, but I want to be with you. Jimmy, I just wish you'd come to me earlier. I could have helped."

"How? You're great at a lot of things, but I wouldn't even let you talk to a guy like Whit. I should have known better myself. I just got so...well, the money, you know?"

"I know." She took my hand in hers, the white gloves the only kind I wanted to see for a while.

"I was saving to buy you a ring," I said. She gave me a sad little smile. "I'm not trying to make you feel guilty or anything. I just wanted you to know. I didn't do it just to have more money to throw around. I don't think I'm a big shot or anything like that."

"I know you don't think like that. It's why I love you."

I kissed her, keeping one eye on the clock. The kiss I got in return belonged to a stranger. Something in her held back.

"Almost time," I said.

As if on cue, Whit's car rolled to a stop in front of the station. I cursed out loud. Lola said, "What is it?"

I pointed out of the darkness to Whit and Vic exiting the car, the driver staying behind with the engine running.

"They must have seen my suitcase," I said. "Put two and two together."

"What took them so long?"

"Maybe they went to the bus station first. They might be checking all the ways out of town."

"So maybe they won't stay."

"Let's hope so."

Whit and Vic split up. Whit kept his gun tucked in his jacket, but his hand also stayed under and I knew his finger danced on the trigger, waiting to teach me a lesson about crossing him. A guy like him, working his way up in the underworld, it must have burned him more than anything to have Cardone beat him to the punch. If he was madder at Cardone than me, he'd already gotten that out of his system.

But if you want the big boys to notice you, you don't leave loose ends to run out of town.

They paced the row of doors for an excruciating minute as I watched the iron hands on the clock grind slowly forward over the Roman numerals. 9:58 and that damn train rolled in right on time.

The whistle blew, and I heard a crackling voice on the intercom announce the arrival of the Chicago-bound train. Lola gripped my hand tighter.

Whit scanned the crowd, his hand still tucked away

but eager to get out. Vic stood and swiveled his gaze around, pounding one meaty fist into another. No gun would satisfy an old slugger like him. When your fists could do the job, nothing else was good enough.

"We have to move if we're going to make that train," I said.

"How? We'll walk right in front of them."

"It's too crowded. They won't shoot."

"It didn't stop them at the fight."

I nodded my agreement to her point. The hands on that clock didn't stop for anyone.

"We've got to try."

I pulled Lola with me out of our hiding spot and walked slowly across the street to the far right door, Vic's side of the blockade. Having changed clothes, there was a decent chance they wouldn't spot me right away. I kept my head down and stayed with Lola between them and me.

"Jimmy," she said.

I turned to her, saw a mask of indecision on her face. I never wanted to see that look again. I'd managed to destroy the most beautiful face I'd ever seen with the doubt and fear I'd placed there.

"What is it?"

A million choices passed behind her eyes. She settled on none. "Nothing. Never mind."

Two cars passed in the street and I ducked us behind them for the last quick steps to the curb. The voice over the loudspeaker called, "Last call for the Number 35 to Saint Louis and Chicago. Track 9."

I moved behind a couple just getting out of a cab and tried to make myself as small as I could. The older couple argued for a moment about money, and the man leaned in to hand over the fare to the cabbie. When he leaned forward, my cover went with him.

Vic looked right at me.

ROUND 15

VIC'S EYES WENT WIDE, and his fists clenched tighter. He charged forward like an angry bull.

I pushed Lola toward the door. "Go, I'll catch up."

Vic crossed the distance between us in no time. He put a heavy hand on the older woman waiting by the cab, and she toppled over her suitcase to the sidewalk. Vic stepped through the pile of luggage and over her body like it wasn't there.

He expected me to run or at least to duck back. Much like in our match at Whit's gym, I decided the way with Vic was to bring the fight to him.

I dropped my bag and made up the three paces between us. With his forward momentum added to mine, I drove my fist into his nose, catching him before he could get any defenses up.

The fight was on.

My knuckles already ached, and the shot to his beak didn't help matters. It was now or never time, though. Vic reeled and I followed him back, swinging another one into his gut. It caught my hand like steel.

Vic staggered, and the fallen woman and her bag finally caught up with him. He tripped over the mess he'd made and went down, the husband now out of the cab and shouting.

"What's the meaning of this?" said the offended husband.

Vic spun on the ground, slammed a sidearm blow into the man's knee. The husband buckled and fell to the floor with a yelp. Vic slapped his palms on the ground to push himself up. No way I was letting that happen.

I dodged a suitcase and put a hard right in his ear. I could almost hear the ringing inside his head. I hated to do it, but I gave him a kick too. No ref, no rules. Only survival.

I looked up to see Whit moving across the sidewalk. The crowd gathering around the fight would keep him back a few extra seconds at least. I spun my head and saw Lola paused at the entrance to the station, seeing me fight dirty.

"Go!" I urged her, but she stood still, watching my bouts to the last.

Vic's massive fist plowed into my thigh. My leg went numb and I slumped, but I caught myself with a knee and remained standing. He got halfway to standing, and I knew my time was running out. I put a hand out, and it landed on top of the woman's smallest suitcase. Makeup, I guessed. She still writhed on the ground, confused by the brutality going on over her head.

I lifted the case and swung up, catching Vic under the chin. His front teeth were long gone, but I heard a few more shattering inside his mouth. No boxer worth his salt resorted to back-alley tactics, but this was me hanging up my gloves.

I dropped the case and laid into him with a left-right-left combo across the cheeks. The dirty tricks had softened him up, but my fists put the K.O. on him. Vic went down, as lifeless as that pile of luggage. For safe measure, I kicked him once in the ear and swung down a hand to lift the makeup case over my head and smash it into his unconscious face, spraying blood on the old woman's fur coat.

A cheer went up from the crowd. The same cheer would have come if it had been my face-down on the sidewalk. Whit had moved in too close for comfort, so I started running—fast.

I snatched my gym bag and made for the door, bracing myself for gunshots. I saw Lola ahead of me. She didn't wait. She turned and moved deeper into the station, a look on her face that frightened me. Fear. Not fear of Whit or Vic—fear of me.

I pounded through the glass door, afraid it might break. I scanned the crowd for Lola and saw her ducking under a sign that read TRACK 9. She moved fast, and I couldn't help thinking she was trying to outrun me. I sprinted across the marble-floored lobby of the station.

The crowd was thin and easy enough to pick through, but no one was in the same rush as me. I nearly crashed into three people as they walked head down looking at their ticket or eyes up searching for the right track.

"Come back here, you rat!" Whit called after me.

People began to turn. I spotted a blue-uniformed security guard. He watched me run past, unimpressed. A guy like him got used to seeing guys like me make a run for a train about to leave.

I heard a porter cry, "All aboard!"

"Lola!" I yelled. She stopped running and turned. Her eyes were scared, her chest heaved with eager breaths. The train blasted a *whoosh* of rushing air, and the metal groaned as all twelve cars lumbered to a slow roll.

"Take any car, just go," I said as I rushed past her. She hesitated, a sliver of doubt playing across her eyes. I almost stopped to plead with her, to tell her this would all be over once we got on that train and headed north, but she started running again on her own. I guess the prospect of the gunman behind her seemed more daunting than the uncertain future in front of her.

The first gunshot clanged into the thick metal hide of the train. People screamed. The train driver sat twelve cars ahead with a steam whistle roaring in his ear. A puny gunshot meant nothing to him and his schedule.

Lola tripped over her high heels and put out her hands to stop herself falling to the platform. Her suitcase went sailing and rolled twice before stopping an inch away from being swept under the wheel of the train.

"Leave it!" I said.

Whit made it to platform 9 and waved his gun out

ahead of him, carving a path through the people standing and kissing loved ones goodbye.

I tossed my bag into an open door on the second-to-last car and gripped the handrail as hard as I could. I turned and held my other hand out to Lola. The train rumbled slow, gaining momentum, so I knew she could make it. The question in my head was, could Whit make it too? I wished for another fistful of broken glass. Anything to slow Whit's charging down the platform.

He fired again. The window beside me shattered, and I heard a yell from inside the train car.

Lola locked eyes with mine, and I saw that look again. She reached for me but pulled back at the last second. Up close, the look seemed less fear than doubt. Doubt I was the man she'd thought I was.

Whit's gun erupted again, and Lola's eyes changed. They read confusion. Pain. Her hand went to her shoulder. Her white glove soaked up the blood.

I jumped off the train, hit the platform, and tumbled. My view of Lola spun, her confused and agonized face rolling in and out of view. I heard two more gunshots and thought surely the worst had happened. Behind me, the train's brakes screeched as the momentum of the massive steel beast ground to a halt. No doubt, a porter watching the action had pulled the emergency stop.

When I stopped rolling and looked up, Lola staggered toward me. I slid up onto my knees and caught her as she fell forward. As her body dropped, I saw Whit behind her, also falling. His arms out wide, the gun sailing through the air and two blooms of red on his chest.

He flopped to the platform and revealed the security guard behind him, gun still pointing straight ahead, smoke drooling from the barrel.

I turned my head down to Lola in my arms.

"Are you okay?"

"My arm," she said and gripped high on her shoulder with that blood red glove.

"You'll be all right." I hugged her. "It's all gonna be all right."

"Jimmy...that man outside. Is he dead?"

"No." I could see more than the pain in her eyes. I held her, yet I offered her no comfort.

"They held the train, Lola." I nodded to the stopped train over my shoulder, brakes still hissing with steam.

"We can still make it to Chicago?"

"If you want to." I left the door open for her to say what I knew she had on her tongue. I always knew a girl like her was too good for me.

"I don't think I ought to travel like this." She tilted her eyes to her bloody shoulder. Something in her demeanor had changed—hardened. It scared me more than anything else had all night.

"Yeah. I guess you better not," I said.

"It's over, though. Right, Jimmy?"

I hoped she wasn't talking about us.

I looked past her to Whit's lifeless body on the platform, the curious crowd gathering around him. "Yeah. All over now," I said, playing dumb, trying not to pick up what she might actually be saying.

A porter from the train bent down to us. "Doctor's on

his way. Be here any second now. You best lay down, miss."

He took Lola from my arms, laid her down using his folded jacket as a pillow. I stepped back and the crowd took over, straining to get a look at the girl who'd been shot.

"Jimmy?" she called.

"I'm here, Lola."

She found my eyes. "You should go. The police are going to want to talk to you, and who knows what they are going to make of this. Go back to Chicago. See if you can settle things with anyone else who might be after you, then make a fresh start." I read between the lines. "You always talked about a fresh start."

"You're right, Lola. I can get a job, a place to stay."

"I won't be long. Couple of weeks, maybe." She winced in pain.

I hoped she was telling the truth. No vision I'd ever had of a new life was complete without her in it.

A man in a long coat and a doctor bag came rushing off the train and pushed through the crowd.

A porter called, "All aboard!" Gunshots were one thing, but the schedule was the schedule.

"Goodbye, Jimmy." Her voice was almost drowned out by the blast of steam and engine churn of the train. The crowd broke apart, people running for their seats. Another story to tell when they got to Chicago, and gossip fodder for the journey. I'd have to hear retellings the entire ride, each one stretching the tale ever taller.

The doctor leaned in close to Lola, her focus on him now as tears rolled down her cheeks.

A second security guard and a cop joined the circle around Whit's dead body. Triumphant over their kill, no one even looked my way. In their eyes, Whit had gotten his target. The girl. They'd figure out why later. For now, I'd enjoy the moment. I knew Lola would keep my name out of it if she could.

I faded back, trying to steal a last look at Lola. I knew in my gut she wouldn't be coming to Chicago. It was easier for both of us to believe the lie. I bought my own lies, telling myself I was taking the money for the right reasons. If she'd wanted me to believe hers, then I owed that to her.

"Best hurry, sir," a porter said to me from the train. I turned and hopped on the steps, spun back to watch Lola fade away from view.

When I got to Chicago, I'd send money every week, come hell or high water, to a certain jewelry store. Then, when that baby was all paid off, I'd have it delivered to Lola, hoping Mrs. Lovell wouldn't swipe it first.

I wouldn't send any note, no letter of apology. Lola would know.

And if she changed her mind about coming to Chicago, then she would come. If not, she still deserved that ring. And a whole lot more. She deserved better than me.

A LOOK AT: PAUL BISHOP PRESENTS... CRIMINAL TENDENCIES: TEN MORE TALES OF MURDER & MAYHEM

Criminal tendencies lie dormant within the labyrinth of all our psyches. Most of us keep them firmly repressed. But what about those individuals who choose to follow their darker impulses?

Bestselling author and crime fiction expert Paul Bishop has again brought together top crime fiction writers and rising stars to share ten devious tales about criminal tendencies too powerful to ignore.

If the dark side of life is your beat, or if your own criminal tendencies are barely restrained, read on...

AVAILABLE NOW

ABOUT THE AUTHOR

Novelist, screenwriter, and television personality, Paul Bishop is a nationally recognized behaviorist and deception detection expert. A 35-year veteran of the LAPD, his high profile Special Assault Units produced the top crime clearance rates in the city. Twice honored as LAPD's *Detective of the Year*, he currently conducts law enforcement training seminars across the country.

As a deception detection consultant, his unique skills make him a valuable resource for private companies faced with potentially damaging in-house data breaches, industrial espionage, or corporate sabotage. His low-key, non-invasive, approach to these challenges has proven consistently successful.

Paul is the author of fifteen novels—including five books in his LAPD Detective Fey Croaker series—and has written numerous scripts for episodic television and feature films. He starred as the lead interrogator and driving force behind the ABC TV reality show *Take the Money and Run* from producer Jerry Bruckheimer.

A regular speaker at writing conferences, he is also an adjunct professor at the University of California Channel Islands, where he lectures on criminal investigation. He regularly presents his popular seminar, *Six-Gun*

Justice—Western Novels, Movies, and TV Shows, at libraries and other community functions.

He is the co-writer/editor of the acclaimed *52 Weeks • 52 Western Novels—A Guide To Six-Gun Favorites And New Discoveries*. Three follow-up volumes (*52 Weeks • 52 Western Movies, 52 Weeks • 52 Western TV Shows*, and *52 Weeks • 52 More Western Novels*) will be published in 2018. His latest book, *Lie Catchers*, is the first in a new series featuring top LAPD interrogators Ray Pagan and Calamity Jane Randall. The sequel, *Admit Nothing*, is due in 2018.

ON THE WEB

www.bishsbeat.blogspot.com
www.elementrixconsulting.com
Twitter @BishsBeat